LADY VIOLET HOLDS A BABY

THE LADY VIOLET MYSTERIES—BOOK FIVE

GRACE BURROWES

GRACE BURROWES PUBLISHING

Cover Design: Wax Creative, Inc.

Cover image: Cracked Light Studio

DEDICATION

This series is dedicated to my nephew, Jackson.

CHAPTER ONE

A handsome, passionate, *inventive* Frenchman was subtly inviting me to sample his charms.

"Perhaps later, St. Sevier."

My traveling companion affected gentlemanly puzzlement. "You give me the look a farm wife aims at the father of her eleven children when I merely suggest we fold out the benches for greater comfort. What is amiss with my darling Violet?"

"I don't feel very darling." The traveling coach rocked along while I pondered my own understatement. My late husband would have called my mood shrewish, but then, *shrewish* was one of many pejoratives for which no exact male counterpart had been invented —yet.

In my present mood, I felt up to the challenge of remedying that oversight.

"You face the prospect of another family gathering," St. Sevier said, settling an arm around my shoulders. "This challenge would daunt Napoleon's bravest cuirassiers. I myself would not venture into the company of the Deerfields without your stalwart escort."

My Deerfield family consisted of my four older brothers, two of whom were married, and my father, the Earl of Derwent. I could also claim some aunties and cousins, as well as a pair of nieces and one infant nephew.

That I knew of. Given my father's propensity for rascally behavior, I might have legions of half-siblings about whom I was ignorant. At least one of my brothers had sired a by-blow, as had my late husband. Papa dismissed his roguish deportment as reminiscent of an earlier era, and I had no reason to believe he'd changed with the times.

Why my thoughts should wander to my father's flirtations I did not know.

"Shall I read to you?" St. Sevier asked. "You can explain Byron to me. He does not translate easily to the French."

"No Byron, thank you." His lordship's verse was exquisitely witty, also savagely bitter. Having not yet reached my thirtieth year, and enjoying great good health as well as the devoted company of a dear man, I was not entitled to bitterness.

Nonetheless, my mood had that acrid, seething quality often associated with bitterness. My appetite had grown indifferent in recent days, and I had neither the energy for much activity nor the ability to sleep well.

"St. Sevier, how does one know if a bout of melancholia is descending?"

Hugh's embrace became subtly protective. He was a skilled physician who'd also done service as a battlefield surgeon with Wellington's troops—despite having French antecedents. I had come to know St. Sevier as more than a passing acquaintance when the time had come for me to emerge from mourning.

I'd found myself barely able to emerge from my own house.

For two years, that dwelling had been more a prison than a refuge. Nonetheless, when I'd finally completed my second year of mourning, I became inexplicably fearful of venturing out even to attend divine services.

Hugh, whose path had crossed mine on one of my rare social outings, had suggested I start by reading at a window, if that was all I could manage. From there, I graduated to taking tea with him on the terrace, and then we'd strolled the garden while we discussed the many books I'd read in the previous two years.

I had known St. Sevier prior to my bereavement as a passing acquaintance, but in widowhood, his strolls with me in the garden had become an escort to church or a carriage ride in the park. Then the blighter had coaxed me into attending some of the less glittering social occasions to which an earl's widowed daughter was invariably invited.

Hugh St. Sevier was tenacious, wily, relentless, and kind. In the year since I'd resumed a life beyond mourning, he and I had shared several adventures and grown close enough that he had asked me to become his wife.

I was tempted. Hugh was everything estimable in a man, as my late husband had not been. Hugh was also affectionate, and I needed that almost more than I'd needed those walks in the garden. My late spouse, Freddie Belmaine, had been cut from the same self-indulgent cloth as my father, for all that Freddie had been an outwardly attentive spouse. He'd offered me his arm when he escorted me. He'd parted from me with a peck on my cheek and shown me reasonable consideration in bed.

I did not miss Freddie, but neither did I hate him. He'd done the best he could, as had I, and no more need be said on the matter.

"One does not always know when a bout of melancholia is descending," St. Sevier said. "Melancholia is unlike a sick headache, where narrowed vision, distorted hearing, or a sensitivity to light can presage the onset of pain. Melancholia is diabolical. It can announce its approach with excessive good spirits, with fatigue, with unexplained tears, with no signs at all. Could you not simply be in the grip of a slight case of dread, Violet?"

Of all the many qualities I loved about Hugh—his humor, his compassion, his integrity—his willingness to simply talk to me was near the top of the list. Then too, he was a fine-looking man at slightly over six feet, with chestnut hair and brown eyes that could shine with humor, ire, or understanding.

"I don't dread my family." Did I dread this gathering? Did I wish the coachman would slow the team from a brisk trot to a walk?

"You regard your family with wary affection. I came to feel something similar for my late wife. I cared for her, I wanted her to be happy, but I suspected that sometimes her happiness and mine had an inverse relationship."

For a man whose native tongue was French, St. Sevier could wield English with impressive delicacy. "She enjoyed making you miserable?"

"We were young, and a jealous husband is a husband showing some regard for his wife. Ann and I married as a result of wartime expedience, and I had hoped we would grow to be friends. I was not the jealous sort, though—I was too tired to be jealous—and this vexed her exceedingly."

St. Sevier did not often speak of his past, which was understandable. As a French émigré who had volunteered to provide medical services to Wellington's army, that past was full of sorrows, conflicting loyalties, and regrets.

His three brothers had served under Napoleon, and not a one of them had survived the war.

"Did you dread your wife's company?" I asked, rather than return to the dreary topic of melancholia.

"I would go through my day in the infirmary and surgery, longing to return to the tent or billet I shared with her. I would grow famished for the domesticity of a meal taken with my wife rather than with the officers. I wove fancies about trading gossip, because men and the women in a military camp gossip differently, and yet, as the sun set, and the time came to rejoin her... I would dither."

"Because," I said, "you and she argued when you should have chatted. The meals were taken in silence, and nothing you did was ever good enough for your spouse. I was relieved when Freddie died."

After five years of marriage, we'd reached a truce that had grown colder with each passing season. Freddie had his numerous frolics, and I had my anger at him for enjoying the pleasures any man of means expected to indulge in. Seventeen-year-old brides were ripe for disillusionment.

Spoiled husbands brought that out in them.

"Ann hated army life," Hugh said, his gaze going to the lovely English countryside beyond the coach window. "Then she was widowed, then she married me rather than become a regimental commodity. I was not relieved when she abandoned me to make her way back to Scotland alone, but neither was I surprised."

"And when she did not make it home?" She'd been killed in an ambush, though details were vague. A French patrol? Spanish *guerrilleros*? Deserters? Brigands? Spain had been a cauldron of violence and shifting alliances for the duration of Wellington's campaign.

St. Sevier left off pretending to study fields, pastures, and endless stone walls. "I was sad to learn of Ann's death, Violet, but to make war is to make sadness, and the sadness in its way can be more deadly than the bullets. Let us turn our conversation to happier topics. Will Lord Dunkeld be on hand when we arrive at Derwent Hall?"

Sebastian MacHeath, Marquess of Dunkeld, was to be godfather to my new nephew. Sebastian had fought in Spain with my youngest brother, Felix, and spent many summers and school holidays racketing around rural Surrey with my siblings.

And with me. War was a less cheery topic than the present incarnation of Sebastian MacHeath, but only just. As a youth, he'd been my dearest friend—my only friend—and his decision to join up had vexed me sorely.

That decision had also vexed his titled uncle, the previous Marquess of Dunkeld, and at the time, I'd thought twitting the old marquess had been Sebastian's sole motivation.

"Lord Dunkeld was making the rounds in London," I said, "hunting a marchioness, no doubt. I've told him he ought to find himself a stalwart Scottish lass to fulfill that office, but he says they know better than to marry a man with a castle."

"Impossible to heat, expensive to maintain." Hugh kissed my temple, the exact sort of casual gesture I usually found so endearing from him. "Tell me of the rest of the gathering. Extended family? Neighbors, in-laws? I want the whole list, and please tell me your lady cousins have declined to attend."

My lady cousins had made St. Sevier's acquaintance on the occasion of Felix's wedding. To say they'd been smitten was an understatement. More accurate to label their reaction to Hugh as stricken with a dire case of hen-witted infatuation.

I had not been infatuated with Hugh, but I had been attracted to him. He had been wise enough to allow that interest to ripen into a deeper regard, one kiss, one embrace, one passionate night at a time.

"I'm not sure who all is expected," I said, "but as godmother, my presence is required. The house will doubtless be mobbed, because this is the earldom's next heir whose arrival we're celebrating."

I was overjoyed for Felix and Katie, who were besotted and not at all high in the instep. They would be loving parents to the boy and prevent my father from meddling overmuch in his grandson's upbringing.

"Is that what has you in such a brown study, Violet? Does the child cause you heartache?" Hugh asked, brushing his fingers along my cheek.

I closed my eyes, enjoying his caress. "Hmm?"

"Never mind," he said. Even with my eyes closed, I could sense the shift in the light that occurred when Hugh drew the coach's shades down. "Have a nap, and by the time you waken, we will be tooling up your father's drive."

Hugh had, in his gentle, oblique way, pointed me in the direction of a painful insight. Freddie had had his light-skirts, his commerce, his clubs, and his wagers. He'd had a by-blow or two, while I had had a household to manage and a husband who'd occasionally visited my bed.

And yet, after five years of marriage and two disappointments, to use the hideously genteel term, my nursery had still been empty.

Always, achingly empty.

~

Papa greeted me at the door, exuding the genial welcome of a patriarch with much to celebrate. He was tall with a mane of white hair and snapping blue eyes, though slight evidence of prosperous living was beginning to accumulate around his middle.

"None of your damned dramas, Violet," he muttered, kissing my cheek. "No intrigue, no uproar. This is a joyous occasion."

"Delighted to see you too, Papa." I treated him to my best Mayfair ballroom smile, all teeth and no charm. "If I recall, the damned drama at Felix and Katie's wedding was the work of one of *your* guests. Offer St. Sevier a civil greeting, or I will sing after supper tonight." The squawking of a broody hen was more attractive than the music I could produce before an audience.

Papa looked as if he'd like to embellish on his opening remarks. Fortunately, my oldest brother, Mitchell, Viscount Ellersby, joined us in the foyer.

Mitchell was a handsome man in the style of the lanky, blue-eyed country squire. He had wavy chestnut hair, a nose worthy of a Roman philosopher, and a formidable intellect. The Almighty had been parsimonious with Mitchell when it came to small talk and warmth, however.

"Violet." He bowed over my hand. "You are looking well. The girls will be delighted to see you, as will Lady Ellersby."

Delight was of course far too untidy an emotion for Mitchell to allow himself. Poor man. He looked tired, and not only in the sense of having missed a night's sleep. Mitchell was something of a mystery to me, having been too much my senior and—as the heir— too dignified to racket about the countryside with me and the other boys.

We younger siblings twitted Mitchell about his serious demeanor, but none of us envied him the role of Papa's understudy.

"I will make it a point to start my day tomorrow by calling on your womenfolk," I said. "If the weather is fair, perhaps the girls can join me in a picnic."

A hint of warmth flared in his eyes. "They would enjoy that, I'm sure, and the nursery staff would be eternally in your debt. St. Sevier, a pleasure to see you again."

The gentlemen exchanged further remarks about the weather, the roads, and the year's hay crop while I awaited a sense of homecoming that never arrived. I had grown up at Derwent Hall, lost my mother here, become engaged here, but I might as well have been at a particularly commodious inn for all the welcome I felt to be back at the family seat.

A well-trained staff never carried luggage in through the front door, and thus I had no idea if my trunks had been taken to the correct room or left to sit in some corridor on the wrong floor. Then too, I craved solitude. St. Sevier was the best of traveling companions, but he, too, would want some time to himself before dinner.

I had written to the housekeeper, Mrs. Stephens, to instruct her to put me in the guest wing rather than in my old rooms. I had made the decision not to bide in my girlhood apartment until the appointments had been updated. The violet and fleur-de-lis wallpaper was faded, the bed small, the cheval mirror speckled.

Besides, in the guest wing, I would have proximity to St. Sevier, which was one benefit of traveling with him. In London, our opportunities for intimacy were limited by propriety, hovering staff, and my own timidity about openly taking a lover.

With connecting balconies, our sojourn in the countryside could be a very enjoyable interlude indeed.

I located my preferred guest room, assured myself St. Sevier had been assigned the one next to it, and found my maid, Lucy Hewitt, already hanging up my dresses.

"Lord Dunkeld is biding on the property next door," Lucy said, "at MacHeath's Ford. Mr. Upjohn left a note for me belowstairs inviting me to a pint and a plate in the village, if that's acceptable."

Lucy was blond, sturdy, and inclined to get above herself. I loved her, because she was also practical, tolerant, and ferociously protective of me.

"You are free to do as you please for supper. I will go down to dine early and ambush my father and brothers in the library. If I wear the sprigged muslin, I can get myself undressed tonight, and you need not wait up for me."

Lucy's smile said she knew exactly who would help me out of my dress. "You'll want the mulberry shawl. High summer it might be, but the evenings can be chilly here in the shires. The last of the guests won't arrive until the day after tomorrow, according to Mrs. Stephens, and Lady Ellersby is in a taking over seating arrangements. Two baronies originating in the same year has her quite vexed."

The order of precedence was a formidable challenge at any large gathering, and Annabelle, Viscountess Ellersby, was expected to play hostess at Papa's grander entertainments. She was also the de facto senior steward at the Hall during Papa's extended jaunts to London.

When Mitchell went up to Town, he usually stayed at his clubs or Papa's town house.

He most assuredly did not stay with me, and for the first time, I wondered why that should be. Mitchell had all but avoided me in mourning and hadn't been much friendlier in the year since I'd put off my weeds.

"Lord Derwent has already warned me not to occasion any drama or intrigue," I said as a knock sounded on the door. I opened the door rather than interrupt Lucy's wrangling of dresses. "A tray. Thank the merciful powers and Mrs. Stephens. She seems quite up to the mark."

Not all of Papa's housekeepers had been, but then, my brothers speculated that not all of those women had been hired for their ability to keep the maids gainfully occupied. Papa had a widower's regrets about his conduct as a husband—he'd confided them to me on rare occasions—but he was also a peer who enjoyed his creature comforts.

My regret was that my mother had not lived longer. Surely Mama would have equipped me with more wisdom where the masculine gender was concerned.

"Mrs. Stephens is a good sort," Lucy said, stacking hat boxes on the shelf that ran around the top of the dressing closet. "She laughs easily, scolds the footmen, and teases the butler. She's either happy with her post, or blessed with a genial nature."

To put up with my father and brothers, she would need a genial nature and regular doses of nerve tonic. I poured myself a cup of tea and one for Lucy as well. We were overly familiar when private, and I had stopped fretting about it.

"Sit for a moment," I said. "The luggage will await your organizational genius while you have a cup of tea and a biscuit."

Lucy hesitated, probably for form's sake. She enjoyed healthy appetites in every regard, though the particulars of her arrangement with Lord Dunkeld's valet-cum-batman were her business.

"Upjohn says Lord Dunkeld had little luck in Town."

Tea and a biscuit in the middle of a very long day was one thing. Gossiping about Sebastian MacHeath was another.

"His lordship's efforts to secure a bride are of no moment to me, Lucy. The marquess deserves every happiness, and he needs heirs." I'd seen Sebastian's ancestral home earlier in the year, a gleaming castle located amid the gorgeous scenery of Perthshire, just east of the Highland line. The views were spectacular, and in Scotland, I'd felt a freedom of soul that my London existence denied me.

Lucy took up the cup and saucer and perched on a window seat rather than use the second wing chair. "The matchmakers were all sniffing at his lordship's heels, but the lady he squired about the most was Mrs. Bonaventure."

I knew Pamela Bonaventure. She was a handsome young widow who didn't begrudge herself an occasional frolic. She struck me as an understandable choice for the post of marchioness, a lady who would accept Sebastian on his own terms and not trouble him overmuch for companionship.

An understandable choice, but... disappointing. Sebastian deserved more than a pragmatic union and was capable of more than that himself.

"Have some shortbread," I said to Lucy. "Supper in the village is a good two hours away, and I can't eat all of this myself."

Though I did set aside two pieces for later. In addition to my troubled sleep and grouchy mood, my appetite was lately indifferent at mealtimes and then came roaring back immediately after. Travel always set me at sixes and sevens, and the tumult of a summer house party would only add to my upset.

I finished my tea and ate a lemon biscuit, because I, too, would not sit down to supper for some time. After I'd had a short lie-down, Lucy assisted me to dress, brushed out and rebraided my hair, and produced the requisite mulberry shawl.

One of the consolations of widowhood was the freedom to wear dark colors. My appearance was nondescript—brown hair, blue eyes, a figure more curvaceous than fashion preferred, average height when I wore heels—and I looked better in richer hues.

Or so Lucy assured me.

"You're going down early?" she asked when I'd donned slippers the same shade as my shawl.

"I am off to ambush my family," I said. "They will share a drink in the library before the guests gather in the parlor for dinner. I do not choose to be excluded from the private Derwent gathering on the basis of gender."

I'd had a lifetime of such exclusion and, out of pure contrariness, wasn't inclined to tolerate it any longer. I was all for leaving the menfolk to their port and pisspots after supper, a sensible enough convention, but my father and brothers were not observing convention when they enjoyed an *aperitif* without me.

I made my way down to the library, passing footmen hurrying this way, maids scurrying that way. They all acknowledged me with bows or curtseys, though I recognized few of them. I was reminded that I had not dwelled at Derwent Hall for nearly a decade, and nothing stayed unchanged forever.

I entered the library without knocking, and came upon the earl and Lord Ellersby as well as my other three brothers: Felix, Ajax, and Hector.

"Looking for a book, Violet?" Papa asked, accepting a glass of what looked to be sherry from Ellersby.

"Looking for my family," I said, "and perhaps a glass of wine to aid my digestion. Sherry will do, an amontillado if we have it."

My father's three youngest sons were good-looking devils, all tall, dark-haired, and lean. Felix managed a smile for me, while Hector and Ajax looked a bit disgruntled. I had not seen them for months, they had not bothered to greet me upon my arrival, and now they stood clutching their wineglasses as if waiting for me to leave.

A fifth man stepped out from between two rows of books. He was the tallest of those present, sable-haired, with cerulean blue eyes.

"Lady Violet, welcome. I was hoping you would join us." Sebastian, Marquess of Dunkeld, held out his hand to me, and I let him take mine, and also wrapped him in a most indecorous hug.

"Dunkeld, you look well." I stepped back and was treated to a genuine, if subdued, smile.

"Ye have been missed, *mo chridhe*." He spoke softly, his Scottish burr evident, then he turned me loose. "Ellersby, get the lady a drink, and, Felix, you can resume rhapsodizing about your prodigy. Not even a year old, and my godson is already quoting Shakespeare verbatim and winning every footrace in the shire."

"He isn't walking yet," Felix said, "but Nurse says he soon will, and not to long for that occasion, because once they start walking, life becomes much more lively. Katie says..."

Felix prattled on, quoting his wife, the nurserymaid, the vicar, and anybody else who had favorably opined about the infant. I listened with half an ear while I inspected Sebastian's person.

This was why I'd come to the library, I realized, because I'd known that as close as Sebastian was to my brothers, he'd likely have been invited to this friendly session with the sherry decanter. I had missed Sebastian in the weeks since I'd seen him, missed him more than I'd missed my brothers, and I was shamelessly gratified to hear that Sebastian had missed me too.

CHAPTER TWO

James Evander Deerfield, in line to succeed Lord Ellersby to the Derwent earldom, had arrived at the earthly sphere substantially less than nine months after his parents' nuptials. Felix and Katie had married in early autumn, and the baby had been born in early spring while I was sojourning in Scotland. His christening was taking place a few months later than most infants were blessed, at a date intended to obscure the proximity of the birth and the wedding.

My father was nonetheless making quite an affair of the occasion, having invited a dozen old friends and parliamentary cronies to join in the celebration. Papa enjoyed the whole political game and always had. He was fond of reminding all and sundry that Pitt had claimed the war with France would be over in a few months.

Papa had known better, *of course*, though nobody could have foreseen the twenty years of unrelieved havoc wrought by the Corsican.

At supper, I was seated with Lord Frampton on my right, a contemporary of Papa's, and on my left was one of the older female guests, Lady Eutheria Anderson. Lady Eutheria was the widowed daughter of an earl, hence the honorific. She'd been married to a local

MP of long standing. She fell into the category of friend of the family, though my aunties grew a bit sniffy at the mention of her name.

Lord Frampton had been a frequent guest of the Hall in my earlier childhood, though I didn't recall seeing much of him in later years. Not every titled man took his parliamentary duties seriously, and I gather Frampton's interest in politics waxed and waned with his fortunes. His lordship had aged well, such that he exuded the dignified good cheer of a spry older fellow.

The widowed Lady Eutheria was an equally entertaining dinner companion. In the parlance of polite society, she had adjusted well to her loss and regaled me with amusing anecdotes from house parties past. She was a handsome woman in early middle age, and her golden hair would pale to flaxen rather than shade into gray.

"And I could tell you stories," she said, "about Sylvanus himself that would render you speechless. Your papa was quite the rascal in his youth. Your poor mother had her hands full with him."

Sylvanus was my father's given name, and almost nobody referred to him thus. "I would like to hear those stories. One wants all the leverage over Papa one can legally acquire."

She patted my hand and glanced past me to Lord Frampton, who was taking an inordinate interest in his glass of claret.

"We will talk," she said. "Tell me about your handsome French-man. He served with Wellington?"

French émigrés had occupied a precarious place in wartime English society. While every fashionable mama longed to brag of hiring French dancing masters, tutors, lady's maids, and fencing instructors for her offspring, the émigrés themselves were suspected of spying, and—worse crime yet—taking bread and jobs from John Bull and his family.

As the shoals of French refugees fleeing the horrors of republican violence had ebbed, most had been quietly absorbed into an English life, but ambivalence toward them had survived the war.

"Dr. St. Sevier did indeed volunteer with Wellington's troops," I said. "He considers England his home, having lived here since early childhood."

Across from me and several seats closer to Papa's end of the table, St. Sevier was in a lively discussion with my brother Ajax about some French painter. My eavesdropping skills were not what they had been when I'd had four older brothers to spy on.

"He's a good-looking specimen," Lady Eutheria remarked, her tone speculative. "The French aren't as hidebound as we English. One learns to appreciate that."

"I treasure Monsieur's friendship," I said, "and have found him to be all that is gentlemanly. This is an interesting claret, don't you think?"

She smiled, for my change of subject had been entirely lacking in grace. Her appraisal of St. Sevier's potential as a frolicking partner had been yet still more graceless, though I knew he would not play me false.

St. Sevier and I had an understanding. We were meandering up to an engagement at a pace set by my hesitance to once again become the property of a husband. My marriage had been trying for all concerned, and I quite liked having the benefit of St. Sevier's attentions without the burden of becoming his wife.

Dinner was informal, and yet, it had the lugubrious quality of a fancier meal. As the courses progressed and the wine flowed, conversations began to cross the table and travel up and down the ranks. The talk turned political. Adjusting to a postwar economy was proving hazardous to many fortunes, and the common folk who had sacrificed much to secure victory were not in the mood to sacrifice yet more.

As the fruit and cheese disappeared, I sent our hostess a pointed look. Time for Lady Ellersby to lead the ladies' retreat to the comforts of the tea tray in the quiet of the guest parlor.

"Have I been such bad company as all that?" Lord Frampton asked. "You are fairly panting to charge from the room, my lady."

"You are all that is charming, my lord, but my day has been long, and I grow fatigued."

"House parties take stamina," he replied as a footman topped up our glasses of chardonnay. "You haven't been that long a widow, but you'll find your balance soon enough. Derwent is a fine host, always has been, and the occasion is well worth celebrating. Have you children, Lady Violet?"

"I have not been so blessed."

"Pity," he said. "You were such a pretty little thing too. Your father doted on you so."

No, he had not. Papa had trotted me out before guests to recite an occasional poem and sometimes let me ride out with him, provided I kept up, but in no sense had he been a doting father.

Dutiful was perhaps a better word for the earl's parenting of me, dutiful and distracted.

Lady Ellersby rose at that moment, much to my relief. Lord Frampton held my chair and would have escorted me to the guest parlor with the other ladies, but I dropped his arm as we gained the central foyer.

"I will make my excuses to Lady Ellersby," I said. "I am truly exhausted and must seek my bed."

"No duets at the pianoforte with your French friend?" Lord Frampton rejoined. "I daresay your brothers will regale us before the evening is over."

Ajax and Hector might perform a pianoforte-and-violin duet, though I would forgo that pleasure. They were quite good, but I was also quite tired.

The rest of the guests meandered down the corridor, and still Lord Frampton hovered at my elbow. "Do you enjoy a morning hack, my lady? I generally do, and I haven't ridden the metes and bounds of Derwent Hall for some time. Perhaps you'd like to join me some day when the weather is fair?"

Through a haze of impatience, I considered the notion that his lordship was flirting with me. But no. Of course not. Frampton was nearly my father's age, had dropped no untoward innuendo into the conversation, and was merely being friendly.

"The true horsemen in the company are my brother Felix and Lord Dunkeld," I said. "They will know the bridle paths far better than I."

I was lying. Bridle paths in rural English surrounds generally dated back to antiquity, some to Roman times if not earlier still. I knew every game trail and bridle path in the neighborhood, but I had no wish—

"Speak of the devil and draw him nigh. Dunkeld, good evening." Lord Frampton smiled and bowed. "I was attempting to inveigle Lady Violet into hacking out with me, but I'm not having any luck. Perhaps you can succeed where I've failed. My lady, I'll bid you good evening."

He jaunted on his way, leaving me to face a marquess whose expression conveyed impatience to equal my own.

"You are dead on your feet," Sebastian said. "I'll light you up to your room."

I considered arguing, but was—well, of course—too tired. A proper row with Sebastian required nimble wits. "I'll permit you to perform that courtesy. I'm in the nightingale room."

Sebastian used the flame of a sconce to light a carrying candle from among those kept on the sideboard in the foyer.

"You hid from me in London," he said as we started up the steps. "Not well done of you, my lady."

"I hide from most of society, and you are intent on finding a bride."

"Are you intent on becoming a bride?" he asked.

And to think I'd missed how refreshingly direct Sebastian could be. "Right now, I am intent on finding my bed and remaining there until such time as my energies are restored. English roads are an abomination. As much as I've traveled recently, I should know that by now."

"There's travel, and then there's travel to the Deerfield family seat. Felix is doing a good job at MacHeath's Ford. The old house has benefited from Katie's attentions, and the property is gradually coming around too. They have years of work ahead of them, but they seem to relish the challenge."

MacHeath's Ford, the neighboring estate, belonged to Sebastian. He'd been banished there in boyhood by his titled Scottish uncle so that the marquessate's heir could learn to make his way among the heathen English. I had formed an attachment to Sebastian before his first summer in England had concluded, and he'd fast become a conspirator in my brothers' adventures.

Upon the occasion of Felix's wedding, Sebastian had offered the newlyweds the leasehold of MacHeath's Ford on very reasonable terms, much to my father's vexation.

"You've met the baby?" I asked.

"Our godchild, you mean?" We had gained the guest wing, where all was quiet and shadows. "This christening will be an ordeal for you, won't it?"

"Yes." The corridor abruptly seemed a thousand yards long, all of them uphill. "I can find my way from here, Dunkeld. Thank you for your escort."

"Pamela Bonaventure sends her regards. She spoke highly of you." Sebastian, of course, remained at my side as we toddled along.

"She and I have not socialized much beyond last year's house parties. We are not that well acquainted." Mrs. Bonaventure had offered me well-intended advice for how to navigate Society as a widow. Pragmatic, almost ruthless advice. "She's quite attractive."

I wanted Sebastian to argue with me, to say the lady's looks were only passable, to report that she gossiped or had a fondness for flatulent lapdogs.

"She is quite attractive and sensible. I prefer sensible women."

You can do better. You deserve better. Pamela Bonaventure, despite her outward sensibility, still grieved for the love of her life, and any subsequent union would be haunted by his shade.

"What did you and Mr. Botham get to discussing so intently?" I asked as my door finally loomed on the left.

"Child labor. He's a reformer, and now that the slave trade has been outlawed, he's turned his sights on other evils."

What good did it do to outlaw the slave *trade* when enslavement itself flourished apace in the colonies? Perhaps I'd ask Mr. Botham that question if he and I ended up seated next to each other. Papa would scowl, Ellersby would send me a pained look, and St. Sevier would take my part in the affray.

Why had I agreed to serve as godmother to this child? Why had I come to another gathering at Derwent Hall when the last one had been so trying?

"I'm glad you're here, Dunkeld." Not an admission I'd planned to make.

Sebastian opened the door to my sitting room and escorted me inside. The fire had been lit, but no candles had been left burning. He tended to a candelabrum on the mantel and opened the bedroom door.

"Shall I light the fire in the bedroom for you, Violet?"

"No need. The night is mild. I'll warm the sheets and be cozy enough."

"Then I will bid you good night."

He set down his candle and took me in his arms, not a fleeting, friendly hug such as we'd shared in the library, but an embrace.

"I will get you through the christening, Violet. The ceremony is short, owing to an infant's ability to create mayhem. I like babies, and I will be happy to hold wee James Evander for the duration if necessary."

"Thank you." For the understanding, for the offer, for the embrace. I breathed in the sandalwood and cedar scent I would always associate with Sebastian and forced myself to step back. "It shouldn't be so hard, Sebastian, but just when I think I've found my balance, I'll see a nanny in the park with twins and think, 'Somebody was twice blessed. Somebody else.'"

"Life, I am sure, has more blessings in store for you, Violet Marie. You are weary and not at your best. Go to bed and dream of summer days spent fishing from the tree house while we dined on bread and jam."

Pleasant memories indeed, and at the time I'd made those memories, I'd no idea how precious they would become. "I'm to picnic with my nieces tomorrow. I'll look forward to that." I would make myself look forward to that.

"If I hear pirates in the woods at MacHeath's Ford, I'll know who's responsible." He kissed my cheek and bowed.

"Dunkeld?"

He paused at the door. "My lady?"

"You did not spend years fighting in Spain just to come home and let yourself be taken captive by the first sensible woman you stand up with. Your marchioness will be the mother of your children. You can spend more than a handful of weeks searching for her."

His brows rose, and then his expression shuttered. "Thank you for that advice. Pleasant dreams."

He closed the door silently in his wake, and I was soon abed, too tired to conjure any dreams at all.

The years had been unkind to my favorite tree house, which looked out over the local river from the majestic boughs of a maple. My girlhood refuge now appeared dilapidated, though I had last seen it only ten years past.

"So much for taking tea in the treetops," St. Sevier said. "Promise me you won't clamber up into the tree house when my back is turned."

Already, he sounded like a husband. "I might climb the tree, but I can no longer trust my brothers' construction. A gardener gave them a few pointers, and they were promptly experts on building tree houses. As soon as I learned of this one, they built another, though this is the best of the lot."

The tree house had a fine view of both the Derwent Hall home wood and MacHeath's Ford on the opposite bank. That had made it special to me, as had the fact that I could climb to the structure without relying on a ladder.

"I hear the approaching infantry," St. Sevier said. "I will leave you ladies to enjoy your outing." He bowed and would have taken his leave, but I stopped him with a hand to his sleeve.

"I missed you last night."

"*Mon coeur*, by the time I escaped from the parlor, you were far gone in the arms of Morpheus. I did not have the heart to disturb you. I will come to you tonight, have no fear."

"See that you do," I said, pleased that he'd looked in on me. Our dealings had progressed to the point that some nights, we simply shared a bed. I treasured the proof that St. Sevier valued my company and not merely our erotic pleasures. "I must protect you from Lady Eutheria's wandering eye."

St. Sevier grimaced. "We need not stay past the actual christening, Violet. I would love to show you my house in Berkshire if you'd rather not return directly to London."

He had not made that offer previously, and St. Sevier and I had traveled the length and breadth of England shut up in the same coach.

"I would love to see it." Though we'd have to be very, very discreet. If we were married, of course no such caution would be needed, a fact St. Sevier was doubtless subtly emphasizing.

"I'm away to the stable," he said. "Your brother Ajax has a new gelding, and we are to try out his paces. Enjoy your picnic."

He strode down the wooded path, taking a piece of my heart with him. Hugh was a lovely, lovely man, and I'd caught his fancy in all my prickly, backward, contrary widowhood. I reveled in his patience with me, needing the reassurance of his steadfastness and needing the sense of control I enjoyed because our dealings progressed at the pace I decreed.

"Auntie Violet! Auntie Violet! We have come for our picnic!" Two little girls thundered over the footbridge from the direction of MacHeath's Ford, both blond, both in pristine pinafores and tidy braids. "We have brought our bears because they live in the woods."

These announcements were made by Sylvie, my older niece, named for my father. She had arrived a decorous twelve months after her parents' nuptials, but alas, she'd been a mere female. Lord and Lady Ellersby's second attempt at securing the succession, little Bella, had followed less than two years later.

Marital discord had arisen since then, though neither party had burdened me with the particulars. Lord Ellersby had at one time been banished from his wife's bedroom, and I had no idea if the warring factions had since patched up their differences.

They had two adorable children to love, and much to my surprise, it was Ellersby himself who was directing the raiding party. Footmen brought up the rear, carrying blankets and baskets, and a pair of nursemaids trundled along beside the footmen.

"Papa, Auntie Violet brought her parasol," Bella said. "When can I have a parasol?"

"I want a parasol too, Papa," Sylvie chorused. "I shall be a lady, and ladies have parasols and carriages and admirers and everything."

Bella ran to me and wrapped her arms around my waist. "I want a bear, like Lord Byron had, or a unicorn."

"I would love to claim a unicorn for my own, too, child," I said, bending to hug her. "Ellersby, good day. Ladies, you must decide where upon this lovely bank to spread our blankets. We want a location both dry and shady, for bears do enjoy napping by a pretty river."

Ellersby bowed to me. "Violet, good morning. My lady wife sends her greetings and thanks. She hadn't thought to send the girls off picnicking, but the resulting quiet is much appreciated."

"We were noisier," I replied as Bella and Sylvie began earnest discussions of the ideal spot for a picnic. I knew where they'd place us, for Sebastian and I had held the same debate many times.

"*You lot* were noisier," Ellersby said, gesturing to the footmen to follow the girls along the bank. "I was born dignified."

I peered at him, then laid the back of my hand to his forehead. "My lord, I believe you have offered a small jest at your own expense. Are you well?"

"Never better," he said as the girls chose the place equidistant between the two largest maples. The ground received enough afternoon sun to be grassy and dry, but at this hour enjoyed dappled shade. Better still, several large rocks protruded from the water within wading distance of the bank. I'd spent many an hour reading on those rocks while Sebastian had fished a few yards upstream.

"I forget how pretty Derwent Hall's surrounds are," I said as a fish leaped from a pool on the opposite bank. "The light is different in the countryside, brighter and happier."

"No coal smoke," Ellersby replied. "How I abhor London in winter for that very reason. I'll leave you to your bears and unicorns. If you look after the girls, Hansom will keep an eye on Dottie, and I can send the footmen back to Lady Ellersby."

Only then did I take particular notice of the two nurserymaids enjoying the shade while the children dickered over the exact placement of the blankets.

"Dottie is still on staff?"

"She likely always will be. We look after our own, and she will always need looking after, though she's also a good worker. I'm off to harangue Papa about the cost of shooting parties, for he's determined we'll have one this autumn. He claims they are the best means ever invented for lobbying reluctant votes in the Commons. I prefer reasoned debate myself, but alas, my wishes do not prevail."

Ellersby made his escape without taking leave of his daughters, which was prudent of him. Children had their own ways of lobbying, and Ellersby's errand was not one I'd have approached enthusiastically. Papa had the traditional aristocratic view of life, which was to say all of creation in his opinion was to order itself to suit his whims.

The earl wasn't entirely hopeless. He grasped that the national interest wasn't served by unrelenting rapine on the part of the peerage, and he was a loyal and generous employer, but he was a Tory to his toes. My late husband, for all his other faults, had taken the time to explain some basic economic facts to me and had ensured I'd have the expertise to oversee my own funds.

Had Ellersby offered his wife those same explanations?

"Auntie Violet, we have decided where to set up camp," Sylvie said. "You must wave a white flag to show us that you come in peace."

I produced a handkerchief and waved it about. "I am Lady Violet of Castle Belmaine," I called. "I come in peace to break bread with my neighbors and the fine bears from Castle Derwent."

Much curtseying followed, along with some prancing about on the part of the little girls. I directed Hansom to take a blanket for her and Dottie some yards off, and we divided up the booty from the wicker hamper. The footmen strolled away in the direction of the dower house, which Lord and Lady Ellersby called home, and we ladies were left to enjoy the summer morning.

"Papa said we were not to climb any trees," Sylvie reported when the bears had declined to partake of the bread, jam, lemonade, and biscuits kindly provided by the kitchen. "I want to see what the birds see, and climbing trees is fun."

"Squirrels climb trees," Bella said. "Bears do too. The bears are not forbidden to climb the trees."

"The bears are tired from rising so early to prepare for their outing," I said. "Perhaps they would enjoy a nap in the sunshine while we go wading."

"Wading!!!" Both girls shrieked their glee, and I exchanged a glance with Hansom. She was a stolid young lady with rosy cheeks and a placid demeanor. Her smile indicated that I would become the best auntie ever in the whole world—for today at least—if wading transpired.

"You will need your table napkins to dry your feet," I said. "And you must be very careful not to splash your hems or to fall into the water."

I had "fallen" into the water regularly and was a decent swimmer as a result. What a hoyden I'd been, and how very much I'd enjoyed my lapses in decorum.

"Off with our boots, my dears," I instructed, "and stockings as well. The water will be very cold, too cold for bears, but we are stalwart explorers looking for lost kingdoms beneath the waves."

Dottie was listening to me, her pretty features puzzled. She had been my companion in the nursery for a time, though several years my senior. In the way of children, I had noticed that she'd preferred to play with dolls long after I'd taken up reading books. I had also grasped that her status was that of servant, though the senior staff always dealt with her gently.

I had lost track of Dottie as I'd endured the finishing-school years, but she'd apparently been assigned to Ellersby's nursery, which made sense. Demands upon nursery staff, while unending, were fairly simple: Keep the children safe, warm, and fed. Keep the surrounds tidy. Try not to curse in front of the infantry.

Though Dottie likely knew no curses. "Dottie, would you like to go wading with us?" I asked.

"Aye, milady, that I would. The water is ever so cool and pretty. I will keep my hems dry too. You'll see."

The four of us were soon toddling about in the shallows, the feel of the stones between my feet rousing long-forgotten memories. Closer to the opposite bank, the stream bed was muddy, perhaps due to how the current negotiated the bend in the river. The murkier water appealed to trout, which meant that Sebastian had succeeded in catching the occasional fish.

Farther upstream, Papa had built an actual fishing cottage, while an old grain mill stood on the MacHeath side of the river closer to the village.

In my girlhood, this little patch of river had embodied a whole world for me, a happy world.

When my nieces had splashed about long enough to declare a mutual case of frozen toes, we dried off and donned our boots. I proposed a hike to the fishing cottage—a distance of several hundred yards—knowing that with children in tow, the cottage might as well be miles off.

We explored the Bavarian wilds, pilfered magic raspberries from the side of the trail, and beat the bushes with stout sticks to waken any lions sleeping in our demesne. By the time the fishing cottage came into view, Bella was asking if Dottie—who had joined our raiding party—could carry her back to the castle.

I turned to admonish my field commander to cease whining lest the enemy pickets hear us, and a flutter of movement caught my eye. A curtain twitched on the upper floor of the fishing cottage.

I had hoped the girls and I might rest on the porch of the cottage, a two-story structure complete with bedrooms, kitchen, and front parlor. Perhaps Hector had sought the peace and quiet of the little dwelling to memorize a play, or maybe maids were tidying up because bachelor guests were sometimes billeted at the cottage when the Hall was full.

More likely the cottage had been put to the use for which I suspected Papa had built it—as a trysting place.

"Come, Sylvie," I said, holding out a hand to her. "I can carry you piggyback to our blankets, and Dottie can take Bella. We have a few more biscuits to gobble up, lest we hurt Cook's feeling by neglecting our tucker."

"Biscuits!!!"

Dottie good-naturedly fell in with this plan—she was nothing if not sweet-tempered—and we were soon tossing crumbs for the birds and demolishing the last of the biscuits. Hansom helped me tidy up our picnic spot while Dottie and the children searched for four-leaf clovers. Then Hansom was shepherding her charges back across the footbridge.

I tarried on the stream bank, debating with myself, then took off my straw hat and made my way up the trunk of the big maple. My destination was not the tree house—I had promised St. Sevier after all —but a sort of crow's nest higher up.

The handholds and branches were still as they'd been, and I was soon perched aloft in the boughs with a clear view of the woods, the MacHeath's Ford manor, and the fishing cottage. Very bad of me, but that I could still climb a tree pleased me inordinately.

My curiosity—or wickedness—was rewarded a quarter hour later when Lady Eutheria and Mr. Botham exited the cottage, her hand wrapped very securely around his arm.

CHAPTER THREE

"How exactly do Hector and Ajax fill their time?" I asked.

Felix paused in our tour of his gardens. On the terrace, Katie was entertaining St. Sevier, who had volunteered to escort me on this call at MacHeath's Ford. Katie and Felix were a love match, and if anything, the passing months seemed to have deepened the marital bond.

I envied them that, but then, in the early months of my own marriage, I had been thoroughly infatuated with Frederick Belmaine.

"Let's sit," Felix said. "You will have to ask our brothers what they are getting up to these days. I am much absorbed with my business and with fatherhood. The boy has started taking a few spoonfuls of porridge, and our nights have grown unsettled. Were you not gracing us with a visit, Katie and I might well be napping."

"Be careful," I said, taking a bench that faced a bed of blooming damasks. "Napping can result in a reoccurrence of fatherhood. You've won the race to secure the succession, and the child is far from weaned."

"There will be no reoccurrence of fatherhood, as you put it, until James is at least a year old." Felix, the most agreeable of my brothers, sounded more stern than I'd ever heard him. "I was with Katie when James came into the world, and I'm convinced every father ought to attend the births of his offspring."

"You were *with* Katie?"

He snapped off a thorny rose and took the place beside me. "Not the done thing in proper circles, perhaps, but Katie wanted me there, and it's the usual course for the common folk. I would never leave her alone to face such an ordeal if she wished me by her side." He sniffed at the rose, a frothy pink bloom whose perfume reminded me of long summer evenings spent reading in the garden. "I did not think it possible to love Katie more, but I do, Violet. With each day, I do."

Such sentiments could be shared with a sister, though they left me torn. On the one hand, I rejoiced for Felix and Katie, because the strength of their union was already impressive. On the other hand, I wanted to warn my brother: Even a young, healthy spouse can be taken from you.

Guard your heart. "Does Katie want more children?"

"Very much. She sees what great good friends Sylvie and Bella are and how Hector and Ajax are thick as thieves. Katie treasures her own siblings and wants brothers and sisters for James."

That Felix knew his wife's thoughts on the matter spoke well for the marriage. As a young bride, I had simply assumed children would "come along," as had my spouse. When disappointments had come along instead, we hadn't known how to speak to each other of matters so close to the heart.

For the first time, it occurred to me that Freddie, while several years my senior, had also been young in wisdom. Social sophistication he'd claimed, but that was a poor substitute for the devotion Felix and Katie shared.

"Katie is lucky to have you," I said. "How fare your stables?" Felix was a horseman to his bones and was trying to make a profitable venture out of his passion.

"Shall I show you this year's foals? We have three fillies and three colts, which was exactly the outcome I'd hoped for. They are all thriving, and I've bred back five of the mares. By this time next year, I could have my own stud colt, and if I choose well, he'll bring in steady revenue. There's an earl about ten miles west of here who specializes in breeding ladies' mounts, and he has a three-year-old colt by Hastings out of My Lady's Riddle. The sweetest young fellow you'd ever want to saddle up and a gorgeous chestnut. The dam line goes back to—"

A woman's laughter floated across the garden, and Felix's whole attention turned toward the terrace. "I love that sound," he said. "I love knowing Katie is happy. James sometimes laughs as well, and when that baby smiles, Violet, it's as if all of creation is smiling with him. If anything were to happen to him..."

"You and Katie would see each other through such a tragedy." I rose, for it was time I faced the challenge I'd set for myself when I'd decided to pay this call. "Will you introduce me to this paragon among infants?"

"Gladly," Felix said, getting to his feet and offering me his arm. "I make a regular nuisance of myself in the nursery, and James is your godson. You will be special to him, so of course you must make his acquaintance."

"Has his godfather made his acquaintance?"

"The marquess was in the nursery within an hour of arriving here," Felix replied. "Did you know Dunkeld has a daughter? I served with him in Spain, and I'm not entirely sure how the child happened. If you can winkle the story from him, I'm dying to learn the particulars. Suffice it to say, I believe MacHeath likes children. He and James were boon companions in no time, much to Nurse's shock."

"St. Sevier likes children too," I said. "For that matter, so do I." Children were generally honest little souls, even when adults wished they weren't.

We collected Katie and St. Sevier and made our way to the nursery. Halfway down the corridor, the peace of the summer day was disturbed by a woman's shouting.

"You stupid girl, put that child down this instant! *Never* waken a sleeping babe. How many times must I tell you?"

"But he were awake, Nurse. I heard him, and if he's wet—"

A loud crack followed, suggesting somebody's face had been slapped.

"Oh dear," Katie said. "Tempers are flaring. We all went short of sleep last night, and having a houseguest—"

The unmistakable sound of a crying baby pierced the air.

"See what you've done? I will tell Mrs. Deerfield about this, Weatherby. You have disrespected my orders once too often."

The crying escalated to the point that I wanted to cover my ears. I could not endure the thought of an infant in misery while grown women indulged in a spat. I opened the door to the nursery and sailed through, going straight to the bassinette in the corner.

"Young man, hush. Please do hush this instant."

James Evander Deerfield was in quite a taking for so small a person. His little face was red, his chubby legs kicking. He roared forth his displeasure, and I had no clue how to comfort him, but knew that I must. He was just a baby, a tiny, innocent baby, and the nurse's temper was no fault of his.

"Come, my good fellow," St. Sevier said, scooping the infant up. "No need for such dramatics. Your mama and papa have brought Auntie Violet to call, and you will make a bad first impression."

The baby, perhaps unused to new people, ceased crying. "Buh." He swung a small fist at St. Sevier's cheek.

St. Sevier tucked the child against his shoulder. "*Bonjour* to you too. The boy speaks French already and offers to shake my hand. Such accomplishments for a mere lad. And such a sturdy fellow, too, with magnificent lungs and rosy cheeks." St. Sevier brushed a finger over those cheeks, gently wiping away the tear stains. "As we are once again in charity with the realm, perhaps some introductions are in order?"

He turned to Katie and Felix, the infant tucked close and apparently happy to be in St. Sevier's arms.

"You will recall," I said, "that St. Sevier is a physician. Crying babies do not unman him." Neither did crying women, as I had occasion to know.

"I adore babies," St. Sevier said, holding James up before him and slowly raising the baby high. "They are precious beyond words and more dear than life. This is a healthy fellow you have here too. Full of himself and clearly enjoying good care."

Nurse, who had watched this exchange with obvious consternation, smiled tentatively. The younger nursemaid, Weatherby, stood at attention, her left cheek a pink contrast to the pallor of her right. She was young, probably not yet sixteen, and painfully trim in contrast to Nurse's more ample form.

"He's my only begotten son," Felix said. "You drop him at your peril."

"When you put him on a blanket, does he roll over?" St. Sevier asked, beginning a circuit of the room with the child in his arms.

"He's trying to crawl," Nurse said, "though only just."

"He rolls handily," Katie said, "from his front to his back, and back to front. He also crouches up like a cat."

"He's still waking in the night?" St. Sevier asked, offering James a finger to grab. The baby caught at that finger and tried to bring it to his little mouth.

"At least once a night," Felix said, exchanging a smile with Katie. "Sometimes more. He's big for his age and very fond of his tucker."

St. Sevier sat on a toy box and started a new game, moving his hand around within James's field of view. The baby followed the movement with his eyes and head and tried again to capture St. Sevier's finger. More games followed, with St. Sevier humming and singing, and James babbling along with him.

To a casual observer, St. Sevier was entertaining a child who had awakened in a fractious mood. I knew better. Hugh was sparing me having to hold my nephew, a privilege I dreaded, and also conducting a medical examination of the baby.

"I pronounce this officer fit for duty," St. Sevier said, rising. "But I fear Miss Weatherby's prediction was accurate. The child wants a change of nappies." He passed the infant not to Nurse but to Weatherby.

She took the baby, sent Nurse a flat stare, and moved off into the next room.

"The commotion has put himself off stride," Nurse said. "He's not used to company in the nursery. Children want peace and quiet. The younger they are, the more that's the case."

In my estimation, James had been thoroughly pleased to have callers. "Is he soon to cut teeth?" I asked, dredging up a snippet from the many pamphlets I'd read on childrearing.

Nurse offered a martyred sigh. "That he is. The Deerfields teethe on the young side, my lady. Master Mitchell were only four months when he started up, though Master Ajax and Master Hector started at five months. I can't say as to how you and Master Felix went on. I was in service with your aunt by then."

We look after our own. I vaguely recalled making Nurse's acquaintance at some point in my childhood. A holiday gathering of all the relatives, perhaps, a wedding, or maybe my mother's funeral? Mitchell was well past thirty, and yet, Nurse recalled when he'd been a teething infant.

"I must pay a visit to you, Nurse, when we have no eavesdroppers," I said. "I want to know every naughty trick my oldest brother got up to."

"He were the sweetest baby, milady. That he were. Not like your other brothers. A pair of rascals, them two."

Ajax and Hector were still a pair of rascals. "Then you must tell me of their misdeeds. An auntie needs to know these things, and nobody else has seen fit to enlighten me."

"The list would be long, Lady Derwent."

I smiled, though Lady Derwent had been my mother. I bore a resemblance to her, inasmuch as a cart horse resembles a champion steeplechaser. Moreover, Mama had probably been more closely acquainted with Hector and Ajax's mischief than anybody else.

"We'll leave you in peace," Felix said, "though I'd like to show James the roses later this afternoon."

Nurse clearly disapproved of that notion.

"A fine idea," St. Sevier said as Weatherby returned with a smiling James on her hip. "Wrap him up warmly and let him enjoy the fresh air and sunshine. He'll benefit from the change of scene, and Nurse can enjoy a cup of tea in his absence."

It took a formidable woman to stand firm against St. Sevier's Gallic charm, but Nurse's frown became a scowl.

"We'll be off, then," Katie said, taking Felix's arm. "Good-bye, sweet boy."

Weatherby curtseyed. Nurse managed a bob and a nod, and my visit to the nursery ended without my having to hold the child. A relief, that. Perhaps I needed to work my way up to such a challenge, though I didn't fancy intruding on Nurse's domain again anytime soon.

We trundled down the corridor in silence until we reached the top of the staircase. The last time I'd seen MacHeath's Ford, the house had been closed up, the furniture under Holland covers. All had been dust and shadows.

Katie had taken the manor in hand, scrubbed it from attics to cellars, and added all the touches that made a house a home—flowers on windowsills, lace runners on the side tables, freshly beaten carpets where only bare floors had been.

I was glad for the house, but I feared the nursery was not yet in such good order. "Will you sack Weatherby?" I asked. The girl had been right to see to the child and had been rewarded for her efforts with a hard slap.

"Nurse Geddes came highly recommended," Felix said. "She's tended Deerfield babies since she was younger than Weatherby."

Katie looked pained at that recitation. "We will not sack Weatherby." She started down the steps, Felix trailing after her. "Shall I order a tea tray on the terrace? The day is so pretty, and it's a pleasure to have callers. Violet, I understand you were picnicking this morning. Felix tells me that's something of a family tradition, though I haven't known Sylvie and Bella to indulge in it previously. Perhaps I ought to picnic with them, given that Lady Ellersby is much occupied serving as the Derwent Hall hostess. Have all of the guests arrived at the Hall yet? The list was impressive from what I recall of it."

For Katie, normally so shy and retiring, that oration should have won her a Speech Day prize.

"The rest of the guests will arrive by the end of today," I said, following my hostess down the steps. "If you do invite the nieces for a picnic, please include me in the invitation. A skirmish with the winged Visigoths enlivens my day considerably."

Felix paused at the foot of the steps. "I thought you banished the winged Visigoths before you put up your hair."

"Of course I did, but like all conscientious Visigoths, they return to sack Rome regularly. Thank you for introducing me to my nephew. He's a splendid boy and clearly very much loved. St. Sevier, shall we brave the haunted woods?"

"Take some roses with you when you go," Katie said. "They are spectacular this year, and the fragrance is exquisite."

She did not intend to escort us to the garden in person. I had the sense husband and wife were about to cover uncomfortable terrain regarding the situation in the nursery and not for the first time.

"I have my trusty penknife," St. Sevier said. "We will raid the roses and then prevail upon Violet's store of magic spells to bring us safely through the woods."

We took only a few roses, which St. Sevier wrapped in a plain linen handkerchief. I held my peace until we had crossed the footbridge and gained the shade and quiet of the woods.

"Nurse needs to be pensioned," I said. "She called me by my mother's name and was much too severe with Weatherby."

St. Sevier ambled along at my side as warblers swooped overhead, and the lush scent of an old forest enveloped us.

"Nurse is also losing her hearing," St. Sevier said. "I asked about rolling over. She replied as if I'd asked about crawling. She did not hear the boy whimpering in his bassinette, and she did not smell that his nappies were damp. Can you say something to Felix?"

I had not noticed the damp nappies, but then, I wasn't a veteran nursery attendant.

"I can say something to Felix." Though I did not want to be drawn into my brother's domestic drama. For that small boy, though, I would speak very plainly to my brother indeed.

"And I will have a word with Mrs. Deerfield," St. Sevier said, "when I return to steal more roses from her garden."

"Why would you do that?"

"To leave a bouquet by your bedside, of course."

We were well along the forest path, far from the view of family or passing Visigoths. "St. Sevier?"

"*Mon couer?*"

"Please kiss me."

"*Bien sûr, ma chère.* I thought you would never ask."

One could copulate against a sturdy oak. Two could, rather, provided the fellow involved was fit and strong. Fortunately for me, St. Sevier was quite fit and very strong, also invigorated by natural surroundings.

By the time we wandered from the home wood into the park spreading from the Derwent Hall garden, I would not have cared if I had leaves in my hair and grass stains on my skirt, so thoroughly had St. Sevier distracted me from the troubles in my brother's nursery. I was relaxed and in charity with the world, and with Hugh St. Sevier in particular.

"Is the French national character inclined to frolicking out of doors?" I asked as we approached the garden's formal parterres.

"I have not had the pleasure of interviewing enough French ladies to know," St. Sevier replied. "I can tell you that soldiers on campaign took advantage of natural surrounds on occasion. In camp, there was no privacy, with most sleeping in tents, even among the officers. Ann and I considered ourselves fortunate if we didn't hear every argument and pleasantry that passed between neighbors on all four sides of our tent."

"I cannot imagine how difficult that was, being newly wed in a military camp." Felix and Katie were close, in part because they had the luxury of private conversations about everything from Felix's broodmares to the staffing in the nursery. How much more difficult would the marital adjustment be when nearly every discussion took place virtually in the open air?

"Newlyweds were commonplace on campaign. Of necessity, widows remarried posthaste. The army made little provision for returning widows to England, and the alternative... Suffice it to say, for most women the alternatives to a hasty marriage were unacceptable, particularly if the lady was expecting."

"You delivered many babies while with the army?"

"Dozens," he said. "Every one a miracle, most of them amazingly healthy. It seems more guests have arrived."

As we passed into the row of pleached limes that formed the garden's central alley, I saw several gentlemen congregated on the terrace. They were hatless, suggesting this was a bit of fresh air taken after coach travel or for the sake of a quick cigar while exchanging greetings.

"You'd think this baby the first born in England after a twenty-year hiatus," I muttered. "Why must Papa make a political gathering out of every occasion?"

"You recognize these men?"

Two of them had their backs to us, but three others were easy enough to discern. "A courtesy viscount awaiting an earldom, an MP whose election Papa sponsors, a wealthy baronet. I suspect the courtesy lord is bound for the hustings as well, unless his papa meets an untimely demise."

"Ironic, isn't it?" St. Sevier said. "War created an abundance of problems. Peace has created still more problems, and the politicians haven't been able to solve any of them."

"Papa says the war was an excuse to hold the populace in check, and what ought to have been freely criticized—the crown's excessive spending, the Regent's philandering, the war profiteering—flourished because John Bull was muzzled by calls for patriotism."

Papa liked his privileges, but he also took pride in the freedoms Englishmen enjoyed even while ruled by a monarch.

"What did your Dr. Johnson say?" St. Sevier murmured. "'Patriotism is the last refuge of the scoundrel.'"

"Dr. Johnson meant the sort of patriotism that requires loud displays and marching about armed on the village green, not the sort of patriotism you, Felix, and Dunkeld showed in Spain."

St. Sevier paused with me at the fountain in the center of the garden. "I was no patriot, Violet. I was a new physician, eager to learn what the battlefield could teach me. The Scottish approach to medicine integrates theory and practice, while the English approach places the theoretical physician above the practical apothecary or surgeon. At war, I saw the whole medical lexicon, from terrible injuries to serious diseases, from imaginary ailments that produced real symptoms, to childbirth. As a mere mortal, I detest war. As a young doctor, I relished the opportunity it gave me."

St. Sevier could make passionate love, then put himself to rights and resume the demeanor of the worldly gentleman. I lacked such facility. I felt I ought to greet the new guests with St. Sevier at my side and endure introductions to any with whom I was unfamiliar, and yet, I hesitated.

"We could detour to the stables," St. Sevier said. "I can show you Ajax's new horse, though I fear for your roses." St. Sevier took a sniff of the damasks we'd cut from Katie's bed of roses.

"We might as well get the introductions over with," I said, accepting the bouquet from him. "I do wonder where Papa has got off to. These are his—"

The fourth and fifth men turned to attend something the

viscount said. I halted on the path and drew beneath the meager shade of the lime trees.

"Violet?"

"The man on the right, with the muttonchop side whiskers." Tall-ish, lean, attractive. As a girl of seventeen, all I had seen was that John Bascomb had been nearly twice my age. He was past forty now and still exuded the confidence and good humor of a wealthy and contented squire.

"He troubles you?" St. Sevier said, his tone mild.

"Exceedingly. I am off to find my father. Thank you for your escort, and if you should ever see me alone in conversation with that fellow on the right, please interrupt. Sprint across the garden, shout at me the length of the gallery, or crash through a window in the library, but do not leave me alone with him. His name is John Bascomb. He owns a property several miles distant, and I haven't seen him since my wedding day."

When he, like half the shire, had presumed to kiss the bride at the open house following the wedding breakfast.

"Has Mr. Bascomb given offense, Violet?" Though St. Sevier still spoke with utmost calm, his gaze had taken on a cool calculation that boded ill for Papa's guest.

"Not for some time. I'm off to find my father, with whom I intend to have a pointed word."

"The flowers," St. Sevier said. "I will find them some water, shall I?"

I handed the roses back to him and marched away past the laburnum alley so I could enter the house through the conservatory and avoid greeting a man I'd hoped to never see again.

I found my father in the stable, in discussion with his head lad about a coach horse that had come up lame. A peer of the realm need not bother with such matters, but Papa was a hounds and horses sort of peer, and the stable was one place where both he and I enjoyed spending time.

For that reason, I waited until he'd concluded his business with the coach horse—a stone bruise was turning into an abscess, alas—and accompanied him on the path back to the house.

"Papa, how could you?"

"Is that a rhetorical question, Violet? How could I invite Lady Eutheria, perhaps? I felt I owed her some sign of my favor—widows are so easily neglected by Society—and the assemblage was short a few female guests. Lady Ellersby wanted to include a pack of silly chits to continue the matchmaking for those who'd failed to bag a husband during the Season. I chose instead to return some favors, hence Lady Eutheria's charming presence."

He ambled along, all lordly unconcern, either unaware of or indifferent to the ire I harbored toward him.

"You presume to lecture me on Society's reception of widows, my lord?"

"No, Violet." His patient tone slipped toward testiness. "I do not presume anything where you are concerned. I dare not offend you lest you give away another water meadow, or otherwise wreak havoc on the father who has loved you since your birth."

"You're still smarting because I deeded that blasted water meadow to Felix?" Felix raised horses, and water meadows were excellent acreage for pasturage or growing hay. The particular water meadow in question had been part of my dowry—the part which, for Papa, had made my match with Freddie Belmaine all but imperative.

"I will never understand why you put such a valuable asset into the hands of a young man who is so regularly inclined to ignore the larger picture. Not well done of you, Violet."

We approached the conservatory side of Derwent Hall, which meant we were out of sight of guests. Here was as good a place to brace Papa on his highhandedness as any.

"Did you invite John Bascomb to this gathering in retaliation for my willfulness?"

Papa stopped on the path, took off his hat, and ran a hand through his hair. "Has all your racketing about with that Frenchman addled your brains, Violet? What *are* you going on about?"

Until I'd married, my father had been able to cow me with displays of temper. In recent years, he'd resorted to sarcasm and feigned indignation.

"You invited John Bascomb to this gathering, Papa. If there's a man I never want to see again, much less attempt civilities toward, Bascomb is that man."

"Because he asked to court you? That was years ago, Violet, and you chose another. Bascomb was the rejected party and had to watch you sashay down the church aisle with the Belmaine pup. Bascomb has set aside his pride enough to join our little celebration. I will have no ridiculous displays of temper from you. You will show the man your most gracious manners."

No, I would not. "I will avoid him, and if I cannot avoid him, I will offer him civilities when others are on hand. I do not intend to encounter him when I am without company, but if I do, he will receive—and deserve—the cut direct. You have bungled this, my lord."

Derwent sighed. He glanced about as if entreating the heavenly hosts to imbue him with even more patience than he'd already shown me.

I wanted to kick the old reprobate. In future, I would ask Lady Ellersby to send me a copy of the guest list before agreeing to join any social occasion at Derwent Hall. No woman should have to take such precautions when visiting her girlhood home, but Papa looked as if he truly had no idea why I was upset.

"Had you agreed to serve as my hostess," Papa said, "then you might have spared yourself the ordeal of being polite to a neighbor. But no, you would rather hare off to Scotland, up to Cumbria, over to Kent. You'll be nipping down to Paris next, but one hopes at some point you will take pity on St. Sevier, Violet. He, too, has the look of a man with courting on his mind."

Papa had neatly sidestepped the fact of his faux pas where Bascomb was concerned, cast me in the role of a rude girl, scolded me for refusing to indenture myself to Derwent Hall as a political hostess, and sailed right on to criticizing my behavior with a man who was a profoundly attentive escort.

"If Bascomb even looks like he's thinking about comporting himself toward me like a suitor, I will geld him."

"Now you threaten violence, in the manner of a hysterical bedlamite. Truly, Violet, I worry for your nerves."

Worry for Bascomb's manhood. "I do not threaten. I promise. Keep Bascomb away from me."

A young man had emerged from the carriage house and stood watching this exchange between the earl and me. He was little more than a boy, blond and sturdily built. Something about the way he held himself was vaguely familiar, but I did not recognize him.

Nor, given the distance, could he have heard us. His presence was a reminder to me that the Hall was full of guests, and guests had servants, and servants had ears and eyes. Fortunately, I had no more to say to my father on the topic of John Bascomb.

"I will see you at supper, Papa. I've met your grandson. He's a fine, darling little boy."

Papa smiled. "They are all fine and darling at that age. Then they begin climbing about, jabbering, and leaving jam stains on half of creation. Marry your Frenchman, and you, too, can present me with fine, darling babies."

He kissed my cheek, as much apology as I was ever likely to have from his lordship, and sauntered on his way.

CHAPTER FOUR

I had brought my mother's diary with me on this visit, and true to my habit, I dipped into it to find the entries that coincided with the time of year of my reading. As luck would have it, Mama had organized a midsummer house party the year before I had been born.

She had faced multiple conundrums, given the guests' various flirtations, jealousies, and past affairs. Papa had decreed the guest list without consulting her, and the potential for petty dramas had challenged Mama exceedingly.

And Sylvanus is proud of himself because the numbers match, Mama had written. *I despair of that man.*

She had despaired of him lovingly on occasion, but the more familiar I became with her journal, the more her frustration shaded closer to anger. Papa had often spent months in London without her, leaving Mama at home with four young boys to raise, endless streams of neighbors to entertain, and a staff to manage.

Her problem, I surmised, had been loneliness. Many wives dealt with the challenges of parenting, housekeeping, and socializing, but for much of the year, Mama had faced those challenges alone. Then Papa would come home, upsetting established routines, countermanding Mama's orders, and expecting to be obeyed in all things by a woman who'd managed his estate and household for him without benefit of a salary.

Her words put me in a contemplative mood. If wives were lonely, and widows were lonely, and young girls were frequently made to feel left out and useless, what did a woman's sojourn on earth amount to?

Lucy interrupted my musings to inform me that the hour had arrived to dress for dinner. The meal would again be informal—thank the merciful powers—as one guest had yet to arrive, and the numbers could not yet be exactly balanced.

"Up, half up, or half down?" Lucy asked when I was seated on the vanity stool and facing my reflection in the folding mirror. She began removing pins from my hair, her touch brisk.

"Up. A simple coronet. How is Mr. Upjohn?"

Lucy didn't smile so much as she took on a glow. "Glad to be away from London. Says the pomp and pageantry in Mayfair put the military to shame, and for what? So young ladies can wear a dress once, and young gents can drink themselves blind while their elders gamble by the hour and make matches doomed to misery. You're sure you want a coronet?"

Mayfair in a nutshell, though Upjohn had neglected to bemoan the occasional duel. "I am certain." Two braids neatly entwined about the head was my preferred style. "I am not out to impress anybody, and a coronet is comfortable."

"Very well, my lady."

An entire sermon lay in Lucy's capitulation, about widows letting themselves go to pot, the honor of the houses of Deerfield and Belmaine, standards, and who knew what else.

"St. Sevier doesn't care how fashionable I am."

Lucy unbraided my hair and used the brush in long, smooth strokes. "Monsieur's devotion is obvious, but when he walks into the room, and all the ladies remark his fine dark eyes and think how delicious it would be to run their fingers through that thick chestnut hair,

aren't you a little pleased that such a striking fellow has chosen to
turn his fine dark eyes on you?"

Being lectured, or perhaps having my hair brushed, had a
soporific effect, for my eyes grew heavy, and a nap before supper
abruptly loomed as an utter necessity.

"I am very pleased to have St. Sevier's notice. What has that to do
with wasting an hour on a hairstyle that will threaten to come down
halfway through the main course?"

"My creations do not threaten to come down, though they might
appear artfully relaxed. Are you going to sleep on me, my lady?"

"Resting my eyes. Travel upsets my sleep." Though I had gone to
bed early the previous night.

"You delight to think that Monsieur's devotion has settled on
you," Lucy said, using a comb to part my hair down the center from
brow to nape. "You are proud to claim him as your own. Why not
turn a few heads yourself, make him proud to claim you as his own?"

"Lucy..." She touched on a more sensitive topic than she knew. "I
have no use for making anybody jealous. Monsieur either cares for
me as I am, or he can flatter somebody else with his notice."

Lucy fell silent, the most effective scold of all, and I deserved it. I
would be devastated if Hugh St. Sevier's devotion attached itself elsewhere, and my dithering over becoming engaged to him was
cowardly of me.

Hugh loved me, I loved him. We thrived in each other's company,
and while we were undoubtedly physically attracted, I also respected
him tremendously, as I'd not been able to respect my father or
husband. More than Hugh's fine dark eyes and silky chestnut hair, I
treasured him for his honor.

Also for his learning, for choosing a calling that aimed at the
betterment of all, for his patience with me, and his humor.

"Half up," I said, "but please not too many pins. If I have to leave
the company to see to my hair, that's less time spent at the table."

"You are awful," Lucy muttered, clearly pleased with my relent-
ing. A quarter hour later, she'd fashioned a coronet with one braid

and styled the rest of my hair so a thick lock cascaded over my shoulder.

"I'm overdue for a trim." For a time, early in mourning, my hair had seemed to stop growing altogether. My body had reacted to grief in other odd ways. I had been too hot, then too cold, unable to sleep despite crushing fatigue, and alternately ravenous and without appetite. I'd stopped driving my gig because my concentration on London's crowded streets had been wanting.

Or that was the reason I had given myself at the time. I'd had no similarly handy excuse for when I'd ceased even walking in my own garden.

"You've spent little time in Town this year," Lucy said. "The fresh air and sunshine agree with you, or perhaps your traveling companion agrees with you."

"Enough, Lucy. I'll want a fichu." The image of John Bascomb on the terrace came to me, smiling genially at his fellows. "Silk, please, not lace. *And* a shawl."

Lucy, having won the battle of the coiffure, graciously complied with my request so that by the time I'd tucked a length of silk into my bodice, donned evening gloves, and chosen a peacock blue silk shawl to wear as a wrap, I felt reasonably well armored against leering squires.

Which, in my father's house, I should never have had to be. I left the guest wing prepared to deliver set-downs to the left and cuts direct to the right. My forward march was halted when I encountered a young girl on the stairs.

"You must be Lady Violet," she said, eyeing my ensemble. "That is a very pretty shawl, and you aren't wearing it as a shawl."

She was twelve, give or take a year. The age was obvious not because she continually tugged her skirts down, nor because of her elfin features and unguarded curiosity. I knew her age because this girl was reaching for the first glimmers of self-possession, pleased with herself for having recognized me, but not yet self-conscious enough to curb every word, thought, and gesture for fear of offending.

I had no wish to tarry with her on the steps, but neither did I hold with treating children as intrusions on the adult world. When the nurserymaids, governess, or footmen caught up with this prodigal, she would be castigated aplenty.

"I am Lady Violet," I said, curtseying. "Who might you be?"

"I am Evelyn Anderson." A coltish curtsey followed. "Mama said you are quietly pretty, and I should watch how you comport yourself. I am not quietly anything. I am a disgrace and almost as chattery as Lady Jersey. I wanted to see the portraits of the previous earls."

The stairwell boasted a number of portraits of Deerfield ancestors, and Evelyn did appear to be interested in them. Lady Jersey, famously and ironically nicknamed Silence, was a patroness at Almack's. For all her tendency to jabber, she was a very powerful woman.

"Someday, Evelyn, you might wield as much influence as her ladyship, and then people will call you an excellent conversationalist. Had I known you were among the guests, I would have invited you to picnic with my nieces and me this morning."

The girl took another visual inventory of the deceased earls of Derwent, then skipped past me onto the landing and ascended the next flight of steps two at a time.

"Sylvie and Bella are to join me in the nursery starting tomorrow. They are very nice, but they are *little* girls."

And *little* girls were clearly the most tiresome company imaginable. My limited patience evaporated on that thought, for though I could sympathize with Evelyn's situation—neither adolescent nor little girl, far from adulthood, and no longer content in the nursery—I sympathized with Sylvie and Bella more.

"Shouldn't you be in the nursery?"

Evelyn offered a sigh vast enough to shake the walls. "I am always in the nursery. Morning to night, unless I'm allowed to read in the garden. Mama says I must learn to comport myself like a lady, but ladies have boring lives. I want to be..."

How oblivious she was to the insult she did me and all of lady-dom. "Yes?"

"I want to be a sea captain, but the only women to be sea captains are pirates, and pirates are hanged if they don't walk the plank."

"Being a lady has many advantages over being a sea captain," I said. "You will never have to subsist on weevily biscuits and grog. You can bathe as often as you like without fretting over low stores of fresh water. You will not be taken captive by Barbary rogues or die in the briny deep off the Cape of Good Hope. You will not die of scurvy."

But you might well die in your own bed after being delivered of your husband's sixth child.

She studied the chandelier hanging over the stairwell, as if mentally counting the candles. Six-hour candles they were, too, for Papa did not skimp on his hospitality, much to Lord Ellersby's despair.

"What's grog?"

"A vile concoction of watered rum. To the nursery with you, child."

Had I been in a kinder frame of mind, I would have referred to her as Miss Anderson. Even *Miss Evelyn* would have shown a touch of respect, but I had shaken a figurative finger in her wayward face by calling her *child*. Better that she return on her own initiative than after the staff had troubled to look for her.

"Good evening, my lady." She heaved another gusty sigh and scampered up the next flight of stairs, her footsteps fading in a rapid tattoo.

She would walk many planks in the years to come, and her dreams and much of her curiosity could well end up in Davy Jones's locker. Her mother took an interest in her, though, and she had a mother on hand, if not a father, to ease the transition to adulthood.

I continued down to the guest parlor, though my encounter with Evelyn stayed with me. Something about the girl was familiar, and not simply because I had made her mother's acquaintance. Lady

Eutheria was blond, while Evelyn was a dark-haired sprite, but both mother and daughter were slender and quick-mannered.

As I paused outside the parlor door, marshaling what passed for my gracious reserve—Freddie's term—it struck me that Evelyn's mannerisms were what I pondered. Something about that girl's martyred sighs and her habit of glancing about in the midst of a conversation put me very much in mind of my father.

My father, who had owed the widowed Lady Eutheria his favorable notice and considered her ladyship an old friend.

Gathering my gracious reserve took rather longer than usual, and when Sebastian MacHeath came along in all his lordly, kilted splendor, I was still in the corridor outside the guest parlor, feeling neither gracious nor reserved.

"You are wearing your Violet-is-vexed expression," Sebastian observed, peering down at me. "Has your handsome Frenchman transgressed?"

I wanted to stick my tongue out at him. Instead, I adjusted my shawl. "St. Sevier is all that is charming and would never be so rude as to insult a lady's expression."

Sebastian was both quite tall and quite muscular. He made an impressive figure, particularly when attired in a kilt. He also had a quality of implacability, of folding his arms as castles raised their drawbridges. His lordly glower was a two-ton portcullis slammed down in the face of an enemy charge, and his chilly reserve was a deep, dark moat of reproof.

He treated me to his Highland fortress scowl. "What's amiss, Violet? If you charge into the guest parlor glaring daggers at the assemblage, speculation will start. Even considering your talent for stirring up trouble, it's early in the gathering for such drama."

"I have solved a few passing problems—with your aid, I might add. For the people who created the difficulties in the first place, that can result in trouble. I am at present annoyed with my father."

Sebastian offered his arm, and I took it. He was right. I was in no fit state to make small talk about the hay crop or the vicar's oldest boy going off to sea. I should have stolen a nap. I should have pleaded dyspepsia. I should have known returning to Derwent Hall was ill-advised.

Sebastian escorted me down the corridor to the music room. The fires had been lit in anticipation of the evening ending with the folding doors pushed back to allow the second guest parlor and music room to serve as one social space.

The candles had not been lit, though, and thus the various stringed instruments hanging against the wall, the great harp beneath its cover, and the closed pianoforte gave the room a haunted quality. Memories of endless hours of practice ghosted about the parlor, as did a faint recollection of playing a simple duet with my mother.

"I am homesick," I said as Sebastian closed the door behind us. "I am home, and I am homesick. How is that possible?"

He made no move to light the candles, thrifty Scot that he was. "One can long for a bygone time or for departed company even when home, Violet."

"I miss my mother." Not a sentiment I could have articulated even five minutes previously. "Coming to Derwent Hall, reading her diary, seeing that her influence on the house is fading... I miss her. We have portraits of every baron and earl ever to curry the favor of a monarch, but of my mother, we have only a few miniatures and a likeness in my father's sitting room. Why is that? Was the mother of four boys too busy to sit for a portrait?"

Sebastian took a seat on the piano bench, making that delicate article creak. "She was your mother too."

"Not for nearly long enough."

Somebody hurried past the closed door. A guest late for dinner, perhaps. The earl's staff would rush only in the event of a dire emergency.

"Heartache is the very devil," Sebastian said as I took the place beside him. "I was sent far from home at too young an age. I was new to England when my aunt Morag died, and she was closer to me than my own mother. For the first year of my banishment, I lived for my sister Clementine's letters, but then she was sent to school in Edinburgh, and I had only my parents' letters from home. They tried not to encourage my homesickness, but their parsimony with details and events only made me miss Perthshire more."

"What did you do?" He'd been such a quiet young fellow that first summer. I'd come upon him reading by the river and had barely been able to understand him, so thick had his burr been.

"I enlisted the aid of my other aunties. Aunt Maighread and Aunt Hibernia took up their pens, and even Uncle Archie deigned to write occasionally, mostly to brag of his fishing exploits, but it helped. I stayed connected long enough to weather the worst of the grief, and they all assured me that one day, I could come home. That home would wait for me, as would they."

I leaned against him, grateful for his solid bulk. Sebastian had been a slender, reserved youth when he'd gone off to war. He'd come home a formidable warrior, and yet, he had compassion for the boy he'd been.

"I want my mama." I rested my forehead against Sebastian's shoulder, knowing I could not have made that confession to another living soul, not sure why I'd confided in him. "I suspect Papa has invited Lady Eutheria here because she is an old flame, and her daughter is my half-sister."

Saying it made the reality worse, particularly when I recalled her ladyship leaving the fishing cottage on Mr. Botham's arm.

"Derwent has ever enjoyed the ladies, Violet. We know this. He's a widower and not given to self-denial."

Derwent was *still* enjoying the ladies. My father's personal correspondence had come under scrutiny on the occasion of Felix and Katie's wedding, and we'd found the earl to be exchanging *billets-*

doux with no less than three women at the same time, one of them not much older than I.

"You are tolerant of his foibles," I said, "considering you hold the earl in contempt."

"I don't have to respect a man to speak honestly of him, nor do I consider it a good use of my energies to carry old grudges against him."

"You need not bother. I can carry enough grudges against Papa for both of us."

Sebastian held his peace, a testament to his generally sensible nature. When I'd left the schoolroom all those years ago, Sebastian had approached Papa to seek permission to court me. Papa had laughed Sebastian to scorn, implying that my response to Sebastian's addresses would be yet worse derision. I had, in fact, had no notion that my friend had made those overtures and only learned of them after completing my mourning period.

Having dashed Sebastian's marital hopes, my father purchased Sebastian an officer's commission and sent him away to war, admonishing him to look after my brother Felix while battling the French. Problem solved.

For Papa.

"Please don't carry any grudges on my behalf," Sebastian said. "Derwent was trying to protect you, and my uncle had remarried a much younger woman. I had gone from a marquess's heir apparent to a poor relation, and I had no business asking to court you."

"Derwent was trying to get his hands on a water meadow, but he might have at least confessed—"

Another set of rapid footsteps passed the door.

"Let it go, Violet," Sebastian said, bumping my shoulder gently with his own. "Let it go, and be happy. That is the best possible revenge on the meddling old rogue."

"Are you happy?"

He rose and offered me his hand. "I am in good health, I am

wealthy beyond what most can imagine, my country is at peace, and I am in the company of a lovely woman. How could I not be happy?"

When had he learned to turn flattery into a scold?

I took his hand and got to my feet. "You are right. I am too easily vexed. Please escort me to the guest parlor, and I will spread sweetness and light in every direction." Meaning upon Papa's cronies, old flames, new flames, and fellow rogues.

Sebastian patted my hand. "If you simply refrain from hurling verbal thunderbolts—"

The door opened, and my brother Hector took three steps into the music room. "Is she in here?"

"I beg your pardon?"

"The girl Evelyn. Lady Eutheria's sprat. Is she in here? Damned chit has gone missing, and Lady Eutheria is threatening hysterics. Ajax bet me that you put the girl up to this, and Derwent has set the guests to searching."

"Evelyn can't have gone missing," I said. "I saw her on the stairs not a quarter hour past. I sent her back to the nursery."

Hector, who was not my favorite brother, glanced from me to Sebastian. "You two have been hiding in here for the past quarter hour?"

"Having a pleasant conversation." I headed for the door. "How is the search organized?"

Hector stepped back rather than impede my progress. "It's not. We're to look in our quarters, and Ajax and I were tasked with searching the public rooms."

"Hector, when we played hide-and-seek, did we hide in the public rooms?"

He glanced behind me into the gloom of the music room. "Not once we grew too big to hide in cupboards. The attics and cellars were your preferred haunts. Please don't suggest we search there until after I've had some supper, Violet. I'm damned hungry."

"And if Evelyn has fallen out a window? Taken a tumble on the attic stairs? Dashed out her brains on the hearth of some darkened parlor because she thought she heard a ghost when it was only conversation traveling up an open flue?"

Many a time, I'd caught my brothers eavesdropping through unused fireplaces.

Hector had the grace to look chagrined. "If you saw her a quarter of an hour ago, she cannot have gone far. You might want to tell her mama that."

Sebastian joined us in the corridor and pulled the music room door closed behind him. "The child is not in the music room. Where is Lady Eutheria?"

"In the guest parlor," Hector said. "Derwent is with her."

"I will search Derwent's office," Sebastian said. "Hector, you'd best take a look on the library mezzanine. I know at least one young lady who used to fall asleep reading up there."

Good idea, but if I had suggested it, Hector would have dithered and complained. Instead, he marched out smartly in the direction of the library.

"Where did you see her?" Sebastian asked.

"On the stairs nearest the guest wing. She was going up…"

An idea tickled the back of my mind. Lady Eutheria had been a frequent guest at the Hall when her husband had been alive. She knew the house well and had maybe even mentioned some of its more interesting features to her curious young daughter.

"Come along." I turned my steps in the direction of the staircase. "I know one place we ought to look."

Before we reached the steps, we came upon St. Sevier. "My lady, my lord." He bowed to each of us. "The company is in something of an uproar over Lady Eutheria's missing daughter. I considered that Violet, having been a girl herself in this monstrosity of a dwelling, might be best positioned to tell us where to look first."

And *that* was why I loved Hugh St. Sevier. "You considered correctly. Come with us. I want to search one place in particular before we turn the attics and lumber rooms upside down."

St. Sevier took a lamp from the nearest sconce and accompanied us up to the blue parlor, a space that hadn't been much used since my mother's time. The room was pretty in the ornate, rococo style of the last century, and no fires or candles illuminated it.

The advantage of this parlor to children was that it was directly above the largest guest parlor and thus a fine listening post for eaves-dropping on the elders. The room held another, more sinister feature too.

"Bring the light here." I ran my hand beneath the mantel until my fingers found the mechanism I sought. I flipped a latch that needed oiling. Sebastian, who well knew the room's secrets, took hold of an unlit sconce and swung back a bookcase built into a panel of the wall.

"Found her," Sebastian said, stepping into the unlit recess behind the bookcase. "Evelyn, are ye well?"

She had curled into a ball in the corner and was shivering, despite the mild temperature of the summer evening. Sebastian helped her to her feet while St. Sevier held the lantern high enough to illuminate whitewashed stone walls and one very pale little girl.

"Your mother will be relieved to know you are unharmed," I said, wrapping my shawl around Evelyn's boney little shoulders. "You *are* unharmed?"

Evelyn nodded as St. Sevier passed her a handkerchief. She looked at him, then at Sebastian, then at me.

"What is it, child?" St. Sevier asked. "Half the household is looking for you, but if you apologize very sweetly for hiding, a missed supper might be the extent of the punishment."

"Punishment?" Evelyn's pointy little chin came up. "I did not hide, sir. I came in here on the way to the nursery, true, but I was pushed into that priest hole, and then whoever pushed me, closed me up in there."

That defiant chin began to quiver, so I wrapped the girl in a hug. "Evelyn, I was once trapped in that same priest hole, and by the time the housekeeper came upon me, I was too upset to speak. You have been very brave, but I must ask more courage of you now."

She clung to me, her skinny arms lashed around my waist, her face mashed to my chest. "Did you think you were going to die?"

"I knew my life was over." After eighteen hours, the only reason I'd been found was because a housecat had kept sniffing and pawing at the bookcase. "But you are safe. We will bring your mama to you here, but you must refrain from saying anything about being pushed into the priest hole. If we're to find out who did this, they must not know what you saw or heard."

"I'll fetch Lady Eutheria," Sebastian said. "And yes, Violet, I'll do so discreetly."

He slipped out the door, leaving me with St. Sevier and one very upset child. I wanted to tell Sebastian to fetch Lady Eutheria *slowly*, for I had questions to put to Evelyn before her memory became clouded by time.

Or by a mother determined to alter those memories into a less terrifying version of events.

"What happened?" I asked, smoothing Evelyn's hair back from her brow. "Please tell us, as best you can recall."

I shepherded Evelyn to a sofa and took the place beside her while St. Sevier pretended to examine the priest hole, the bookcase, and the latch under the mantel.

"Mama told me about this parlor, about how it's the best place to listen in on the guests. I was leaning against the mantel when I came upon the little switch thing set into the wood. I pressed it, and the bookcase clicked away from the wall about half an inch."

"And you were curious?"

"Yes, but I only had the light from the corridor to see by. I dragged the bookcase back and couldn't make out what lay on the other side. That's when somebody shoved me into that stone closet and pushed the bookcase closed behind me."

"Did you hear footsteps before you were shoved?"

"Only one or two. I noticed the light change behind me, but thought that was simply somebody passing by in the corridor."

St. Sevier was listening to this recitation while leaning against the mantel. "Tell us, Evelyn, did you smell anything?"

"Smell anything?" She scrubbed at her cheeks with his handkerchief. "The fireplace smells like coal. You are French."

"And you have a good ear," he said, smiling. "I am Monsieur Hugh St. Sevier, a friend of Lady Violet's, at your service. Did you smell anything other than coal? Lemons, for example, roses, cedar, pine, cigars, horses... anything?"

I heard my father's voice in the corridor, his tone the forced good cheer of a host soothing an upset guest.

Evelyn's brows knit while she studied St. Sevier. "I might have—"

"Evelyn, you naughty girl!" Lady Eutheria burst into the parlor. "How could you do this? We talked about decorum before I allowed you to accompany me here, about what is expected of young ladies, and the deportment they must at all times—"

"Ma'am." I touched Lady Eutheria's arm as Evelyn shrank against me. "Your daughter was the victim of a nasty prank. On her way to the nursery, she detoured in here to admire the old-fashioned appointments of the room and inadvertently tripped the latch that opens the panel. Somebody else came along and pushed her into the priest hole. You must not scold the child for being the victim of a very mean joke."

"Pushed her?" Lady Eutheria's expression underwent a series of shifts, from indignant, to disbelieving, to worried. "Sylvanus, what is Lady Violet saying?"

"I have no idea," Papa muttered, taking Lady Eutheria's hand, "but it sounds as if we have a mishap on our hands or a footman in need of sacking rather than a wayward child. Come, girl." Papa waggled his fingers at Evelyn. "We'll see you up to the nursery, where you will stay, and then we will have no more excitement for the duration of this gathering."

He sent me an unreadable look, and once again, I wanted to stick my tongue out at a grown man.

"Evelyn," St. Sevier said as mother, daughter, and earl headed toward the door. "About my question?"

Evelyn shook her hand free of her mother's. "Starch, Monsieur. I smelled starch, and whoever it was muttered that I was a beast, which is not true." Her mother all but whisked her out the door, with Derwent bringing up the rear.

I patted the place beside me. "Sit with me, St. Sevier. We must make a list."

St. Sevier stayed right by the mantel. "We must join the other guests and assist Lady Ellersby to restore order and calm."

"First, we make a list. You were in the guest parlor downstairs. Who was there with you for the fifteen minutes before Evelyn was noted to be missing?"

St. Sevier's ambled away from the mantel, took the place beside me, and sighed. "Every male guest is wearing a starched neckcloth, Violet, as are the footmen. The maids wear starched aprons and caps."

"So let's eliminate as many possibilities as we can as soon as we can."

He rubbed his forehead with his fingers. "This was a prank, as you said."

He'd never been shut up in that vile, frigid hole, never known the terror of absolute darkness closing around him hour after hour, never held his bladder until he couldn't any longer.

"Give me the names, St. Sevier, and please give them to me now."

CHAPTER FIVE

"To the extent possible, you will please keep Mr. Bascomb away from me." I wanted to pace and shout, but because I addressed Annabelle, Lady Ellersby, my hostess and sister-in-law, I kept my seat and spoke calmly. Then too, this was not the topic I had intended to discuss when I'd made my way to the dower house that morning.

Her ladyship was in some ways a perfect foil for my brother Mitchell, both of them being serious, conscientious, and dull company. And yet, two dull people had somehow managed to argue their way to a marital stalemate.

"Has Mr. Bascomb given offense?" Annabelle worked at her embroidery, creating a fantastic border of foliage, birds, and flowers, embellishing maroon satin with brilliant jewel tones.

"His transgressions occurred years ago, but he never apologized or acknowledged the wrong."

Annabelle took another measured stitch. "Do I sense, Violet, that even if the gentleman had professed abject remorse, you would still dislike him?"

Annabelle was the classic English beauty—willowy, blond, blue-eyed, and quiet. She hadn't always been so aloof, but the passing years had added to her dignity while subtracting from her warmth.

"I would loathe him. That Papa invited him appalls me, and I've already said as much to the earl."

Annabelle's needle paused. "And how did his lordship respond?"

"He informed me that I am ridiculous, addled, the next thing to a bedlamite."

The needlework resumed. "Derwent uses the same ammunition on Ellersby. Shows a want of imagination to reuse insults, or perhaps the diminution of powers that can come with advancing age."

She stitched away at her gorgeous creation, the epitome of domestic serenity, and yet, she had just offered Papa—albeit remotely—precisely the set-down he deserved.

"I wish I had thought to say something along those lines. I changed the subject."

Annabelle's smile was slight. "One learns to change the subject frequently with Derwent, or to look attentive and nod periodically while mentally laying out next year's flower beds."

I took a visual inventory of Annabelle's private parlor, which held framed specimens of elaborately stitched samplers, intricate cutwork, and a few oil portraits of cats—smug, fluffy, arrogant felines occupying velvet pillows and satin coverlets.

The samplers were so elaborately bordered and decorated that the verses thereon were obscured by impressive needlework.

For a just man falleth seven times, and riseth up again: but the wicked shall fall into mischief.

An odd choice, though beautifully rendered. Hanging next to it was a more familiar excerpt from Proverbs. *She is more precious than rubies: and all the things thou canst desire are not to be compared unto her.*

"You are a fraud, my lady. You comport yourself like a prim and dutiful wife while harboring a wit worthy of Byron's satires." And an artist's eye for color and composition, in oils, no less, which young ladies were seldom taught how to use. I decided to take an informal tour of the rest of the dower house to inspect what Annabelle had done with a dwelling more neglected than treasured.

"I am a prim and dutiful wife. I don't suppose you will tell me what Bascomb did to earn your ire?"

I had never told a soul, and I lacked the courage to start with my sister-in-law. "I would rather not."

Annabelle tied off her thread and snipped it free. "You might think that 'prim and dutiful' means I never speak to my husband other than to ask him to pass the salt. Ellersby and I are not so far gone as all that—not yet. If Bascomb is a social liability, I will warn Ellersby accordingly, just as Ellersby suggested to me privately that Lady Eutheria should have a bedroom in the family wing. His lordship and I are out of charity with each other, but we are not enemies."

Never in my wildest imaginings could I have anticipated such candor from Annabelle. "I'm sorry. I know Mitchell can be difficult, but I'm sorry." What else was there to say?

Annabelle tucked her embroidery into a workbasket. "So am I. I tell myself that Ellersby lacked a good example of how to be a father and husband, and I know we were not a love match, but I did think I had his esteem."

"I'm sure you do." How did I know that, though? Freddie had been an attentive and doting husband to appearances, but he'd also been profligately self-indulgent and had, in fact, died in the company of his mistress. One of his mistresses, rather.

"I envy you," Annabelle said. "I envy you the ability to verbally send Derwent to Coventry. I ought not to admit that, but I am apparently to transgress all manner of rules of propriety today. A gathering to christen the next Derwent heir has both Ellersby and me at less than our best. You will please ignore me, and I will do what I can to see that you are not subjected to Mr. Bascomb's company."

"Thank you." My relief was inordinate. "If it's any consolation, I envy you too. You have two gorgeous and delightful daughters, Ellersby clearly loves them, and you manage not one but two households without ever losing your composure. Papa implied that I should become his hostess, and were you not here..."

Annabelle stood and went to the window, raising the sash enough to let in a breeze scented with honeysuckle.

"I don't want to be here," she said. "Derwent takes Ellersby for granted, ordering him about like a glorified land steward, then dragging him off to Town for months at a time to deal with all the parliamentary whatnot. I tried going up to Town with them, but I missed the girls, and the girls missed me, and to be truthful, I saw almost nothing of Ellersby unless I presided over one of Derwent's command performances..."

She stood at the window, gazing out on a garden approaching its summer glory. The dower house had a much smaller back garden, but Annabelle had taken great care with it, such that each walkway was awash in color and scent, unlike the formal parterres at Derwent Hall itself.

For years, she'd managed the myriad social obligations of an earl's household—Papa did enjoy rural entertaining—and very likely kept an eye on estate matters when the earl went larking about in the Lords.

"My mother would have liked you," I said. "She would have understood your frustrations."

Annabelle faced me, her smile wan. "I have the sense that you understand them too, my lady."

"Certainly not all of them, but Freddie Belmaine was a less than ideal spouse. I was too hidebound, too... innocent, I suppose, to be the sort of wife he needed." Too naïve.

Annabelle regarded me, and I kept speaking, though I knew she'd learned that trick of building a silence from my brother.

"John Bascomb presumed on my person." Polite words for intimate violence. "Papa gave him permission to court me without informing me of Mr. Bascomb's request. Mr. Bascomb might have believed his overtures were welcome, though I made it plain..."

I had all but pummeled the man, and I should have pummeled him. I hadn't known how at the time. I did now.

"Was it rape, Violet?"

I had never heard that tone of voice from Annabelle. Her question was patient and gentle, as a mother was patient and gentle with upset children.

"Not rape. He got his hand where it didn't belong, under my skirts." Where a lady was damnably vulnerable. "The sight of him makes me bilious." This recitation made me bilious, also furious. I should not have to be civil to such a man, should not have to fear he would sit across from me at breakfast.

"I'm sorry," Annabelle said, her gaze sympathetic. "I am so sorry. Derwent has Bascomb in mind for the magistrate's post, and Bascomb is widowed, so he's frequently called upon to make up the numbers."

"Widowed?"

"He has twin boys. His wife died trying to deliver a daughter. She would have been all of about twenty-one at the time. Because I knew Lady Eutheria was bringing Evelyn, I invited Bascomb to bring the twins, but he declined, which leaves Mr. Botham's son quite without an ally until Pritchard's boy arrives. I tasked my nursery staff with preparing accommodations for Bella and Sylvie at the Hall so Evelyn will have some female company."

I rose and pretended to study the quote about the just man, which as magistrate, Mr. Bascomb would assuredly not be. "Evelyn claims she was pushed into the priest hole, and I believe her."

Annabelle's maternal warmth faded into maternal skepticism. "She's a dramatic child, Violet, and has learned from her mother how to command attention."

Even dramatic children deserved to be safe. "I have been shut up in that priest hole myself, Annabelle. It's very hard to pull the panel closed from the inside. It takes strength and height, by design. Evelyn has neither."

My discussion the previous evening with St. Sevier had been unsatisfying. He had been newly introduced to many of the guests gathered before supper, and memorizing who was present and who was absent hadn't been on his mind at the time.

His impressions had been vague and incomplete. Annabelle, as hostess, would have been keeping a closer watch on who was in attendance, hence my private call upon her.

"Derwent's theory is that a footman played a nasty prank," she said, joining me before the quotes. "I am inclined to agree."

"Why would a footman risk his post to prey on a child?" Why would any adult be that cruel? I had resigned myself to the notion that my own imprisonment had been a fraternal prank that became too serious to own up to, but no other child had been underfoot to treat Evelyn so badly.

Annabelle still looked unconvinced. "We have brought in a lot of extra help for the duration of the house party. Some yeoman's son thought to play a trick at the expense of a hapless girl."

A yeoman's son who knew his father's tenancy was at the earl's sufferance would never mistreat a guest at the Hall like that, or so I hoped.

"Perhaps a footman is to blame, but can you recall who was in the guest parlor for the quarter hour before Evelyn went missing?"

Annabelle gave me a measuring look. "Ellersby is stubborn too. He looks like the consummate gentleman, all decorum and lordly indifference, but once that man makes up his mind, Napoleon's armies charging with fixed bayonets could not change it."

"I am worried for a young girl, Annabelle. It was a cruel and dangerous thing to do."

Annabelle went back to the window, this time opening a drawer in an ornate Queen Anne escritoire. She withdrew a piece of paper and considered it.

"Almost everybody had arrived, save a few stragglers. I noted your absence, of course, as well as..." She gazed off into the distance.

"Concentrate on the men."

"Ajax hadn't made an appearance. One thinks of him and Hector almost as a couple. Derwent was there, of course, as was Monsieur St.

Sevier." She rattled off more names. A few barons and their ladies, the marquess's son, the viscount... I purposely let her ponder rather than convey to her the list St. Sevier had come up with.

"Derwent kept looking at the door and glancing at the clock. I assumed he was concerned for you. St. Sevier held the attention of the wives." She frowned at her list. "Mr. Botham was yet abovestairs, as was Mr. Bascomb. Ellersby had not joined the party, but then, he detests the small talk. Lord Pritchard isn't expected until tomorrow, so I suppose..."

Her recollection was confirming St. Sevier's list to a person: Ajax, Bascomb, Botham, and Ellersby had been the absent gentlemen.

"Thank you," I said, rising. "You've been very helpful." Also very kind.

"You have been helpful as well. The girls are in raptures over their picnic, Violet. You have secured favored-auntie honors, which is no mean accomplishment."

"My mother occasionally picnicked with me." The memory had sprung into my head as Annabelle had spoken. "She said we ladies deserved a respite from the company of rogues."

"I will remember that," Annabelle said. "Are you off to charm Monsieur St. Sevier?"

"He and I are to go for a hack this afternoon. I want to show him the estate's prettier corners while the weather holds fair."

"Of course you do." Her tone was so droll I realized I was being teased, and by Annabelle of all people. "He's quite comely."

"He's quite patient, good-humored, intelligent, and *healthy*. He has asked to pay me his addresses, though I haven't made that known to anybody in the family save you, and I hope you will hold my admission in confidence."

Annabelle put away her list and escorted me from the parlor. "I will, of course, but even I can tell he's smitten. You deserve an honorable man, Violet. A man who delights in your company."

A just man falleth seven times, and riseth up again. "Is there anything I can do, Annabelle?"

"About Ellersby? I think not, but thank you for asking. Marriage is work, sometimes more work than other times, but the rewards are worth the effort." She hugged me as we reached the back terrace, the first time I could recall her embracing me.

"My mother was lonely at Derwent Hall," I said. "She never says it outright in her diary, but she wanted for friends. I'm sorry if I've neglected you, Annabelle, and I promise to do better in future."

Just men were not the only souls charged with rising up after a fall. I was nonetheless horrified to see that my comment had brought tears to Annabelle's eyes.

"I'd like that," she said. "So would Sylvie and Bella. Ellersby has worried for you, too, but he doesn't know how to show it without sounding lordly."

"I know." We shared a smile of immense understanding, and I made my way down the terrace steps, pleased with the call. My mother would have liked Annabelle, that was true, but much to my surprise, I liked her too.

"Annabelle?" I called. "One other thing?"

"Yes?"

"You might want to give orders that the fishing cottage is to be kept locked if extra staff is underfoot. It has its own pantries and cellars, after all, and its privacy can be a temptation."

She wrinkled her nose. "Not a bad idea. I doubt anybody will be doing any fishing. Oh, and, Violet, add Dunkeld to your list. His lordship had yet to join us when Evelyn went missing. I'm sure that's a coincidence, but one wants to be thorough."

"Thank you, and yes, one does." Though not *that* thorough. If there was one man—besides St. Sevier, of course—who would never, ever harm a child, it was Sebastian MacHeath. On that truth, I would stake my life.

～

"Aurora, my love, you look beautiful."

Aging, but as beautiful as an old horse could be. The mare who'd carried me so gallantly from my girlhood to my come out was in good weight and sporting a coat gone snow-white with the passing years. She'd been a dappled gray when we'd first met and as sleek and elegant as any unicorn in a fairy tale.

Her back dipped slightly now, and her eye held both the wisdom and the contour of the equine pensioner.

"No mad gallops, your ladyship," the head lad said. "Herself is sound, but she leads a placid life now."

"No mad gallops." A brisk canter might nonetheless figure on our itinerary, if Aurora was willing. I settled into the saddle from the lady's mounting block and picked up the reins. "Monsieur, at your convenience."

The blond, youthful groom I'd noted earlier led out a big, handsome chestnut gelding for St. Sevier. The boy patted the horse's neck while St. Sevier adjusted the stirrups, and I was once again struck by the sense that I knew the boy from somewhere.

He stepped back as St. Sevier swung aboard.

"Lead on, my lady. I've a mind to put some distance between myself and the other guests this afternoon."

In deference to Aurora's advanced years, we toddled out of the stable yard at a walk, our mounts side by side. The day was gorgeous, if warm, so I began our hack in the shade of the lime alley that arched over Derwent Hall's drive. My objective was the same as St. Sevier's —to elude the other guests for a time and enjoy a pleasant hour with my darling.

We trotted over the wooden bridge at the foot of the drive and onto the lane that led to the estate village.

"What has changed since you were last at Derwent Hall?" St. Sevier asked as I turned Aurora onto the bridle path that ran beside the river.

St. Sevier was asking me to make comparisons between last autumn and now. "You and I have become lovers."

"A very great change for the better, I hope. What has changed about the Hall?"

He could not know how great a change for the better, but I resolved to tell him some fine and courageous day.

"The staff grows older," I observed. "What staff I recognize. Not much else. Papa's goal seems to be maintaining the manor as is rather than making improvements."

"Improvements cost money, as Lord Ellersby had no doubt reminded the earl."

Oh dear. "Mitchell and Papa got to arguing over the port?"

"English gentlemen never argue before company. Suffice it to say, fulminating glances were exchanged. Ajax and Hector seem more restless to me."

Interesting comment, and accurate, now that I thought about it. "They aren't as joined at the hip—or the flask—as they were last year. I suppose Felix setting up his nursery has the middle brothers thinking of their own futures."

I hoped so. A year ago, Papa had been after Felix to stand for a seat in the House of Commons, which would have ensured Felix's misery. Hector struck me as having the requisite cynicism for political office, while Ajax had the charm. To see both brothers elected would take considerable coin and influence, a challenge Papa might relish.

If he could afford the extravagance.

"How are your finances, St. Sevier?"

"Thriving, thank you very much." He rattled off figures from his estates in Berkshire and Kent, a rental property in London, an annuity left him by the aunt who'd raised him, and—oddly—some nominal income from a Scottish property he'd inherited through his late wife.

"Where is this property?"

"Perthshire. Good farming land. Ann's cousins have a tenancy in name, though I intend to leave the land to them so it can revert to family hands. Shall we let the horses stretch their legs?"

Aurora had walked long enough, though my dearest Hugh—who had regaled me with his income to the penny—was dodging when it came to this property in Scotland.

"Let's walk to the next bend in the river. The path widens after that. How did a soldier's widow inherit profitable land?"

St. Sevier adjusted his reins. He settled his hat more firmly on his head. "The Scots and the Irish contributed disproportionately to Britain's enlisted ranks. They joined the militias in droves, and as the war dragged on, many were forced by economic necessity to transfer into the regular army. Once the campaign on the Peninsula got under way, they were the first to see battle."

"And thus the first to die. Ann lost more than a husband, then?"

"A brother, two cousins, and from the cousins, the property came to her, and from her, to me. You are about to ask me why I did not take the time to go see it when we were in Perthshire."

St. Sevier was the most equanimous of souls. His temper was a rare and magnificent, if arctic, display, and yet, my curiosity about this property had turned him testy.

"I ask you a rude question about your finances, which no lady ought ever to ask, and you disclose all to me. Earlier this year, we traveled within the same county as your most distant property, and you didn't bother to look in on the place. When I ask about it, you are abruptly ready for a steeplechase. You are upset, and that concerns me."

"*Je ne suis pas énervé.*"

His French could translate to *I am not annoyed*, and his tone suggested the very opposite. I remained silent, rather than insist on the obvious.

St. Sevier muttered something about *Anglaise têtue.* "Scotland was full of red-haired women who spoke in that particular burr common to the area northwest of Edinburgh. The food, the attitudes, the plaids... I was put much in mind of Ann when we traveled in Perthshire, and that unsettled me."

Stubborn Englishwoman that I was, I did not let the matter drop.

"You and I became lovers in Scotland." Had that unsettled him too? St. Sevier had courted my intimate trust with more patience than anybody had ever shown me previously—and more determination. I suspected even he had been surprised when I'd surrendered to his charms.

"I have no regrets where you are concerned, Violet. None. That you seek to know the details of my financial situation encourages me to hope that I will soon graduate from lover to something more."

"You are much more than a mere lover, St. Sevier. You are also my friend and companion." He was my confidant, which was probably why I kept babbling out my thoughts. "I suspect part of why I dislike London so is that I was Freddie's wife there."

The bridle path widened out into more of a cart track, and now I was ready to gallop halfway to the coast.

"Is there more to say, Violet?"

So much more. "For months after his death, I'd think I heard him coming in the front door. Once or twice, I saw men across the churchyard who I thought were him, but of course, most gentlemen dress alike at services, and Freddie was neither unusually tall nor unusually portly. And then I would not know what to feel. Was I frightened to think he might yet be alive? Hopeful? Resentful?"

I drew Aurora to a halt as the water burbled along peacefully to our right. "Freddie was everywhere and nowhere. I would pass the tobacconist's shop where he'd purchased his pipes and have to argue with myself about whether to stop in to sniff the blend he'd preferred. His clubs, his little love nests, the glovemaker he patronized, Almack's where I first waltzed with him... London was his town, not mine. Never mine."

And still not mine, nor did I want it to be.

"The mind has its own sense of time, of when one season ends and another begins. We will return to London by way of my property in Berkshire, *non*? I will be curious to know what you think of it. My indoor staff is mostly émigrés, so you can practice your French to your heart's content."

St. Sevier offered me a reprieve, acceptance, and understanding. "I'd like that. Shall we have a canter as far as the footbridge?"

The bridge to MacHeath's Ford lay some distance upstream, and the path was deserted. Many a time, Aurora and I had galloped this stretch, often with Sebastian pounding along beside us on his gelding.

"You ladies set the pace," St. Sevier said. "We gentlemen will follow."

Aurora tried. She labored determinedly at the canter, but the sheer glory of a heart-pounding gallop was beyond her. Had she been kept in regular work, the years might not have taken such a toll, but she was a lady's mount, and the grooms had probably made a low priority out of exercising her.

By the time we slowed to the walk at the bridge, she was heaving mightily.

"I have overtaxed my mount," I said, patting her sweaty neck. "We should walk back to the village."

"The heat takes a toll. Let's cross the stream, shall we?"

Felix would certainly not mind that we used his drive to return to the village. The way was shady and winding, and another path long familiar to me. The peace of the afternoon was broken only by the *clip-clop* of our horses' hooves and by Aurora's puffing.

"Do you practice medicine when you are in Berkshire?" I asked, hoping the question would be less fraught than memories of red-haired women in Scotland.

We passed the unused water mill. The stone structure was kept locked now, a place to store extra grain for Felix's herd. The building still had the quality of a fortress, of a structure that would stand for centuries while pretty manor houses fell to ruins.

"When I am in Berkshire," St. Sevier said, "I practice medicine casually if the staff or a neighbor seeks my counsel. I have considered setting up an office in London. The émigrés would consult me, and they understand medicine as the Scots practice it, for that is also the Continental model."

St. Sevier and I had been distantly cordial since shortly after my marriage, but nearly two years ago, I'd renewed my acquaintance with him at a musicale. Another widow had discreetly informed me that he'd call upon me at my residence, if I was in medical difficulties. With Lucy badgering me, I'd sent for him. By then, I had not left my home for two weeks, and Lucy was growing alarmed.

As was I.

St. Sevier had made those calls pleasant for me, mostly social, not the professional inquisitions I'd anticipated. I'd found him skilled not only regarding ailments of the body, but also regarding miseries of the mind. As my anxieties had eased, I'd allowed him to step into the role of escort.

He *should* be practicing medicine, for himself and for all the suffering souls who could benefit from his knowledge.

"What has prevented you from establishing a practice?" I asked. "I saw you with my godson, St. Sevier, and I have numbered among your patients. Medicine is your calling, and you've said you'd particularly like to treat children and mothers."

He stood in the stirrups and settled back into the saddle. Hugh St. Sevier made a picture of masculine pulchritude in his riding attire, and I abruptly wished we'd returned to the manor by way of the wood. But alas and welladay, I was wearing a riding habit. No frolicking for me.

"You do not care for London," he said. "I care for you. Therefore..."

I drew Aurora to a halt. "Don't do that. Don't give up a dream on my account. You would not ask that of me, and I will never ask that of you."

His gelding shuffled to a stop as well. "But if you marry me, Violet, you could well be giving up the dream of having children. I suffered several illnesses at war that could have diminished my functioning. You should know this."

St. Sevier had explained to me that many of the diseases rampant in military camps—measles, mumps, chicken pox, smallpox, and others—could leave a man sterile. No amount of military might had found a way to defeat those foes, and most men marched off to war unaware they risked not only their lives, but also their procreative abilities.

"So why do you withdraw when we are intimate?" My husband had never withdrawn, and when Hugh had first shown me that courtesy, I had been somewhat taken aback.

"Because medicine is an inexact science, Violet, and I would not use a child to entrap you. We know you are perfectly capable of conception, and one does not tempt fate unnecessarily. Then too, withdrawing is not a foolproof precaution."

I urged Aurora forward, glad that St. Sevier and I had had this private outing, though it wasn't the flirtatious interlude I'd hoped for. So much about becoming a couple benefited from frank conversations, and prior to my first marriage, Freddie and I had discussed none of it.

CHAPTER SIX

"I want you to be happy, St. Sevier," I said, as our horses ambled along. "I want you to practice medicine. To treat children and expectant mothers, as you would love to do. If that means dwelling in London, well, I've lived there since I was eighteen. To share a household with you would put a very different and much happier face on matters."

He sent me a patient, measuring look. "You and I have only an understanding, Violet. Unless and until you are my wife, I will not establish a practice in London. I could just as easily ply my profession in Berkshire or Kent or up in Scotland, where the need for physicians is great."

I was reminded of Annabelle's observation that marriage was work. I hadn't understood that as a bride. I had expected to be in love with my spouse and to wake up every day pleased to behold him at the breakfast table.

"We will discuss this again," I said. "If you weren't smitten with me, you'd already have your medical practice."

"If you weren't smitten with me, you'd have left London when your mourning concluded."

"I did leave London. My tyrant of a physician ordered me to attend a house party, then he insisted on escorting me to a wedding... I have been leaving London regularly ever since."

"And you are no longer that retiring, unhappy widow, are you?"

St. Sevier had the knack of confronting me with the truth while avoiding anything like a scold. He teased, he flattered, he commiserated, and somehow, I found the courage to acknowledge what I'd rather avoid.

"I am a woman who has earned and reciprocates the love of a good man, Hugh St. Sevier. I am abundantly happy and looking forward to greater happiness still."

St. Sevier enjoyed a full complement of *amour propre*, but my words had him looking away and resorting once again to French. *Now she tells me,* or words to that effect.

I had not intended to use this outing to declare my feelings, but I should have offered St. Sevier the words sooner. "I do love you, St. Sevier. I know not how or when this ailment befell me, but the case is serious, and I have no interest in a cure. Regular applications of passion, affection, and companionship should keep the condition from abating."

The horses plodded along as we neared the end of the drive, and my heart felt light. I could not give St. Sevier a wedding date—not quite yet—but I could give him my honest sentiments. He and I would somehow forge a good life together, despite London, despite babies or a lack thereof, despite my meddling family and all the losses in our past.

I knew him, loved him, and trusted him in a way I had never trusted my husband. I could, from the perspective of a woman truly cherished by Hugh St. Sevier, feel compassion for the bride I'd been —hopeful and ignorant and then despairing and not as ignorant—and also for Freddie.

He had been just another man who hadn't known what to do with me, poor fellow.

"Is that Ajax?" St. Sevier asked, shading his eyes against the afternoon sun. "That looks like his new gelding."

Brothers. They appeared when unwanted and were least in sight when needed. "Ajax without Hector. Again. Annabelle confirmed your list of absentees from the guest parlor, and she also named Ajax."

"Violet, leave it alone. No harm befell the child. Evelyn won't be listening at chimneys or tarrying in unused parlors for the rest of her visit at Derwent Hall."

"I will have to leave it alone. I'm not in a position to question male guests regarding their whereabouts. Then too the situation did resolve itself quickly." I would not question Bascomb, though I'd have a word with Mr. Botham, if the opportunity presented itself.

Ajax waved to us, and as we drew nearer, he turned his horse to fall in beside Aurora. "I underestimated the heat. Should have taken Perseus out earlier in the day."

Perseus was a handsome bay of about seventeen hands. His coat was matted with sweat, and he, at least, had clearly had a good gallop.

"Walk with us back to the manor," I said. "Aurora needs to cool out." I wanted to ask Ajax where he'd been before dinner the previous evening, but suspected St. Sevier would chide me for it. My own brother had no motive for mistreating a child.

But he did know of the priest hole, which Bascomb and Botham might not.

As we ambled through the village, we drew a few curious glances. The publican's wife offered me a smile and a wave, and I nodded in return. Ajax knew and greeted nearly everybody, while St. Sevier had gone silent.

We had almost reached the bridge at the foot of the Derwent Hall drive when St. Sevier halted his horse. "Deerfield, if you would please see Lady Violet home, I'd like to tarry in the village for a moment."

Maybe St. Sevier was giving me an opportunity to question Ajax after all. "Don't trust the inn's summer ale," I said. "It goes down much too easily on a hot day."

An ornate traveling coach lumbered past us, matched grays in the traces. The coach turned to cross the bridge, creating a prodigious racket of iron-shod hooves against sturdy wooden planks.

"Violet, I will see you at supper." St. Sevier touched his hat brim with his riding crop and guided the horse in a neat pirouette back in the direction of the village.

"Will you put yon Frenchie out of his misery soon?" Ajax asked while he and I waited for the coach's dust to settle.

"None of your business. Has Papa offered to sponsor you for a seat in the Commons?"

Ajax fiddled with his reins. "Hector wants to become a fencing master. He'd be the better politician. He's logical, whereas I just want everybody to be happy."

"You didn't push Evelyn Anderson into the priest hole yesterday, did you?"

Ajax gave me a look brothers had been aiming at sisters since siblings were invented. "No. I was with Papa's valet at the time, arguing over which knot to tie in my cravat. As a future politician, I'm to cultivate understated style, whatever that means."

If Papa had imposed his valet on Ajax, a seat in the Commons could not be far behind. "Tonight's meal will be formal, brother dear, if that was Lord Pritchard's coach. You'll need something fancier than a plain mathematical."

"Pritchard is on the guest list?" Ajax said, urging his horse forward. "Why am I not surprised? He's the consummate perennial everything. Speaks politics with Papa by the hour, accompanies the wallflowers when they grace us with their arias, always in demand as a partner at whist, and the waltz was invented to show off his lordship's grace on the dance floor. Crying children become wreathed in smiles when he passes and doves coo in three-part harmony. St. Sevier's hopes with you are doomed until Pritchard goes smiling and bowing on his way, which cannot happen soon enough for me."

Gracious heavens. "You are jealous."

"I am agog, Violet. Prepare to observe your first mass swoon, for Lord Pritchard has arrived."

Ajax nudged his horse to the trot, while Aurora and I kept to the walk. I had no wish to interfere with the entrance the incomparable Lord Pritchard was making at the Hall.

Far from it.

I regarded napping with wary unease. In mourning, the quiet rhythm that normally anchored my days and weeks had slipped from my grasp. I had slept badly at night, often falling into bed exhausted, only to waken three or four hours later unable to get back to sleep.

Napping, which then loomed as an inescapable necessity in the afternoons, had contributed to more misery after midnight.

I had thus not planned to nap before dinner, though my energies were at low ebb after returning from our ride. I'd slipped in through the conservatory and avoided the commotion Lord Pritchard's arrival had caused. A tepid hip bath had been a divine indulgence, and then I'd curled up with Mama's diary.

And promptly fallen asleep on my balcony, only to waken when Lucy arrived with a tray.

"It's the heat," she said, setting the tray on a low table beside my chair. "Takes the starch right out of a body. Summer hasn't been too bad until now, but the butler says we're in for some hot days."

"Summer is supposed to be hot." Summer in London also boasted an unbelievable stench off the river most years.

Lucy leaned against the railing and fanned herself with a table napkin. "The kitchen is an inferno with all the baking for the fancy meals." She had brought me lemonade, a bowl of cherries, and slices of toast topped with what appeared to be half-melted Stilton.

I was abruptly famished and very grateful that Lucy Hewitt was my maid. "Cook hasn't moved operations to the summer kitchen?"

"Summer kitchen is going nineteen to the dozen, but with all these guests, that's not enough. What are those fools getting up to?"

My balcony faced the shady path that led to the stable. A group of men had assembled beneath the maples, and two of them had their shirts off.

"A fencing exhibition, apparently." Doubtless, maids and female guests all over the house were lingering by windows to enjoy the view. Among the men encircling the combatants, I saw the sort of nods and handshakes that confirmed bets were being placed.

A lot of bets. "Hector is more impressive than I'd imagined." My brother had the sort of ropy, lean muscle that I associated with the athletes at Astley's Amphitheater. He was both limber and strong. I also knew him to have a calculating turn of mind, which meant superior speed or strength alone would not best him.

He and his opponent saluted with their foils, and my gaze fell for the first time on the other man. He was, indeed, a paragon. This fellow had perhaps an inch or two of height on Hector, and Hector was on the tall side himself. Whereas Hector was dark, the opponent was golden-haired, his mane swept back à la Byron.

He could have been the Apollo Belvedere's handsomer older brother made flesh, so perfect were his proportions. His smile when he saluted was at once jocular and arrogant, that of a happy predator, hunting for the joy of the kill rather than to fill an empty belly. My late husband had worn the same sort of smile when he'd maneuvered a business rival close to ruin, and the poor fool had yet to realize his peril.

"Lord Pritchard has arrived," I murmured.

"Aye," Lucy said, crossing her arms as she regarded the spectacle. "The maids were drawing straws to see who'd change his sheets. He's known to be friendly to the help, but then, his kind always are. What will you wear for your first meal with the great man?"

Pritchard was a mere baron, but a highly skilled fencer. Hector showed himself to good advantage as well, drawing his opponent in, then driving him back with lightning flourishes and a relentless arm.

Pritchard battled back, and the spectators called encouragement or taunts depending on whom they'd bet upon.

The spectacle was engrossing, as a nightmare is engrossing, when one wants to waken but cannot. A roar went up from the crowd, and combat ceased as Ajax came forward to wrap white linen around a cut on Hector's arm.

"They haven't tipped their swords," I said, rising and taking up the tray. "I have no wish to see more."

"The arm's not a fair hit, for foils," Lucy said. "Only the trunk counts."

How could she know such a thing? "It's an exhibition, Lucy. Fencing-hall rules might not apply." More than that, my brothers were involved. Who knew the extent of the foolishness they could get up to? "Let's dress with the heat in mind. One of the muslins, jumps rather than stays, and one petticoat."

Lucy left the French door open as she trailed me into the bedroom. "Jumps?"

"I'm a widow. I can place comfort above a perfect shape when the weather is disobliging." My shape fell far short—and wide—of the willowy Grecian ideal. No amount of boning in a corset could change that. Then too, St. Sevier had firm opinions about the ill effects of excessively tight lacings.

So much to love about that man.

While Lucy laid out my clothing, I did justice to the tray, being sure to leave enough that Lucy could enjoy an ample snack herself. When the kitchen was in an uproar, the servants' hall would offer a cold buffet and a barrel of ale, if that.

After the usual arguments concerning my hair, some dithering over the choice of shoes, and a debate about whether my necklace should be a garnet or sapphire drop, Lucy pronounced me fit to join the company for the evening meal. I wasn't ready to go down yet, though.

Let Lord Pritchard make yet another grand entrance, for surely such a specimen in formal attire deserved to hold center stage for at least the first quarter hour.

I made my way to the nursery and found Evelyn, Bella, and Sylvie explaining the finer points of the Battle of Hastings to two boys—one blond and one little fellow with blazing-red hair. Hansom stitched away in a rocking chair while horses, infantrymen, archers, and a stray dragon were moved about on the carpet. Dottie stood by the window, rapt at Sylvie's description of poor doomed Harold Godwinson's misfortunes. Dottie still looked to me like a child playing dress-up, though she was an extra pair of hands, which Hansom would need with this many charges.

"But Harold was *English*," the red-haired boy said. "The English won."

"No, they didn't," Bella retorted. "William the Conqueror conquered the Saxons, and the Saxons were English, so the English lost."

This news apparently upended the younger lad's entire grasp of English history. He stared at the forces deployed on the carpet, his little brows knit in consternation.

"Tell him, Auntie Violet," Bella said. "Tell him William won."

"William won the battle," I said, "but the Saxons had their triumphs too. William tried to impose the French language on us, for example. He lost that battle. He tried to impose French styles as well. Another defeat. At court, the high and mighty toadied to him, but in the shires, he won little more than that single battle. Rather than fight us again, he encouraged intermarriage between Saxons and Normans, and that worked much better than a lot of fighting and bashing of heads."

The children, Hansom, and even Dottie were regarding me with puzzlement. "Ask the Earl of Derwent if you don't believe me," I said, for it was my father's version of history I put forth.

"I will do just that." Lord Pritchard himself stood in the doorway to the corridor. "You would be Lady Violet Belmaine, if I'm not mistaken. I have the honor to be Pritchard, at your service."

He bowed and I curtseyed. Hansom scrambled to her feet—a courtesy she'd not shown me—and Dottie was repeatedly bobbing over by the toy chest as she stared at the battlefield.

"Papa, did Harold lose?" the red-haired boy asked.

Pritchard aimed an apologetic smile at the lad. "Afraid so, Henry."

The boy weathered that blow with manful stoicism. "I want to change my name to William."

"Your second middle name is William," his father said. "We could call you Henry William Manfred Harold Fortnam. Would you like us to use your full name?"

The child shook his head. "Just William."

"You can't just change your name," Evelyn said. "That's *silly*."

"I can change my name if I want to, can't I, Papa?"

I waited to see which way his perfect lordship would lean—toward truth or toward humoring a child's daunted feelings.

"Many people aren't called by the names they are given at birth," Pritchard said. "This gorgeous young lady here is called Bella, but her name is Annabella, after her lovely mother. That young lady,"—he nodded at Dottie, who had ceased bobbing—"is called Dottie, but her given name is Dorothy. I did not name you after the ill-fated Harold Godwinson, Henry."

I was impressed. This was neither cold reason nor needless parental indulgence.

"For whom did you name him?" Evelyn asked.

"Good King Hal, of course. Henry VIII cast off the yoke of Rome and dispelled corruption in the Church. He is considered the father of the English navy and vanquished the Scots in the Battle of Flodden. Henry was an accomplished musician, an excellent horseman, and,"—Pritchard aimed a smile at me—"he was very successful with the ladies. Harold is included among your names as a nod to my dear old grandpapa, who was a very wise fellow indeed."

Apparently, sending two wives to the gallows and setting aside two others did not tarnish a man's reputation for success with the ladies—in Lord Pritchard's opinion.

"Then call me Hal," Henry said. "My name is Hal."

"That's a nickname," Evelyn retorted. "That can be your nickname, but your name is still Henry."

Pritchard picked up his son and hugged him. "Keep us honest, young *Evvie*. We gents benefit from the guiding hand of the ladies. Wish me luck, son."

"Good luck, Papa. Are you riding into battle?"

"In a manner of speaking. I must run the gauntlet of polite society. If I should inadvertently burp at table, my fortunes are doomed."

I had the sense this exchange was not for my benefit, but a genuine expression of paternal affection.

"Papa, what if you fart—"

The little girls went off into peals of giggles while Lord Pritchard put gloved fingers to his son's lips.

"Manners, *Hal*." He put the boy down. "We must moderate our speech in the company of the fairer sex. And speaking of ladies... Lady Violet, may I escort you down to supper? I know we haven't been introduced, but Derwent has sung your praises to me so often that I feel as if I already know you."

That was complete balderdash, of course, but so clearly intended to charm that I could not take much offense.

"You may accompany me down to supper, my lord. Enjoy the battle, children. You might also find it interesting to speculate on why the contest ended as it did. Was Harold's death the deciding factor? William's cavalry and archers? If William had had to wait another week to cross the Channel, and Harold's forces had had more time to recover from the Battle of Stamford Bridge, would the outcome have been different?"

"Harold needed a dragon," Bella said.

Evelyn rolled her eyes. "Dragons are silly."

Sylvie dropped to the carpet and began arranging soldiers behind the dragon. "Not when they're breathing fire, they aren't."

"Hansom, you will not permit any insurrections at bedtime," Lord Pritchard said. "Dottie, I bid you good evening." He offered me his arm, and we were soon in the shadowed corridor, making our way to a battlefield of another sort.

"Neatly done," I said, "to bring Good King Hal into the discussion." Also neatly done to make allies of the nursery staff, though he'd likely done that with one charming smile.

"But," his lordship said, "you are about to tell me that King Henry was a despot, a despoiler, and a tyrant."

Not now, I wasn't. "He actually strengthened the role of Parliament at the expense of the nobles, though I would not have wanted to be married to him."

"We will get on famously, Lady Violet, for I'm not too keen on marriage myself. While I esteemed my late wife greatly, and adore my son, I am not keen to stick my boot in parson's mousetrap again. Tell me, what am I to make of Lady Eutheria Anderson? Has she an older daughter to launch, or is her campaign to win my favor on her own behalf?"

I was supposed to find that audacious sally disarming, the confidential overture of an ally amid hostile forces. Pritchard took the time to look in on his son and knew the nursery staff by name. He had a sense of humor, was exceptionally pleasant to look upon, and he was bothering to charm me.

I found him tedious, and what a joy that was.

"You should ask Lady Eutheria herself, for her designs upon you are of no interest to me whatsoever. Her only daughter looks to be barely twelve years old."

Lord Pritchard laughed, and he managed to do even that charmingly. When we reached the guest parlor, I fobbed his lordship off on Sebastian. I put myself at St. Sevier's side and remained there until Lady Ellersby summoned us into dinner.

Where—drat the luck—I found myself seated right beside Lord Pritchard.

CHAPTER SEVEN

Dinner had passed agreeably enough, with Lord Pritchard providing an effortless stream of *on dits*, asides, and quotes from Byron's wittier poems. His lordship had touched my arm twice and the rest of my person not at all.

Not a stupid man, then.

Because I'd had a nap, I had the stamina to endure until the evening ended. Then I was all too grateful to snuggle into St. Sevier's arms. He had made no amatory overtures, and I reasoned that without a nap, the day for him had been long indeed.

I fell asleep, treasuring the increasingly dear comfort of his embrace.

He took himself off for a morning hack shortly after dawn, and I, like a fool, went down to breakfast without an escort. I was famished, else I might have exercised more caution.

John Bascomb was the breakfast parlor's sole occupant. Not even a footman stood by the sideboard. My first impulse was to withdraw and ring for a tray, but the staff was already overtaxed, and I was in my father's house.

Unlike Bascomb, I had done nothing wrong.

"Lady Violet." He rose from the table and bowed. "Good morning."

You have choices, Violet. St. Sevier had begun his efforts to draw me back into the world with that observation. When my spirits had been at their lowest ebb, he'd reminded me that I could choose whether to read by the window or on the terrace. I could choose to forgo a nap, to wander the garden. I could choose not to attend a formal ball for three hundred guests, and if I pleased to, I could choose to enjoy a cup of tea on the terrace with a friend.

I chose to neither charge nor retreat. "Mr. Bascomb." I did not curtsey. My plan was to fill a plate and take it to the conservatory. I opened the sideboard cupboard to retrieve a tray, and Mr. Bascomb came around the table.

I was safe. I knew I was safe, and not five steps from the parlor door, but still my heart sped up and my breath grew short as he approached. I could upend a platter of hot eggs on him, cosh him with a teapot, or simply scream, all of which would cause talk and make me look foolish.

But I was in no physical danger. "Come no closer." I held the tray like a shield over my middle and picked up a fork. As weapons went, a fork was no lethal pike, but it apparently conveyed my ire adequately.

Bascomb glanced at the open door behind me. "You aren't willing to let bygones be bygones."

"I am not willing to let an intimate and unprovoked assault, a betrayal of a very young woman's trust, and a complete abdication of gentlemanly honor be a bygone."

He smiled, and I was reminded that Pritchard was not the only handsome fellow at this gathering. Bascomb was edging toward middle age, but doing so handsomely. His brown hair had yet to sport any gray, he was trim, and he took care with his appearance. He was the country squire with a bit of dash, and more to the point, he was considerably taller and stronger than I was.

"I've been reading up on the law," he said. "Derwent has me in mind for the magistrate's post. Do you truly believe I 'intentionally applied force to the person of another'?"

"I absolutely *know* you did, and unless you keep your distance from me for the duration of this gathering, I will acquaint my father, among others, with the particulars of your misconduct."

He took another step closer. "Violet, it was years ago. Courting foolishness. We're adults now, and I have no wish—"

"*Lady* Violet," I all but snarled at him. Had he apologized, or simply bowed and left me in peace, I would not have been so enraged, but this arrogant cajolery was beyond the pale. "You hurt me intimately, you frightened me, and you abused my trust. Either apologize or leave this house party."

I hadn't planned to make that threat—I was not the hostess and thus had no authority to eject a guest—but I could not stand to look upon the man.

I felt movement behind me, and Bascomb's demeanor underwent a subtle shift. His smile faded, his posture became straighter, and he retreated two steps.

"Ye heard the lady," Sebastian said, his burr quite thick. "Apologize or depart."

"I will happily escort you to the end of the drive, Bascomb," St. Sevier added, coming up on my left. "Assuming there's anything left of you to escort when Violet's brothers finish with you."

A gratifying flicker of fear showed in Bascomb's eyes. "Her brothers?"

"You English are great observers of protocol," St. Sevier said. "Though there *are* four of them, aren't there?"

"Ellersby is the one to take most seriously," Sebastian added. "He had to keep three younger brothers coming at him at once in line. He's devious and determined. His pugilism has *science* to it. Must be some Scot in him from way back."

Bascomb swallowed. He studied the carpet. He tugged down his waistcoat and met my gaze. "Lady Violet, I am sorry to have given offense. You did nothing to provoke my overtures and—"

"Your assault." I willed my words to have the effect of a poker aimed between his legs.

A hint of mulishness came into Bascomb's gaze.

"*Soyez prudent, monsieur,*" St. Sevier said quietly. "English law has many quaint characteristics. For example, no conviction results when the entire case is merely the word of one witness against that of another. You doubtless chose the moment for your crime against her ladyship with that fact in mind. Her brothers, and I daresay I myself, will choose our moments similarly when we discuss the inadequacy of your apology with you."

"I don't have discussion in mind," Sebastian said. "So unless you want to be sent to your knees with the aid of my fists, make a proper job of it and get out of her ladyship's sight."

"My lady." Bascomb bowed. "I am abjectly sorry to have offended you. I was wrong. I have no excuses for my behavior."

He had a million excuses, but he'd done the minimum that honor required. I pointed toward the door. "Don't so much as look at me, Bascomb. Don't gaze upon my hems. Leave the other women here alone, or *I will geld you.*"

"I will provide her ladyship the dullest of knives for the operation," St. Sevier said.

"And I," Sebastian added, "will ensure the blade is filthy and stuff your balls down your throat when she's done with you. *Go.*"

Bascomb left the room at a forced march while I sank onto the nearest chair. "Thank you both. I don't know what I would have done if you hadn't come along. I did not realize he was alone in here, and I should never have..."

"Never have held him accountable?" Sebastian said, pouring me a cup of tea and adding cream and dollop of honey. "On the one hand, you knew Bascomb to be capable of violence, so perhaps provoking him without us on hand was foolish. On the other hand, you knew help was one shout away, Bascomb behaved unforgivably toward you all those years ago, and the matter wanted addressing."

Now that the confrontation had passed, I marveled at my audacity. "I should have waited until others could observe from a distance."

"And then," St. Sevier said, "you would have pulled your verbal punches for fear of causing a scene. Bascomb will behave now, or we shall kill him." He set a plate of toast before me, both slices slathered in butter and jam. Raspberry, my favorite, something Hugh would pay attention to, even as he issued death threats on my behalf, charming fellow that he was.

"I am torn between the urge to cry and the urge to lecture myself about excessive dramatics."

Sebastian filled a plate for himself, and St. Sevier did likewise. They chose seats on either side of me, and some of my upset subsided. I was safe, Bascomb was gone, and he would not presume to approach me ever again.

"If you mean every word, it's not dramatics," Sebastian said. "St. Sevier, could you brew up a purge to slip into Bascomb's morning tea?"

"*Bien sûr*. And I could teach Violet to make the tisane herself. One never knows when a strong purgative will prove useful. Perhaps Violet and I will discuss this as we join the day's hike to the ruins. The teapot, please, Dunkeld. All this justice so early in the day has left me parched."

He and Sebastian chatted about Ajax's horse, the heat, and yesterday's fencing exhibition while I nibbled my toast and gathered up the tattered threads of my composure. St. Sevier's word—*justice*—stuck with me as my nerves gradually settled. On my own, I would not have been capable of holding Bascomb accountable for his assault.

And yet, he had not been sent to prison or publicly flogged, as he deserved to be. His reputation was in such good repair that Papa had him in mind for the magistrate's post, of all the ironies. Had my brothers not started arguing outside the parlor door when Bascomb had treated me so badly, I might have been forced to marry the next thing to a rapist.

My safety mattered, but we had not come close to seeing justice done where Mr. Bascomb was concerned. Not yet.

"I should change into a walking dress if we are to hike to the ruins this morning," I said, rising. "Gentlemen, thank you again for your assistance."

"Two pieces of toast will not sustain you until lunch," St. Sevier replied, bowing over my hand. "I will find the estimable Miss Hewitt and have her procure a snack for us to take along. Dunkeld, thank you for a pleasant outing. Violet, please finish your meal."

He bowed and withdrew, taking a piece of my heart with him. Death threats, raspberry jam, a snack to bring along, nasty tisanes... He was a lovely and formidable man, and I would not find his like if I searched every corner of the realm and all of France.

"You should tell him," Sebastian said, spooning a third of his eggs onto my plate. "If you won't marry him, at least give him the words, Violet."

I sat back down. "I suspect I will marry him." I had not admitted that to anyone else, but Sebastian seemed the appropriate party in whom to repose my confidences.

"But," he said, putting a slice of ham on my plate, "you are enjoying the pursuit, and well you should. Was Bascomb why you fell so easily into Belmaine's arms?"

I thought back to the year of my come out and to the sequence of events as they'd unfolded that spring. Sebastian had left to take up his commission in Spain, and our parting had been awkward for reasons I had not appreciated at the time. Reasons having to do with my father's meddling.

I hadn't known until after Sebastian left how much I'd depended on his friendship, on his terse and insightful letters, and his epistolary lectures and musings. He'd been my closest friend growing up. All I'd known when he'd departed was that he'd been determined to join up without telling me why.

Matters had deteriorated from there. "I accepted Freddie's proposal within a fortnight of Bascomb's assault, and yes, the notion that other suitors might attempt similar liberties did inspire me to get the whole courting ordeal over with."

Sebastian used a triangle of toast to sop up the egg yolk on his plate. "Did Belmaine know of Bascomb's behavior?"

I shook my head. "Nobody knew. I hardly had words to describe what he did, I was so shocked. I did not comprehend his objective until he'd accomplished it."

"Rape?" Sebastian asked, as one might ask to have the salt passed. He and I had always had this ability to discuss anything without artifice or pretense. Even with St. Sevier, I was often inclined to choose my words carefully, and I sensed he showed me a reciprocal courtesy.

"Something close to rape," I said. "With his fingers." Just saying the words brought back all the shock and horror I'd experienced at the time. Bascomb had shoved his wretched damned fingers inside my body while half lying atop me and holding his forearm across my throat. The prospect of rape had frightened me, but the prospect of asphyxiation had terrified me witless.

"And now Bascomb is Derwent's choice for magistrate?"

"Apparently so."

Sebastian finished his breakfast without further comment while I ate eggs and ham I did not taste. I was tempted to beg off from the day's activities, but that would have been cowardly. Besides, Sebastian and St. Sevier would keep an eye on me, and I hadn't been to the ruins in ages.

The walk would do me good, or so I hoped. I finished my food and managed a second cup of tea, though the greater sustenance was from Sebastian's simple company.

"Leave Bascomb to me," Sebastian said when we'd risen from the table. "I'll make an early wedding present of him to you and St. Sevier."

"No violence, Sebastian. Vengeance solves nothing, and St. Sevier and I merely have an understanding."

"You did not spend enough time in the Highlands, my dear. Vengeance, properly carried out, solves much. Change your dress.

I'm donning my kilt and filling my flask, because the ladies do so love to admire my knees."

The image of him in his kilt, pleats swinging with each stride, came to mind. "It's not your knees they're admiring, Dunkeld. Or not exclusively your knees."

"Be off with ye." He kissed my cheek and turned me by the shoulders. "Ye have a Frenchman to torment. I'll see Bascomb dealt with, and he will rue the day, Violet. My promise to ye on that."

Sebastian always kept his promises. On that comforting thought, I went upstairs and changed my dress.

I sought to use the outing to the ruins as a time to simply enjoy the bucolic splendor of my father's estate and to stretch my legs. In London, a lady did not walk if she could avoid it. She used her coach, or she sent servants. If she was older, she might resort to a sedan chair rather than set her foot upon the walkways.

So why, when I had developed an appetite for rambling in the out of doors early in life, had I allowed myself to be confined to the metropolis? I looked forward to seeing St. Sevier's manor in Berkshire, though the fact that his dreams were more easily pursued in an urban setting was not lost on me.

London boasted an abundance of sickly children and expectant mothers, and St. Sevier had no need to extract coin from his patients. He sought to establish a practice mostly for the betterment of the species, for which I admired him.

"Evelyn begged to join us," Lady Eutheria said, coming up on my left. "She was alternately peevish about missing your picnic the other day and dismissive of little girls' tea parties. Perhaps you might consider scheduling another outing?"

Lady Eutheria had enjoyed my father's escort on the way to the ruins. For the walk back to the Hall, the company was less organized and making slower progress. We had partaken of a meal al fresco amid the remains of the ancient Derwent abbey, using the detritus of tumbled granite walls as our chairs and tables.

The more daring among us had climbed the sole tower still standing and admired the view, which in summer was pleasant indeed.

"Evelyn is at a difficult age," I said as Lady Eutheria and I wandered along the river's edge. "When she would love to practice putting up her hair with girls a bit older than she is, she's instead closeted with stuffed bears and toy soldiers."

"And,"—Lady Eutheria lowered her voice—"with a pair of *little boys*." She smiled at me as if small boys were the greatest tribulation a young lady could bear, which—as I had occasion to know—they sometimes were. "Your mother worried that you had no sisters, Lady Violet, but she delighted to have a daughter among her offspring."

Vague memories stirred of Lady Eutheria and Mama taking tea on the terrace while I played with my own toy beasts.

"You and the countess were friends?" Mama had socialized with half the shire, as a lady of the manor was expected to, but her diary had given me no sense that she'd had particular women friends among her neighbors and callers.

And how odd was it that Mama's former acquaintance was now housed in the family wing? That had to be by Papa's decree, conveyed through Ellersby's diplomacy.

"Our husbands were well acquainted," Lady Eutheria said, "and friendship between wives makes such situations ever so much easier. Are your brothers feuding?"

Ahead of us, Ajax and Hector were engaged in a heated discussion. No voices were raised, but then, even those two had enough manners not to engage in pitched battle before Papa's guests.

"You saw the fencing exhibition, I take it?" Had Ajax lost coin when Pritchard had defeated Hector?

"I allowed myself that indulgence," Lady Eutheria replied. "I felt bound by loyalty to root for our Hector, but Pritchard prevailed, as he is so habitually wont to do."

Her ladyship wasn't smiling now.

"You don't care for the incomparable Lord Pritchard?" He was somewhat younger than her ladyship, but not so much younger that they moved in different social spheres.

"Pritchard has matured, I'll give him that, but he had a great deal of maturing to do. Heirs tend to be overindulged, and while he's a handsome man, he was a beautiful youth, and he's had charm to spare since he was in leading strings. Much was forgiven him that another young man would not have even attempted. Oh dear. Should you make peace between your brothers?"

Hector had shoved Ajax hard enough that Ajax stumbled.

"They would join in mutual resentment of my efforts and without resolving their own difficulties. My father's approach to raising boys was to let them sort themselves out, unless broken bones or hanging felonies were involved." And sometimes, Papa had not interceded even then. Frustration with his parenting numbered among the most frequent laments in Mama's diary.

"I wish your mother had lived to see what fine young people her children grew up to be," Lady Eutheria said. "She loved you all to distraction, and you most of all, my lady."

Lady Eutheria probably meant those words kindly, but they hurt. "I miss her terribly. More since losing my husband." Mama would have liked St. Sevier, and she would have *approved* of him. She would have also rejoiced to know that I'd renewed my friendship with Sebastian, but then, if Mama had been on hand, that friendship might not have flourished as it originally had.

Papa had been a distant parent to his sons. He'd been even more remote to his daughter.

"Widowhood is not for the faint of heart," Lady Eutheria replied. "As Evelyn threatens to become a hoyden of the first water, I realize how much better my husband understood the girl than I do. They were conspirators against Mama's tyrannical rules, and I fear—"

The first footman trotted up the path, out of breath and red-faced. In the gathering heat, his livery would be stifling.

"Beg pardon, my lady, my lady. I'm looking for the earl."

"Lord Derwent is some way behind us," Lady Eutheria said. "Perhaps Lady Violet can aid you?"

Dawkins looked torn. He'd hustled past both Hector and Ajax, but then, they'd been spatting.

"Tell me, Dawkins. Derwent was debating some detail of an old treaty with Lord Rowbottom, and they could be all day at it."

Dawkins ran a finger around the inside of his neckcloth. "The nursery is in another uproar, milady. Hansom says the young miss has disappeared again. We looked in the blue parlor, but she weren't to be found. With the whole house at sixes and sevens and the earl off to the abbey—"

"Miss Evelyn has gone missing again?" I asked.

"Hansom said we must fetch the earl, for the child is a guest of the house, and her mama will be tore up something fierce."

Lady Eutheria looked more annoyed than torn up. "I am the child's mother, my good man, and my suggestion is that nobody even acknowledge her absence. She made herself the center of attention by disappearing once before, and she's pouting because I would not let her join an adult excursion this morning. Resume your duties, and tell Hansom to do likewise."

Dawkins looked unconvinced. He was one of eleven siblings and had joined the staff at the Hall as a boot-boy at a tender age. He'd climbed ambition's ladder, serving as potboy in the kitchen, helping out in the stables, becoming an underporter, and then winning a coveted position as an underfootman.

In another five years, if he comported himself well, he might become an underbutler, and five years after that, butler.

He had not run in search of the earl in this heat merely to gratify Hansom's whim.

"Who saw the girl last?" I asked. "And are the other children accounted for?"

CHAPTER EIGHT

I had to see for myself that Evelyn had not taken a wild notion to hide in the priest hole. After my mishap, my brother Mitchell had shown me how to work the latch from inside the hiding place, though shoving the bookcase open at that age had taken all my might.

I had purposely not offered Evelyn the same explanation, because I wanted her to avoid the priest hole altogether, and because she was not an acknowledged Deerfield. The priest hole was a family secret, the only real secret we had—as far as I knew.

Rather than argue with Lady Eutheria about the proper response to Evelyn's disappearance, I made my way alone to the nursery. I found a distraught Hansom being comforted by the tutor who'd accompanied Mr. Botham's son and the governess who'd come along with Lord Pritchard's boy.

Dottie stood by the card table, supervising two rounds of a game of patience. Sylvie played against the Botham boy, while Bella opposed Henry. The children seemed oblivious to the upset adults around them, perhaps because Dottie's usually placid demeanor was firmly in evidence.

Any minute, my father, my brothers, or some other helpful man would intrude, and Hansom's anxieties would blossom into hysterics.

"Hansom," I said in my best her-ladyship-demands-composure tones, "we must remain calm. The child's own mother claims the girl is quite dramatic. If we must search for Evelyn, we have a house full of guests all too eager for a scavenger hunt with an element of excitement. When did we last see Evelyn?"

The Pritchard governess, Miss Oakes, spoke up. "I offered to sketch some fruit with her. She went back to the classroom to fetch her sketch pad, and she never returned."

"Miss Oakes and I got to talking," the tutor said. "About perspective." Mr. Harkness was youthful as tutors went, slender, and dark-haired, and the gaze he turned upon the petite, blond Miss Oakes suggested he was also smitten.

Fast work, but then, this was a house party, and Miss Oakes was quite pretty. She blinked at Mr. Harkness, sighed, wrung her hands, and worried her lower lip between her teeth. Sarah Siddons herself could not have embodied the damsel in distress more winningly.

"Have we looked to see if the sketch pad is still in the schoolroom?" I asked. "If Evelyn took a notion to sketch the folly, she might well be perched on some rock, pencil in hand, fascinated by the swans on the trout pond."

Like many English estates, Derwent Hall had a number of water features. Most of the boundaries for the manorial acreage were streams, ponds, or ancient irrigation ditches. The water meadow was bounded on one side by a dyke that made up part of the banks of a shallow ornamental lake. Close to the home farm—in the direction of the abbey—the second earl had had a trout pond built.

On a hot summer day, water would have appealed to my younger self, but then, I'd learned early in life how to swim. Not an accomplishment most girls aspired to.

"Dottie keeps the schoolroom tidy," Hansom said. "Dottie, go see if Miss Evelyn's sketch pad is still in the cupboard."

Dottie looked up from the card table, her gaze uncertain. "How am I to know which sketch pad is Miss Evelyn's?"

A sensible question. "I'll go with you, and we will know by the quality of the drawing." Surely Evelyn's artistry was more accomplished than that of the other children?

"Evelyn likes to draw trees," Bella said, turning over two sevens in succession. "Trees and trees and trees."

"Sometimes with birds in them or birds in the sky," Sylvie added. "Great big birds." She flapped her arms, and the two little boys exchanged a girls-are-hopeless look. "She is good at trees, but I do not care for her birds."

"Go with Lady Violet," Hansom said, waving a hand at Dottie.

Dottie and I made our way down the corridor, and I realized I had an opportunity I might have otherwise overlooked.

"Where do you think Evelyn has got off to, Dottie?"

Dottie shrugged. "She's lively, that one. She hasn't much sense. Thinks she knows all, but she don't."

Coming from Dottie, whom everybody acknowledged to be of limited understanding, that was an impressively sagacious answer, though not particularly helpful.

"She's young, Dottie. Most of us lack sense when we're young." Some of us lacked sense later in life as well. "Did you and Hansom take the children out for some air at any point?"

Dottie shook her head quite firmly. "I might get my pinny dirty if I sit in the grass. Hansom scolds me when my pinny is dirty, because I must put on a fresh one, and that is more work for the laundresses. Miss Oakes and Mr. Harkness took the children out on a nature walk yesterday. Hansom and I had a nice cuppa tea, and Hansom put her feet up for a bit. She does that a lot. Puts her feet up when we have tea."

We reached the schoolroom, a place I'd had no reason to visit in years. The globe in the corner, decades out of date in my childhood, was yet still more out of date now, but then, the print was too small to read without a quizzing glass. The best use of the globe was simply to spin it and see what country lay beneath one's finger when the spinning stopped.

I went to the cabinet where the drawing supplies had been kept in my childhood, and right there they were: sketch pads, pencils, charcoal, gum erasers, and even a pair of penknives. Those knives would be too dull to do more than scrape a point onto a pencil. On the next shelf down, the painting supplies were neatly arranged, and the bottom shelf held spare paper, ink, rulers, and other writing implements.

I doubted Lady Ellersby had had the classroom shelves stocked solely for the house-party guests, but why hadn't this room ever been cleaned out and shut up? I had been the last Deerfield child to use the classroom, and I'd left its confines well over a decade ago.

"Let's look through the sketch pads," I said, passing one to Dottie and taking the next half dozen for myself. There were at least a dozen, but the bottom half of the stack looked too venerable to have seen recent use.

"This is Miss Bella's," Dottie said, showing me the first page. "She do love her pony."

I was struck by an urge to sketch Dottie herself. Something about the simplicity of her mind had preserved her features from the marks of time obvious on my own countenance. She was attractive as a young girl draws the eye, not only for her youth, but also for her innocence and her goodness.

The very young are usually strangers to bitterness. Their acquaintance with regret is a fleeting thing, however passionate. Dottie still had that youthful quality of living in the present and allowing past and future to remain undisturbed by her emotional peregrinations.

Simple she might be, but she'd also been given a certain style of wisdom.

"Have the children gone to the stable in the past few days?" I asked.

Dottie again emphatically shook her head. "Lord Ellersby said he'd take Miss Sylvie and Miss Bella to see their ponies tomorrow. Not today. For a visit only, not to ride, because the young ladies do not rise while the morning is still cool, and ponies grow heated very easily."

Dottie was all but quoting Ellersby. On the one hand, I was surprised that Mitchell had thought to take his daughters for an outing. On the other, ponies were well able to tolerate the exertion of a short outing, no matter the weather.

Mitchell had exercised parental guile. I was impressed.

I opened the sketch pad I had taken from the stack and found a scene executed with some skill. The perspective struck me as a nursery-eye view of the Derwent Hall formal parterres, with the park stretching beyond the garden to the river. The home wood in full summer foliage sat to the left and the conservatory to the right. An outsized full moon hung over the whole scene, and some great bird swooped low near the river.

Not an owl, for the creature had the hooked beak and sleek body of a hawk. And yet, this raptor had a smaller bird clutched in its talons, reminiscent of the hawk's habit of hunting songbirds. The image was fanciful—hawks hunted at dusk, but not in full darkness— and oddly violent for a young girl's choice of subject.

"That's hers," Dottie said, crowding close to me. "That's Miss Evelyn's. I wish I could draw like that."

I was unused to an employee being so familiar with my person, as Sylvie or Bella might have been. Dottie even bore the chamomile and fresh-laundry scent that characterized the younger girls.

"I haven't much skill with a drawing pencil," I said, turning the page. "I can draw flowers, cats, and horses and not much else. I do better with needlepoint."

Male voices sounded in the corridor, and the thump of boots passed the classroom door. Dottie shrank against me.

"They'll be mad as hornets, them. Miss Evelyn ain't here, and they'll be powerful mad."

"They will be worried," I said, "but for all we know, Miss Evelyn took a notion to visit the stable, and she's reading away her afternoon in the hayloft. You must not worry, Dottie."

Dottie hugged me. "I like you, Lady Violet. You were always nice to me. I like Lord Ellersby, too, though he tries to be stern all the time. He were a sweet boy."

And perhaps Dottie was a bit daft. Ellersby was honorable and hardworking, but I didn't know as anybody else save his old nurse would have characterized him as a sweet child. I eased away, for I did not want anybody—my father, for example—upsetting Hansom, much less the other children.

"We know Evelyn never retrieved her sketch pad," I said, "so let's put these away, shall we?" I kept Evelyn's handiwork, curious as to what else she might have drawn.

Dottie beamed at me. "I will put away the toys. You can be on your way, Lady Violet. I shall tidy up. I am good at tidying up. I tidy up the toys, and Hansom puts her feet up." She smiled at me, a dazzling display of self-assurance and pride.

Life for Dottie proceeded along well-ordered lines. She knew her place, she fulfilled that place marvelously well, and she made a valuable contribution in the process. What did it say about me that I envied Dottie her contentment?

I left her sitting among the sketchbooks, tracing a slow finger along the simple lines of Bella's pony. Dottie might be quite good at tidying up, but she also had sense enough to avoid the drama inevitably unfolding in the nursery.

She took a seat at a desk and gave me a little wave. I turned my steps in the direction of the raised voices coming from the playroom.

~

"When did Papa develop a tendresse for Lady Eutheria?" I asked.

Ellersby sauntered along beside me, though his gaze was on the undergrowth and trees that bordered the river path.

"What makes you think Derwent has a tendresse for her ladyship?"

"Because she calls him Sylvanus, and he allows it. Mama rarely used Derwent's given name before us children and never in front of company." Lady Eutheria had also commanded Derwent's escort all the way to the ruins, and there was that business about her rooms being in the family wing.

"I daresay you would like to call him something other than Sylvanus."

"He upset the children, Mitchell." Bella's chin had gone all quivery when *dear Grandpapa* had begun a tirade about the foolishness of allowing children at house parties. Mitchell, oddly enough, had picked the child up, perched her on his hip, and explained that dear Grandpapa was tired after his morning's exertions, and tired old grandpapas could be quite grouchy. One mustn't think anything of it if Grandpapa forgot his manners from time to time and grew a bit *hysterical*.

The nursery had gone as quiet as a chapel at midnight, and the topic had turned to organizing a search.

I had volunteered to search this path, in part because it was mostly shady and in part because, as a girl, I had spent many an hour along the river. Ellersby had appointed himself to escort me, but I also had the sense he simply wanted to be away from the tension in the nursery.

Papa had assigned Lord Pritchard and St. Sevier to inquire of the village shops. Mr. Botham and Lord Rowbottom had been sent off to the home farm. Various other parties were inspecting the home wood, the stables, and the myriad estate outbuildings. Sebastian had been dispatched to do likewise across the river at MacHeath's Ford.

"Speaking of upsetting people," Ellersby said, "when will you announce your engagement to St. Sevier? You torment Lord Dunkeld with the suspense."

I halted a half-dozen yards downstream from the picnic spot. "I beg your pardon?"

"You and that Frenchman can't take your eyes off each other. If Hector's fencing hadn't already cost half the gentlemen dearly, they'd be wagering on an announcement of your engagement by the end of the gathering."

"Hush, my lord, or I will push you into the river, and don't think I'm too small and ladylike to manage it." I was too small, probably, but I could not fathom what Mitchell was saying. "Firstly, I do not exchange unseemly glances with St. Sevier in public, and secondly, Dunkeld spent the spring searching for a marchioness in London. He wishes me well and considers St. Sevier a friend. He is the least-tormented man I know."

Not quite true. Every former soldier carried a few torments among his memories.

"But Dunkeld did not find a marchioness, did he?" Ellersby picked up a rock and sent it bouncing over the water. "Try to beat that. It skipped four times."

"Three." I found a suitable skipper and managed to do as well. "You are daft to think Dunkeld is jealous of St. Sevier."

Ellersby resumed walking, and I fell in step beside him. "Dunkeld is not jealous of the Frenchman, but he is in love with you, Violet. Always has been. Because he is in love with you, he wants you to be happy. Ergo, he encourages the Frenchman's suit."

If anybody had told me over supper that my oldest brother would use the term *in love* to describe the behavior of a man acquainted with me... I did not consider even St. Sevier to be *in love* with me. We were passionately attracted, devoted, fond, loyal, compatible, and many other wonderful things, but *in love*? I would have to consider that possibility. I loved Hugh—madly—but I was not infatuated with him.

Never that. Never again that, and what did it mean to be in love, if not to be infatuated?

"Dunkeld was somewhat taken with me long ago," I said, "as a boy far from home is smitten with the only girl he knows well. We were friends, and he... he talked himself into something that wasn't of any moment."

Mitchell strolled along beside me, and it occurred to me that this was probably the first time he'd rambled around the property in years. Maybe his daughters could help him remedy that oversight, for nothing compared with the beauty of the English countryside in summer.

"Dunkeld asked one thing of me before he joined his regiment all those years ago," Mitchell said. "One thing only, upon my word of honor."

"I do not want to hear this."

"You need to hear it. You are not a seventeen-year-old schoolgirl, helpless to thwart Derwent's machinations."

We passed the picnic spot, which was cast in full sun at this time of day. Across the river, MacHeath's Ford sat on its majestic rise, looking more spruce and imposing than it had in years. Why had Sebastian hung on to that property all this time? Why had he let it out to Felix only last year?

"What did Sebastian ask of you?"

"I had to promise to look after you. Only that. I gave Dunkeld my word that I would not allow Papa to match you up to any gouty old baron or miscreant rake. I was to ensure you married a man who cared for you. How I was to manage that feat, I did not know, but Dunkeld—merely MacHeath at the time—was desperate to wrest that promise from me."

"Freddie cared for me." In his way. "He wasn't gouty or old." But he had absolutely been a rake. I was still supporting some of the evidence of his raking and would be for years.

"Dunkeld cared for you more, and he still does. He thought you had rejected him when he went off to Spain, and he still did what he could to safeguard your happiness. That is devotion, Violet. That is selfless devotion."

We wandered up the path, past the fishing cottage set back in the trees, and on toward the sweeping green expanse of the water meadow.

"That was all a long time ago," I said. "Dunkeld is no longer a brooding young fellow of uncertain prospects. He can have his pick of the young ladies, and any woman would be delighted to gain his notice."

Ellersby stopped to pick raspberries growing from thorny bushes bordering the path. "God, these are delicious." He'd found a patch the girls and I had neglected on our battles against the Visigoths.

"You should take your daughters for an outing to pick some." I popped a succulent berry into my mouth, tasting all of summer's abundance in one bite. Sweet, tart, luscious... and the canes were full of fruit. "We're supposed to be searching."

"We will resume our efforts shortly. I daresay the girl took a book into some venerable climbing tree and will present herself, complete with a fresh crop of freckles, before supper."

The berries stained my fingers, and I wished I'd brought a bucket for picking. Sebastian and I had picked berries by the hour. Read poetry by the hour. Fished by the hour without catching anything.

A truly horrifying memory popped up. The summer of my sixteenth year, I'd demanded that Sebastian allow me to practice my kissing on him. All the girls at school had become obsessed with kisses, some going so far as to accost the underfootman, though he'd been spotty and had rabbit teeth.

"Mitchell, has Dunkeld said anything about my interest in St. Sevier?"

"They are both gentlemen. Nothing need be said, but I know the look of a man hopelessly in love with a woman who cannot see that he treasures her. Such fellows are sad creatures, and dignity is their only comfort. What's this?"

He hunkered down to examine the dusty path.

"A boot print," I said, noticing several others. I put my boot beside one of them, and the marks in the dirt were smaller than my own. "A child's boot print." Though I was certain Bella and Sylvie hadn't traveled this stretch of the path.

Ellersby produced a penknife that happened to match the length of the boot print exactly. "Any village girl or boy might have come this way."

I considered the distance we'd come and the fact that the path was visible from the MacHeath's Ford manor house. "Not likely. Raspberries also grow much closer to the village, and taking produce from Derwent Hall property is technically stealing. No yeoman's child would steal from the earl, not when the theft was in plain sight of a manor house. Whoever made these boot prints tarried here long enough to leave plenty of evidence."

We searched farther up the path, but the track turned grassy closer to the water meadow. Down the path, we had some luck—another boot print—and headed back in the direction of the Derwent Hall home wood.

"This proves nothing," Ellersby said, gaze on the river, which was deep enough in some places to drown a child who could not swim. "The trails and bridle paths in this area are all considered common rights of way. The farmworkers use them, the tenant families... The vicar's children are regularly at large, and nobody thinks anything of it."

He was worried, as only the father of two young girls could be worried, when viewing the perils of rural life for heedless children.

"We have learned that Evelyn is not wandering the path along the river at present," I said. "We can ask in the nursery if yesterday's nature walk came this way."

Ellersby left off scanning the woods. "A nature walk?"

"Miss Oakes and Mr. Harkness took the children on a nature walk while Hansom enjoyed a cup of tea in peace." I kept to myself the observation that all of the boot prints were the same size. If five children and two adults had passed this way, that would not be the case.

Ellersby's frown suggested he had reached the same conclusion.

"I don't like this, but we've covered the ground we were assigned. Let's report back and hope somebody else has found the girl asleep in the home farm's hay mow or dozing beneath some shady oak."

The ground beneath oak trees was usually peppered with acorns. Not even a fairy-tale princess could manage to fall asleep on such a bed.

We partook of a few more raspberries, then made our way back to Derwent Hall, retracing our steps, but finding no more boot prints. I pondered a question as we walked along in the afternoon heat:

How did Mitchell, Viscount Ellersby, know the look of a man *hopelessly in love with a woman who cannot see that he treasures her?* Was he describing Papa and Lady Eutheria? I thought not, and then it occurred to me that Mitchell—awash in dignity—might be describing himself.

But was the woman he treasured his wife, or some other female?

⁓

Two things became apparent when the company gathered in the library before changing for dinner. First, we hadn't found Evelyn.

Second, not even my father thought a disappearance of this duration a childish stunt.

"St. Sevier inquired of the shopkeepers and at the forge," Lord Pritchard said. "I questioned the publican and the vicar. Nobody has seen an unaccompanied child matching Evelyn's description, and the only strangers in the village came through on the stagecoaches."

St. Sevier apparently had nothing to add to that recitation, for he remained by the library window, gaze on the terrace, the drink in his hand untouched. I crossed the room to stand beside him, and too bad if anybody noticed.

Dunkeld was still at MacHeath's Ford and would not return to the Hall until supper, which of course was of no moment whatsoever.

"You are worried for the girl," I murmured as Mr. Botham reported on the home farm and Mr. Bascomb on the outbuildings.

"Miss Evelyn is either pulling a grand prank," St. Sevier said, "or she's in danger."

I wanted to lean against his taller frame, but of course I did not. "Or she's dead. Toppled into the trout pond from a slippery bank, swept off her feet by the river's current, lying in a tangled heap at the foot of a tree not as sturdy as she'd thought."

St. Sevier's smile was slight. "The river's current isn't that strong, barring torrential rainfall."

"You think my only bad experience with the river was the result of a coaching mishap last autumn," I said, slipping my hand into his. I stood such that my boldness wasn't visible to the other guests. "I nearly came to grief once as a girl too."

He squeezed my fingers, then let my hand drop. "Tell me."

"I was wading, and something brushed my leg under the water. A fish, no doubt, but the sensation was horrid and unexpected. In my upset, I bolted not toward the shore, but toward the middle of the river. The bottom dropped off steeply, my foot got caught in some submerged branches, and I was in a very bad spot."

"Dunkeld rescued you."

"How did you know?" I could still feel the blessed relief of Sebastian's arms coming around me. *I have ye. Cease thrashing, ye daft girl. I have ye.*

"He might have mentioned this mishap last autumn over a brandy or two. When you were upset, angry, or afraid as a girl, Violet, where did you hide away?"

I had been upset frequently as a girl. "I hid in my room, mostly. I hid in books. I hid on the back of my mare. My family was happy to let me hide in those places."

"Where else?"

"In the tree houses, the hay mow. I'd visit the gamekeeper's granny, who always had a slice of bread with jam for the earl's headstrong daughter. I think she moved to the village when her son married."

Behind us, Mr. Harkness was reporting that various tenants had not seen Evelyn at large, nor any girl matching her description. Ellersby had yet to disclose the boot prints we'd found, probably because he was hoping for more encouraging news from another quarter.

I crossed to the sideboard and poured myself a glass of cold lemonade. "Mr. Harkness, you and the children took a nature walk yesterday, did you not?"

"With Miss Oakes, my lady. The boys in particular were rambunctious and needed some fresh air."

"Where did this walk take you?"

He reported a route that started at the terrace doors, ran through the garden and into the deer park and horse paddocks. The children had wanted to see the year's crop of foals, then rambled down the drive to throw stones into the river from the bridge near the gatekeeper's cottage.

The wanderers hadn't gone anywhere near the raspberry patch.

"And then the children were tired," Mr. Harkness said, "so we came back to the Hall by way of the front drive."

That route passed the gamekeeper's cottage at the edge of the deer park, the gatekeeper's cottage at the foot of the drive, a folly in the deer park, and many good climbing trees.

"I know this much," Lady Eutheria said from a seat near the unlit hearth. "Evelyn might have a penchant for drama, but she's a good girl. She would not hide for hours out of sheer deviltry. She knows I expect proper behavior from her."

"She will turn up," Papa said, patting her ladyship's shoulder. "If she's twisted an ankle or taken a wrong turn on some bridle path, we'll find her. The weather is mild, the nights are short, and we've sounded the alarm. Try to remain calm, and all will be well."

Soothing words. Had Papa offered them to me, I would have been hard put not to tell him what I thought of such condescension.

Dinner was informal and a subdued affair owing to the day's upheaval. Lady Ellersby presided over the meal as graciously as if no little girl had gone missing, but I saw the looks she exchanged with her husband.

I was seated beside St. Sevier, thank heavens, and yet, we had little to say to each other. Hugh loved children, and a child was in peril. What mattered the weather, the race meets, or the Regent's latest extravagance compared to that?

As the fruit and cheese were served, I noticed Dunkeld regarding me from the place at Lady Ellersby's right. His expression was unreadable, as only a Scotsman's expression can be. His physiognomy might well have been carved of the cold granite that formed so many Highland strongholds.

Then he smiled and lifted his glass in my direction, and it was as if that frigid, lordly indifference had never been. Which face was he showing London Society? Which face did he show Mrs. Bonaventure?

"Will you forgive me if I retire early tonight?" St. Sevier asked me as Lady Ellersby signaled that the women were to withdraw.

"Of course," I replied. "The day has been long and fraught. I'll join you at the earliest polite opportunity."

"I will await you in slumber."

"Will you accompany me on a visit to the nursery tomorrow morning?" I posed that question while the assemblage sorted itself into a crocodile for the purpose of seeing the ladies escorted to the guest parlor.

"You want to interrogate the children?"

I wanted to question the children when my father wasn't on hand to make the exercise pointless. "Yes, and to have another look at Evelyn's sketchbooks. They might tell us something about her travels around the grounds before Sylvie and Bella joined her in the nursery."

We tarried in the dining room while the rest of the guests shuffled ahead of us into the corridor.

"Much of today's effort was wasted, Violet." St. Sevier, normally so self-possessed and urbane, sounded nearly despairing.

"Why do you say that?"

"Because we are in the English countryside. Lord Pritchard is all that is charming, but I saw him attempt to question the innkeeper. The innkeeper's wife had her daughters out of the common before Pritchard had so much as removed his hat."

I tried to sort my biases as a member of the Deerfield family from what St. Sevier had observed.

"The publican and his wife didn't care as much for a missing girl as they worried about a fancy lord troubling their daughters," I said, "because that's what fancy lords do."

"Some fancy lords, in any case. His lordship is not precisely awash in reserve."

Two footmen hovered by the sideboard, clearly anxious to begin the cleaning up. I left the dining room on St. Sevier's arm, my unease growing as I pondered what he wasn't saying.

"Pritchard is a fancy lord and a stranger," I admitted, "and you are worse than that—a Frenchman and a stranger. The shopkeepers wouldn't tell you if they'd seen Evelyn dancing on the village green."

"Because," St. Sevier said as we approached the foot of the steps, "all Frenchmen are spies for Napoleon's brothers or nephews or cousins. You and Dunkeld should have asked questions in the village. Your brothers should have inquired of the staff and tenants. Instead... we are bungling this search, Violet."

We, meaning my father. "Is that all that troubles you?" Or had Hugh's mind gone to where my own had, to Bascomb's propensity for forcing himself on the unwilling, and Evelyn's inability to protect herself? Bascomb knew the house and grounds well, and even knew some of the neighboring properties.

The rest of the party trundled down the corridor to the guest parlor while St. Sevier and I remained at the foot of the staircase.

"I am tired," he said. "I am unsettled because of this missing girl and unsettled to be at your family home, and in the capacity of something other than gentleman escort."

I had the sense Hugh was concocting an explanation rather than facing the real source of his upset. "I've agreed that we have an understanding, sir. Is that what ails you? You enjoyed the pursuit, but as you come closer to catching your quarry, you lose interest in the chase?"

Something had upset him beyond the upheaval of Evelyn's disappearance, though Hugh was hardly the sort to put a personal matter ahead of a missing child.

He took my hand in both of his. "I was regarded with suspicion and even hatred, Violet. I was viewed as a possible French spy, and I had not anticipated that reception. We cannot trust the answers I was given, and I sense that for some reason, Pritchard was regarded with even more suspicion than his charm warranted."

I tended to romanticize the countryside, to see it in contrast to the inbred, backstabbing, glittering Society to be found in Mayfair. But the countryside, particularly in the south of England, had borne a disproportionate share of the burdens caused by twenty years of war with France.

All along the coast and in villages with no connection to the sea, press gangs had snatched able-bodied men from families and loved ones, and many of those men had never returned. Farmers' sons had been required to join militias, and those militias had transferred thousands of soldiers into active service.

The poets, fashionable ladies, and lords could all delight in visiting Paris once more and hire émigrés to teach French to their children, but the average Englishman would view a curious Frenchman, at best, with skepticism.

"I'm sorry," I said, longing to hug St. Sevier. "I should have gone into the village with you. Perhaps tomorrow, I will."

"Tomorrow," he said, "we start in the nursery. We should also speak with the governess who looks after your nieces."

"Ellersby and I found a child's boot print along the river," I said, lowering my voice. "I cannot imagine why he hasn't disclosed that development to the others." He'd tell Papa first, was my guess, and I hoped he already had.

"Violet, you aren't thinking clearly." St. Sevier gazed down at me, his countenance as serious as I'd ever seen it.

The point he'd refrained from making became clear to me between one beat of my heart and the next.

"Somebody among the searchers," I said slowly, "might well be responsible for the mischief that has befallen Evelyn."

My suspicion fell immediately upon Bascomb, though just because he'd pressed his advances on a young lady fresh from the schoolroom didn't mean he posed a risk to a mere child—did it?

"You see the nature of the problem," St. Sevier said. "Nobody is above suspicion."

The men began to file back down the corridor to the dining room, and I looked into their faces with a new sense of dread. We had agreed to restart the search at first light, but would that be soon enough?

"We don't have a motive," I said softly. "Who would want to harm a perfectly innocent young girl?"

"Only monsters prey on children." St. Sevier kissed my cheek and took himself up the steps on that extremely unsettling observation.

CHAPTER NINE

I enjoyed the day's first cup of tea on the balcony, the morning air already promising a warm, humid day. The hay crop was in, and thus rain would have been welcomed by the farmers.

I thought of Evelyn and prayed the rain held off. The outdoor staff was already fanning out along game trails and bridle paths, and I dearly hoped we'd find her in the next hour.

"Good morning, my lady." St. Sevier, a cup of tea in hand, regarded me from two yards down the balcony. He was in riding attire minus his jacket and a fine sight to behold. "You look well rested. May I join you?"

In Scotland and Cumbria, he had known he was welcome, but then, in Scotland and Cumbria, we had treasured any opportunity to pass the night in the same bed.

"Please have a seat," I said. "I missed you last night."

He settled onto the nearest chair, his hair still damp and tidily combed. Hugh St. Sevier was a gorgeous man, but the merciless morning sun also revealed him to be a tired man.

A troubled man, as well.

"You chose not to join me last night, my lady. Are your courses upon you?"

Hugh was blunt about discussing bodily functions. I suspected that would be the case even were he not a physician, and I actually liked that about him—usually.

"Summer's heat often disturbs my bodily rhythms. I left you in peace last night because you looked so utterly exhausted. Sometimes, a man needs his sleep."

He sipped his tea and made even that mundane activity a display of masculine pulchritude. The elegant little cup in his grasp, the exact contours of his lips, the way he traced the gilded rim with a single finger... the morning abruptly grew warmer.

"I can contain my urges, Violet. Sometimes, in the dark of night, a man needs simply to hold the woman he adores."

"Perhaps I cannot contain my urges where you are concerned."

This confession earned me a smile. "You flatter me."

"Not entirely." Hugh's embrace could be simply comforting, and I was much in need of comfort. What must Evelyn's mother be feeling, and from whom could she derive comfort?

St. Sevier's smile became less naughty and more fond. "My lady will please explain herself."

Birds were chirping a greeting to the day, the sun turned the dew-laden grass into a sparkling expanse of green, and a mare whinnied from the direction of the paddocks. The day was beautiful, and I was starting it with the man I loved.

That Hugh and I shared sunrises as well as the occasional bed meant much to me, and I wanted to explain to him how much, before the anxieties of the day parted us from each other again.

"When I was married, I followed my husband's direction regarding our intimate arrangements. For the first year, we shared a bedroom, then Freddie decided we were no longer newly wed, and we moved to adjoining bedrooms."

"You learned of his extramarital liaisons."

I sipped my tea and let bitter recollections find me. "I suspect

Freddie felt guilty for deceiving me, because I was determined to adore my husband. He left the usual receipts where I would come upon them, and Freddie was not a fellow to make a mistake like that casually."

"Jewelry?"

"Jewelry. Also dresses, hats, gloves... every little detail of a woman's wardrobe, which in a way was worse than a mere bracelet. When he suggested I might enjoy better sleep in my own quarters, I acceded to his wishes. I still spent most every night in his bed, hoping he'd appreciate having me there. If I retreated to my own quarters—whether because of my courses or in a fit of pique—he never brought it up. I might have been a spare pillow, for all the difference it made to him."

"You were eighteen years old. You doubtless excelled at acceding to male wishes."

A kind observation, also accurate. "I did not realize until I had my own quarters that Freddie also banished something precious from the marriage when he established our separate bedrooms. The late-night chats, the casual affection beyond lovemaking, watching him shave in the morning, helping him choose a cravat pin... all gone, because I was in his room at his sufferance. He sent me on my way—'Don't let me keep you from your day, dearest'—and I toddled off like a good little wife."

St. Sevier set aside his tea, rose, scooped me into his arms, and resumed his seat. "All gone, because Belmaine chose shallow pleasures over true wealth. Young men are fools. Young Englishmen are particularly foolish."

I snuggled close, at peace in a way that had nothing to do with good sleep. "Young Englishwomen aren't much better. I wonder now if Freddie wasn't challenging me to unbanish myself, but what did I know of waging marital battles? I came home from some inane social call a few weeks after the second miscarriage and found my things had been moved back into Freddie's quarters. He did not always come home of a night, and he still went off on his supposed shooting parties, but we once more shared a bed, unless I decided otherwise."

A robin flitted onto the balcony railing, peered at us as if assessing whether any toast crumbs were to be had, then flew away.

"You were older and wiser by then," St. Sevier said. "You knew Belmaine was admitting defeat of a sort."

How I loved the feel of Hugh's arms around me, loved that he and I could simply *talk*. "Freddie remained the victor. He decided we were to again share a bedroom, just as he had at the start of the marriage, and I acquiesced. He decided when and how we were intimate, and for the most part, I acquiesced. I refused some of his more outlandish sexual games, but the only real power I retained was the power of passivity."

St. Sevier's chin rested on my crown. "I do not like this power. It sounds lonely."

"Or English. I never importuned Freddie for his intimate attentions. He had to initiate all intimacies, and if I was victorious in any sense, it's because I made it plain I could survive without his lovemaking, and survive cheerfully. I never decided outright to be sexually reticent, and I enjoyed his attentions more or less, but I made no overtures and thus never risked rejection."

The robin came back, its bright eyes demanding something of us, but I was too comfortable even to toss toast crumbs at the little creature.

"Am I then to take all the risk of rejection, Violet?" St. Sevier asked.

"No, but I ask for your patience as I learn to negotiate discussions such as this one, where we are honest with each other about difficult and personal matters. I haven't much experience with this sort of conversation, but with you..."

The bird flew away, and Hugh shifted his hold on me so I was pressed closer to his heart. "With me?"

"You are my friend as well as my lover. Also my companion and my confidant. Sometimes, you are my conscience and sometimes my dear opponent in a battle of wits. I am inebriated by all the ways you find to be close to me, and this embarrassment of riches has me at a loss. I honestly missed you last night, and I honestly thought you needed a night of undisturbed rest."

Hugh sighed, and a physical tension went out of him. "I am overwhelmed as well, Violet, in a good way, but still overwhelmed. We shall be overwhelmed together, but let us agree to always, come what may, be friends."

"I can agree to that." And perhaps that had been the element missing from my marriage to Freddie. He and I had never achieved the status of friends. But then, my only example of friendship with a male had been Sebastian. In a decade of trying, Freddie would have been hard put to measure up to that standard, and he hadn't been interested in trying.

I wanted to ask Hugh if he and Ann had grappled with similar issues, or had Freddie and I been the only dunderheaded couple in creation? I refrained from posing the question, in part because Hugh and Ann had been married for months rather than years and in part because my courage had limits.

"Shall I take you to bed now, Violet?"

"You tempt me."

"But," he said, lips close to my ear, "the staff is up and about, the indomitable Miss Hewitt will soon be underfoot, and a locked door would cause scandal. Also not the done thing when a little girl is missing, and we are determined to find her. Let's away to the nursery, then, and speak to the children before breakfast."

"I also want to look again at Evelyn's sketch pad."

"And perhaps you and Miss Hewitt will wander the village shops before the day grows too warm?"

"Excellent suggestion, if only I did not have to leave your lap to effect it."

He rose and deposited me in my own chair. "I will await your summons." He bowed and withdrew, and I shamelessly enjoyed the sight of his retreat.

I finished my tea, crumbled up half a slice of toast for the birds, and went to find the coolest ensemble I could don for the morning's activities.

～

A missing child ought to turn a household upside down, and the oppressive weather was also taking a toll. As St. Sevier and I made our way to the nursery, we encountered no other guests and only one maid, already pink-cheeked under her linen cap.

"The heat makes us all miserable," I muttered, taking the final flight of stairs up to the nursery suite. The air on the upper floor was stiflingly close, though we found Dottie opening the window at the end of the corridor. She had a light, crocheted shawl draped over her arms—despite the heat—and it kept slipping down as she struggled with the sash.

"Allow me," St. Sevier said, tucking her shawl up over her shoulders and easily raising the window. "Humidity plays havoc with old wood. Were you on your way out?"

Dottie blushed, which was understandable. The friendly attentions of handsome men were a rarity in the life of any nurserymaid, doubly so, perhaps, for a nurserymaid in Lord Ellersby's employ.

"I come from the dower house, sir. I bide there in my own room, where my own things are." She bobbed a needless curtsey or two, though she regarded St. Sevier in a manner nearly approaching flirtatious.

Good heavens, Dottie was pretty, and though her intellectual powers were modest, she grasped very well how to smile at a handsome fellow.

"A lovely morning for a walk," St. Sevier said, politely ignoring the dampness marring the hem of Dottie's skirt. "Wise of you to open the window. The day will be quite warm, will it not?"

"Very warm, sir, and all the cows and sheep will gather beneath the shade trees. Then we will have a storm, and the trees might be hit by lightning if they are very tall. We lost a tree at the vicarage to lightning before I was born."

Her gaze turned solemn to contemplate such a momentous occasion, though I'd forgotten about the old tree at the vicarage. In my childhood, nothing had remained save a charred stump and the tales of the old women over their pints in the posting inn's snug.

A tremendously loud crack, they recalled, then the tree had become a fiery column of biblical portions, and all agreed the harvest had been very good that year despite such an omen.

"We thought to visit the children, Dottie," I said, "and I'd also like to have another look at Evelyn's sketchbook."

"The children will be at their porridge," Dottie replied, leading us down the corridor. "I like porridge with butter and honey. We can have a dash of cinnamon on Sundays and holidays, though cinnamon is ever so dear. Cinnamon smells mysterious."

On that insightful observation, she opened the door to the playroom, and we found Hansom presiding over the porridge.

Little Bella sprang from her chair and charged me. "Auntie Violet!" She wrapped her arms around my waist. "Can we have another picnic? *May* we? If we have a picnic, then Evelyn might come out from wherever she's hiding and join us."

"You didn't say excuse me," Sylvie chided, rising and offering us a curtsey. "You should say 'scuse me when you leave the table, Bell, and you didn't ask permission."

Bella stuck her tongue out at her sister. "I don't need permission to hug Auntie Violet."

The boys traded an amused glance and kept at their porridge while Hansom looked worried. "Come back to the table, Miss Bella. You'll wrinkle your aunt's skirts."

Bella gazed up at me. "May we have another picnic, Auntie? *Please?*"

She broke my heart with her big blue eyes and spontaneous affection. As the youngest and the sole female child, I had spent years trapped in the nursery, only a governess and a lot of moralizing old books for company.

"Perhaps later this afternoon we can make an outing to pick berries," I said, "but we will need to bring Miss Oakes and Mr. Harkness along as well." I had no intention of being the sole supervisor for four unruly children on a hot day near the river.

"I can come too," Dottie said. "Hansom can put her feet up and have a cuppa tea."

"Child," Hansom said, "you forget yourself."

Dottie's expression turned mulish. "I will help look after the children. I always help look after the children, and you can put your feet up."

"I'm sorry, my lady," Hansom said, looking weary. "The excitement from yesterday has us all at sixes and sevens. Dottie doesn't mean to be rude."

No, but like a child, Dottie meant to get her way. Perhaps that wasn't a bad thing. "Bella and Sylvie can come to the classroom with me now, and we will look over the sketchbooks. We will reserve a decision regarding the berry picking depending on the weather and on a nursery full of children on their best behavior. Does that suit?"

Hansom looked skeptical, or perhaps she hadn't heard me.

"We will behave," Sylvie said. "All of us will behave, even the boys."

The boys, from what I'd seen, had been perfect little gentlemen. "St. Sevier, perhaps you'd teach the young fellows how to say 'my pony is faster than your pony' in French?"

St. Sevier pulled a chair away from the table, turned it backward, and straddled it. "*Bonjour, mes jeunes amis. Finissez votre porridge.*"

Henry—Hal—looked fascinated. "Finish our porridge?"

St. Sevier helped himself to a spoonful of Bella's abandoned breakfast. "Young Henry, you are a genius among Englishmen. Finish your porridge indeed."

The girls and I left the menfolk to their linguistic amusements,

Hansom subsided into her rocking chair, and Dottie took the place at the table Sylvie had vacated.

"Dottie isn't very smart," Bella said when we'd found the stack of sketch pads in the classroom. "But she's nice, and we must not make fun of her."

"We shouldn't make fun of anybody," Sylvie said, flipping through the sketchbooks and withdrawing one, presumably her own. "We make fun of the boys when they are rude, though."

I retrieved Evelyn's drawings from the cupboard and took up a perch on a window seat. "Why is it allowable to make fun of rude boys but nobody else?"

"Because we mustn't cosh them as they deserve," Bella said. "I miss my pony."

"Draw me a sketch of your pony."

"I shall draw my pony too!" Sylvie announced, taking up a desk. "I will soon be too big for a pony. Papa said."

"I don't want to be too big for Galahad." Bella took up another desk and wrapped her legs around the legs of the chair.

"You aren't supposed to sit like that, Bell."

"I draw better sitting like this. Mind your own business, Syl."

I flipped through Evelyn's sketchbook, finding more images of raptors flying through the night sky. She'd also done a number of studies of a long-haired ginger cat, whom I did not recognize, and some of the flower still lifes every young lady was expected to do.

My nieces bickered and sketched, and I envied them the pleasure of having a sister to bicker with. Brothers weren't the same, but then, Sylvie and Bella had no brothers, so perhaps fate had been even-handed with us.

Sylvie and Bella did, however, have two devoted parents.

I flipped the page and came upon a sketch of a building I did not recognize. "Ladies, I have a question." I turned the sketchbook so the drawing faced out. "Do you know this building?" The structure was small, smaller than a fishing cottage, not much larger than an enclosed folly.

"That's our summer cottage," Sylvie said. "Mama and Papa used to take us there for picnics when we were little, but Mama says Papa is too busy now, and Papa says Mama has much on her mind. Hansom says it's too far to tramp for old bones, but it's not that far."

"When would Evelyn have seen it?"

Bella spoke up. "She came to stay with us when her mama first arrived at Derwent Hall, because the nursery at the Hall hadn't been tidied up."

Or because the earl had wanted a quiet interlude with Lady Eutheria, free of children and the servants children required? I vaguely recalled the summer cottage, though it lay in the woods along the river on the far side of the dower house and upstream from MacHeath's Ford.

The girls went back to their sketching, and I flipped through more of Evelyn's handiwork. She had ability, particularly with faces. She'd caught my brothers Hector and Ajax in discussion, and while fraternal resemblance was apparent, so was the testy nature of the conversation.

When had she seen this, and where had she been at the time? Was one of my brothers involved in her disappearance? I was reminded that Ajax had only a valet's alibi for the time when Evelyn had been shoved into the priest hole.

I turned one more page, and what I saw chilled me. Evelyn had sketched John Bascomb, his hair windblown, his smile fond. The perspective was from below, a child's perspective, and Bascomb loomed like a dashing cavalier surveying some distant clime. He needed only Byron's turban or a flowing silk scarf to add an air of the exotic.

This was a flattering, even adoring, portrait of an adult male, drawn by a girl who hadn't even put up her hair.

"What's wrong, Auntie Violet?" Bella asked. "You look afraid."

"Auntie is not afraid," Sylvie retorted. "Papa says she's 'trepid."

"Papa said she's *in*trepid."

Ellersby had said that about me? "I am worried for Evelyn." The blasted, understated truth. "What do you two suppose has happened to her?"

A look passed between the sisters. "We did something," Sylvie said. "Something we weren't supposed to do."

Visions of pushing Evelyn out of a tree or locking her in the wine cellar danced in my head, though the staff had searched every room, pantry, and closet of the Hall.

"What did you do?"

"We snooped," Bella said. "Only a little."

"Because you were concerned for Evelyn?"

Sylvie closed her sketchbook. "If somebody steals you away, you don't take a spare dress and stockings, do you?"

Dear God. From the mouths of babes... "Not unless the somebody knows where to look for your clothing and intends to keep you for a time. Where did you snoop, ladies?" Why hadn't I thought to snoop as well? Alarming myself with sketches was all well and good, but why not search the nursery suite for proper clues?

"We each brought a satchel with us from the dower house," Sylvie said. "We put our own clothes away because the staff is run off its feet."

"Not *really*," Bella added, "but the maids were busy because of all the guests. We each picked out two drawers from the bureaus and put our clothes away very neatly. Dottie helped, and she said my drawers were perfect. Evelyn needed three drawers because she brought *a lot* of clothes."

My heart began to thump against my ribs. "And some of Evelyn's things were missing?"

"Yes," Sylvie said, "and not dresses she wore, so they aren't in the laundry. She took clean clothes."

"Or somebody took her *and* her clothes," Bella said, her voice small. "I hope we find her soon."

"We will, Bella. This is actually good news."

Sylvie looked skeptical. "Why? Either Evelyn has been very foolish, or somebody stole her and her clothes."

"The missing clothing suggests Evelyn has not fallen out of a tree or come to grief in the river. We can eliminate misadventure from her possible fates."

Neither Sylvie nor Bella looked much comforted by my observation, and neither was I. We could eliminate misadventure, but running away was now more likely, given the missing clothing.

As was kidnapping.

CHAPTER TEN

"In Scotland, we'd claim a ghoulie or a bogle was at work." Sebastian said quietly. "Let's take this discussion elsewhere." He'd found me in the classroom, apparently thinking as I had to speak with the children early in the day.

"We must collect St. Sevier from down the corridor, my lord. He's conducting impromptu French lessons with the boys."

Sylvie and Bella weren't even pretending to sketch, but rather, goggling at Sebastian. He was attired in a less formal version of the kilt, and the girls were clearly impressed.

"Come along, ladies," Sebastian said, holding out his hands. "We mustn't let the lads have all the fun." He was seized by a pair of giggling little girls and dragged toward the door. "If the boys think to enjoy French, then I will teach them some Gaelic that puts the French to the blush."

I followed more slowly and took Evelyn's sketchbook with me. When we returned to the playroom, St. Sevier was explaining to the boys how to say *good day* and *good night* in French, and Dottie was moving her lips in unison with the boys.

"What about 'my pony is better than your pony'?" Stephen, Mr.

Botham's boy, asked as St. Sevier rose from the table. "Lady Violet said you can teach us that."

"*Très facile*," St. Sevier replied. "*Mon poney est meilleur que ton poney.*"

The boys took up the chorus in robust voices while Dottie repeated the words more quietly, gaze upon her lap. I had vague recollections of her sitting through some of my earliest schoolroom lessons, but wondered if she'd been given any formal education at all.

"Lads," Sebastian said over the din, "you mustn't shout in the nursery, or you won't be seeing much of your ponies for some time. Lord Pritchard and Mr. Botham would not like to know that you've cost Hansom her hearing."

"They've healthy lungs," Hansom said. "Never a question about that."

Sebastian, St. Sevier, and I left the nursery as a footman arrived to collect the breakfast dishes. I had a word with him—I did not know his name—and then led my escorts along the corridor and down one flight of stairs into the family wing.

"We won't be disturbed in here." I pushed open the door to my old rooms and moved through the parlor to the French doors. "This side of the house doesn't get much morning sun, so it should be reasonably cool, and I've asked to have a tray sent up."

"You found something among the sketches," St. Sevier said, taking out a handkerchief and swatting at a wooden bench along the balcony wall.

I took the proffered seat while the gentlemen lounged against the balcony. "Have a look for yourselves, especially toward the back."

They perched side by side and leafed through the pages, Sebastian darker and slightly taller than St. Sevier, both men quite striking, and both so very dear.

"Not a bad portrait of Bascomb," Sebastian muttered at length.

"Not a good portrait," I retorted. "When did he sit for it, and why was Evelyn so flattering?"

"He's an attractive man, Violet," Sebastian replied in patient tones. "What motive could he have for making off with a girl child who happens to be at a most troublesome age?"

"Whatever his motive, it's nefarious." Of that, I was certain. Did he know of the summer cottage? I was abruptly in a tearing hurry to conclude this discussion and visit the cottage myself, though Evelyn's sketchbook might be entirely irrelevant.

St. Sevier passed me back the drawings. "Bascomb apparently considers himself a disappointed suitor where Violet is concerned. Perhaps he talked Evelyn into pulling a prank, and he will redeem himself in Violet's eyes when he rescues the child."

That theory made a sort of sense, and thus I did not care for it. "Except that I gave him a chance to make his peace with me, and he declined it."

"Pride goeth..." St. Sevier muttered, taking a seat at the opposite end of the bench.

Sebastian turned to face the dense woods across a short expanse of park. "What we aren't saying is that Bascomb could have taken the girl to do sexual harm to her, and we might never find her."

"How old is she?" St. Sevier asked.

"I'd say twelve, at least, though I don't know for certain. I can ask her mother."

Sebastian sent a glance over his shoulder at St. Sevier.

"Whatever it is, out with it," I said.

Sebastian returned his gaze to the tangled woods. "The age of consent for females in England is twelve. The army had occasion to impress that fact on its more unruly soldiers."

"Some of whom," St. Sevier said, "ignored even that law."

"Bascomb was married," Sebastian said. "He has children not much younger than Evelyn."

St. Sevier rose and paced the length of the balcony. "You know that makes no difference, Dunkeld. Comstock was married and had two daughters, for God's sake, but no young girl was safe around him."

"Who was Comstock?" I dreaded the answer, but had to know.

"A lieutenant," Sebastian replied. "To the casual observer, he was a well-liked, gallant officer. Then the other officers' wives noticed patterns. Comstock was so good with children, especially the shy young girls. He was always happy to take them up before him in the saddle when we moved camp. He read to the children on Sunday afternoons... And yet, whenever a siege broke, he became a monster in regimental scarlet, making straight for the convent schools."

"What became of him?"

A silence bloomed as a hawk soared up from the trees.

"He did not survive the campaign," St. Sevier's tone would have frozen that hawk in midflight.

The footman arrived with the tray, and for a few minutes, we busied ourselves making sandwiches of toast, ham, and omelet. I'd asked for cold lemonade rather than hot tea. Even on this shady, breezy balcony, the day's heat was beginning to intrude.

"Do sit, Dunkeld," I said, patting the bench. "You loom over me like a disapproving nanny."

St. Sevier had resumed his place at the far end of the bench, and thus Sebastian took the place between us. While he munched his sandwich, he resumed leafing through the sketchbook.

"I've seen this cat," he said. "Big fellow. I can't think where I saw him, though. Shall I have a look around the summer cottage?"

"Please, and as soon as may be," I replied, holding the cold glass of lemonade to my cheek. "When a suitably discreet and private moment presents itself, I will let Ellersby know what we've found." I would create such a moment in the next hour.

"Not Derwent?" St. Sevier asked oh-so-casually.

"Not Derwent. His job is to look after Lady Eutheria and the other guests."

Neither man argued with me.

Sebastian turned another page. "Any idea what Hector and Ajax are arguing about? I heard them going at it in the stable yesterday afternoon."

"They are always bickering." Though what did I truly know of them? I had not shared a household with my middle brothers for nearly ten years. I was closest to Felix, who was only a couple of years my senior. Ajax and Hector had always been closest to each other.

Which had left Ellersby precisely where?

"They were having a contentious discussion over the port the other night," St. Sevier said. "All whispered admonitions and fuming silences. They are out of charity with each other."

I finished my lemonade and poured myself another half a glass. "If I were to ask them what was amiss, they would be insulted that I implied less than perfect harmony between brothers."

"Felix beat them in the race to secure the succession," Sebastian said, rising and passing me the sketchbook. "That has his brothers all quite peevish."

"Not peevish enough to stage a kidnapping just to disrupt James's christening, Dunkeld. Don't be ridiculous."

Sebastian bowed. "My apologies, my lady. I meant no offense. I'm off to enjoy a constitutional in the vicinity of the summer cottage. A pleasant day to you both."

St. Sevier slid down the bench to the place beside me and took a sip of my lemonade. "I want to resent the marquess, but he's too decent. I suspect he knows how that vexes me and takes delight in my misery."

"Now you are being ridiculous." Though I grasped St. Sevier's point. Sebastian knew me of old, and I trusted him without reservation. He'd grasped without being told that I'd head for the nursery this morning, for example.

He was also correct that my brothers were discommoded by James's arrival, and that *was* ridiculous.

"If we are to *enjoy* the village shops before the worst of the day's heat, do you need to change your dress?" St. Sevier asked.

"This is a walking dress. Did you learn anything from the boys in the nursery?"

St. Sevier finished his breakfast and dusted his hands together. "The boys were in awe of Miss Evelyn, and I gather they are secretly relieved that she's no longer on hand to correct, chide, insult, or harass them."

"They did not care for her?"

"Hansom allowed as the young miss demanded a great deal of attention."

"God forbid a young girl not be silent and invisible for the convenience of all around her, but we have come across another clue, St. Sevier. Sylvie and Bella tell me some of Evelyn's clothes are missing."

His gaze narrowed on the forest canopy. "Either Evelyn had sense enough to gather up some belongings before she decamped for parts unknown, or somebody knew where her clothing was kept."

"And the somebodies who might know that include both Botham and Pritchard, because they have children in the nursery."

"As do Lord and Lady Ellersby. This grows complicated."

I leaned against him, because complicated was a euphemism, and somewhere nearby a young girl was doubtless much in need of rescuing, if she was still alive.

To avail ourselves of shade and draw less notice, St. Sevier and I decided our walk to the village would follow an indirect path, through the woods, across the river to MacHeath's Ford, and down the drive through the Ford's park.

We tarried in the woods long enough to indulge in a protracted, close embrace. I was tempted to detour to the fishing cottage to make another search, except that I'd suggested Lady Ellersby lock it rather than encourage wanton behavior among the guests.

I knew where the key was, of course, but I also knew that questioning the shopkeepers was urgent.

"I should part from you at the posting inn," St. Sevier said. "I will linger over a cool pint while you visit the shops."

"Then who will carry my parcels?" Because I intended to

purchase this and that in the interest of loosening tongues and jogging memories.

"The shopkeepers will speak more freely if I am not at your side, Violet. You are a widow, and thus you need no maid or chaperone to accompany you on your errands. Have your parcels delivered to the inn, and I will carry them for you when we return to the Hall."

We walked along the dusty drive as the morning took on the heavy stillness of a hot summer day. Not even the birds exerted themselves overhead, though the river burbling along to our right was cool and lovely music.

St. Sevier was up to something, being gallant or delicate or devious. I applied my mind to the conundrum as we approached the end of the drive.

"You plan to inquire regarding passengers on the stagecoach. Where would Evelyn get the money for the fare?" Children did travel unaccompanied frequently, particularly boys off to school or apprentices given leave to visit family.

"Evelyn might not have been traveling alone."

More delicacy. "St. Sevier, must I be severe with you?"

He ambled along beside me, all relaxed male grace, his stride easily keeping pace with mine. "I do not want to upset you."

"I am upset over a missing child. I doubt you can exacerbate that unfortunate state of affairs."

"I overheard a pair of footmen grumbling on the terrace below my room this morning."

We turned right at the gate, taking the lane in the direction of the village. "Out with it, St. Sevier."

"Bascomb sent his valet home to collect the twins. He claimed he hadn't realized Pritchard's son would be on hand, or the Botham boy. He did not want to add to the staff's burdens, but as the footmen quoted him, 'What's another couple of boys when the nursery already has a pair on hand?'"

"Clearly, Bascomb does not understand the math of boys."

"Or he needed an excuse to send his valet away, possibly with Evelyn in tow."

I asked the logical question. "Was Bascomb's carriage missing?"

St. Sevier heaved up an aggrieved sigh as we approached the church at the edge of the village green. "I made an inventory of the carriage house this morning before joining you on the balcony. I know not which carriage belongs to Bascomb, and my casual inquiries met with raised eyebrows and prevarications."

I considered that report and considered that most of my father's staff had lost loved ones at some point in the twenty years of hostilities with the French. That French families had suffered even more grievous losses would not have occurred to the footmen and grooms.

St. Sevier had, in fact, lost all three of his brothers, not to mention a wife in the course of the war.

"Here is how we will go on in the village," I said, linking my arm through his. "You will escort me from shop to shop. I will beam at you. You will smile at me. When I ask for your opinion, you will provide it in a manner that flatters my vanity."

"You have no vanity."

"St. Sevier, we shall *bill* and *coo* and *dote* and *flirt* before the local populace until they grasp that you are my dear, darling friend and entirely worthy of their trust. They either accept you, or they will earn my disfavor. If that means the footmen must catch us cavorting on the stairs, then so be it."

Without making a sound, my dear, darling friend was laughing at me.

"Trust, *mon coeur*, must be earned, present company being an example of same. Far be it from me to miss an opportunity to dote and flirt, though. I will bat my eyes at you and slobber upon your hand, shall I?"

"Slobbering will not be necessary. Ought we to stop in at the vicarage?"

"Pritchard called there yesterday. If anybody was likely to be forthcoming with his lordship, the local parson would be."

"To the shops, then."

The village was organized in standard English fashion, with a large green where markets and outdoor gatherings were held. The blacksmith's forge stood opposite the apothecary and lending library. Other establishments included a store that sold fabric and dress-making sundries, a general store, a bakery, the posting inn, and, set back some way, a horse-powered grain mill that also traded in agricultural supplies.

I knew the families associated with each business, but had not ventured near the forge in years. A lady risked hearing profanity, breathing cigar fumes courtesy of the men loitering about the place, or seeing the blacksmith without his shirt (a magnificent sight, as best I recalled). The smithy had always loomed in my imagination as a place of mystery and alchemy.

Tools arrived broken and left once more serviceable. Bars of metal became horseshoes and fire tongs. Men spoke in a strange dialect around the forge, an earthy, humorous, vulgar tongue I did not comprehend. I'd spent many an afternoon perched in the branches of a maple in the yard of the bakery, watching the goings-on at the blacksmith's.

"That's Ajax," I muttered, "and that's his new gelding."

Ajax had apparently brought his steed to be shod, and Hector had accompanied him. They stood on the green across from the smithy, the horse cropping grass while Ajax and Hector bickered. I caught "foolish" and "cork-brained" from Ajax, while Hector tossed out "stubborn" and "miserable sod."

The men at the forge were mostly ignoring this behavior, though on the steps of the posting inn, the publican was spending an inordinate amount of time watering his potted salvia. The horses were taking note, as indicated by pricked ears and alert eyes.

"My brothers are making a scene. This is not good."

"Shall I interrupt?"

More aspersion crossed the green on a sultry breeze. "Doomed to the shires" from Hector and "bloody daft" from Ajax.

"If either of us intervenes, the hostilities will simply resume as soon as we've been told to mind our own business. The dressmaker's is the logical place to start our errands."

Hector swiped his hat off and brushed back his hair and, in so doing, caught sight of me. He waved, smiled, and went right back to arguing with Ajax.

I waved back and all but dragged St. Sevier into the dressmaker's shop. I made small purchases in each shop, and St. Sevier and I enjoyed a picnic luncheon of fare provided by the inn. No matter how delicately I inquired, no matter how much St. Sevier flirted, stood too close to me, or smiled at the shopgirls, nobody had seen a half-grown girl of Evelyn's description.

Not on her own, not in the company of a strange man, not getting onto the stagecoach. Not anywhere.

"We've learned little, though I suppose it's a relief that Evelyn didn't depart by coach," I said when we emerged from the inn into the early afternoon heat. "I hope Dunkeld has something encouraging to report regarding the summer cottage."

"Will you take it amiss if I also explore this summer cottage on my own, Violet?"

We wandered past the green, this time making for the bridge that led onto Derwent Hall land. "I have promised the children an outing to the berry patch later this afternoon," I said, "fool that I am."

"You are not a fool. You are a favorite auntie who will earn the undying devotion of the nursery staff." St. Sevier stopped walking in the middle of the lane. "I just recalled something, though it's probably of no moment."

I was preoccupied with the fact that my brothers had made a public spectacle of their differences. What could possibly goad them into such a display?

"What did you recall?"

"This morning in the nursery, Dottie's fingers were berry-stained."

"Dottie is taller than I am. I doubt Ellersby and I saw her boot prints by the berry patch."

"Coincidence, then. She must have made a stop on her way over from the dower house, and who wouldn't avail themselves of such bounty if they could do so undetected?"

St. Sevier parted from me at the Derwent Hall stables, intent on inspecting the summer cottage. I knew I should accompany him, except that I was hot, and my afternoon would include yet another outing. I also wanted some peace and quiet to consider the day's developments, discouraging though they were.

CHAPTER ELEVEN

The outing to the berry patch was a sweaty, sticky ordeal that culminated in a high-spirited berry battle. To my great consternation, I was left to preside over the warring factions alone while Miss Oakes and Mr. Harkness "sought some shade for a moment."

I shamelessly eavesdropped on the children, who seemed fairly compatible outside the watchful eye of the nursery staff. Dottie had begged off, "owing to the heat and all," though I suspected she wanted a break from the children more than she wanted to escape the nursery.

Why weren't the children more upset about Evelyn's disappearance? Perhaps the poor girl had rubbed everyone the wrong way. I knew how that felt and was thus constantly scanning the woods for any sign Evelyn had passed the berry patch. Contrary or not, she needed to be found.

I took care to surreptitiously compare footprints left by Bella and Sylvie with those Ellersby and I had found earlier. The mystery boot prints were slightly larger than my nieces' impressions, though not as large as my own, strongly suggesting they indeed belonged to Evelyn.

"We should have brought Dottie," Bella said, flopping down on the grass beside the river. "She likes raspberries."

Sylvie came down beside her sister. "She eats everything she picks."

"So do you."

Sylvie grinned, her lips rosy with berry juice. "I saved some to repel the Huns."

"We're the Roman army," Henry said, taking his place on the grass. "We're conquering Britannia."

"You conquered the berry patch," I said, "and thus it's time we were getting back to the Hall."

Stephen Botham was the last to give up on the berry picking. "I'm tired."

"We will take our time returning to the nursery," I assured him, "and keep to the shady paths in the wood."

"Can we come again tomorrow?" Sylvie asked. "We had ever so much fun, Auntie Violet."

"Please," Bella chorused. "Dottie didn't let us pick berries when we came this way from the dower house, and she was forever ordering us not to go in the river. I don't want to go in any beastly old river."

"We could go wading," Henry said, "if Papa gave permission."

"Not here." I grasped Bella's hands and hauled her to her feet. "The water is too deep here, but closer to the water meadow, the river is shallow enough to cross on foot most of the time, hence the name of Uncle Felix's home, MacHeath's Ford."

"MacHeath is Uncle Sebastian's name," Sylvie said. "He wears kilts."

So Sebastian had earned honorary-uncle status? That thought made me happy, though it surprised me.

"Kilts are stupid," Henry declared, getting to his feet. "Papa says so. Why would a man want to show off his knees like that?"

Because his national dress meant the world to him, and he'd been banished from his homeland as a mere boy.

"I like kilts," Bella countered, "and I like that Uncle Sebastian has lemon drops in his sporran."

Stephen, I noticed, remained above this verbal affray. Mr. Harkness and Miss Oakes rejoined the party only as I was herding the children back in the direction of Derwent Hall. I had mostly left the infantry to their berry picking—or berry eating and berry pitching—while I gathered up enough fruit to make a pie for the nursery.

What Miss Oakes and Mr. Harkness had got up to, I could not say, but whatever shade they'd found had left the young lady quite flushed and the gentleman's hair in disarray.

And in this heat.

The children's suggestion that we wade in the river stuck with me, and thus I pleaded fatigue at dinner—not a headache, because the genuine article plagued me all too frequently. St. Sevier had nothing of note to report about the summer cottage, which was a mere three rooms and a wide porch facing the river. Its outstanding feature, from my recollection, was that the slope of the land and overhang of the porch meant enterprising children had been able to scramble onto the roof.

"You didn't happen to see a large, long-haired ginger cat on your travels?" I asked St. Sevier when he looked in on me before supper.

"I did not." He took the place beside me on the sofa, where I'd been reading Mama's diary. "You are honestly only tired?" He perused me with a physician's keen eye and a lover's concern.

"I am tired of worrying, St. Sevier. At supper, Papa will try to be cheerful without being obnoxious, and he will only half succeed. Lady Eutheria will be brave and quiet. Lord and Lady Ellersby will try to keep the conversation engaging without shading into inanity, and Bascomb will be seated halfway down the table. He will pointedly ignore me and I him, so I will spare us both the effort."

To be fair, Bascomb had searched as hard as anybody for Evelyn, but that was exactly what a monster would do, had he kidnapped the girl.

St. Sevier wrapped an arm around my shoulders. "Thank you for dragging me about the village today, Violet. You made it very plain you were showing me off."

"You are well worth showing off." Not that we'd made any headway winning the trust of the village folk. They'd been polite to St. Sevier, but their gazes had still held suspicion. "Rome was not conquered in a day, and the dressmaker's approval of my prospective spouse does not signify."

"I'm a prospective spouse now?"

"People who enjoy an understanding with one another are generally contemplating marriage, St. Sevier."

He withdrew his arm. "So they are. Right now, I had best contemplate how to listen to Bascomb's droning on about the direct route from reform to revolution."

I shuddered to contemplate such a discussion. "He's a staunch Tory?"

"Or he's intent on convincing your father he is." St. Sevier rose with the air of a man facing a difficult penance. "I do not dare point out to Mr. Bascomb that it was precisely an unwillingness to effect reforms that resulted in the bloody alternative coming to pass in France. Far be it from me to explain French politics to an Englishman of no particular education."

I got to my feet and hugged St. Sevier. "Engage Lord Ellersby in the discussion. He is a man of relentless moderation, and he can challenge Barsomb's conceits without provoking a lecture on the more sanguinary points of French history."

St. Sevier pressed his forehead to mine. "I will miss you."

"Would you miss me less if I chose a date for our nuptials?"

He drew back to peer down at me. "I will miss you more than ever knowing you seriously contemplate speaking your vows with me."

He kissed me, the sweetest, most tender, languid, cherishing... oh, Lord. The man could kiss.

"I will have to travel to the dinner table by way of a cold bath," he said, stepping back a moment later. "You put me in a state, my lady."

I patted his chest and then slid my hand lower. A state indeed. "I will count the hours until we can be in a state together."

He kissed my fingers, bowed, and withdrew.

I had offered to set a wedding date, and St. Sevier had not pressed me to do so. Was he being gentlemanly, coy, shrewd... or something else?

～

To say St. Sevier had left me hot and bothered was only partly figurative. The sun had set, and the summer twilight turned the world beyond my window to shadows. The moon would not rise for another hour, and I was seized by an impulse. I could resume my place on the sofa, re-reading the words of a woman long dead, or I could treat myself to the sort of small adventure I'd enjoyed frequently as a girl.

I gathered up what I needed and slipped down the maids' stairs to the side garden. From there, I made my way the short distance into the trees and along a path to the river.

The water gleamed darkly in the fading light, insects sketching trails on the tranquil pools near the bank. A frog offered his homely song to the evening air as I spread my blanket and peeled down to my oldest chemise.

If I were a bolder woman, I'd have left the chemise on the bank. Instead, I eased into the water—lusciously cool near the bank, colder still where the current ran more strongly—and struck out for the opposite side.

The pleasure was exquisite, to be cool, to be comfortable, to be free of confining clothing, bonnets, parasols, garters, shoes... A tepid bath could never compare to the utter joy of cavorting in a living body of water, and as I luxuriated in the cool currents, I blessed the fact that I had four older brothers.

Stubborn little creature that I'd been, I'd demanded that they teach me how to paddle about safely in the water, where they disported by the hour like otters. My governess had been horrified when she'd learned that I knew how to swim, my mother resigned, and my father—I dared hope—proud.

I found the stony river bottom with my toes and stood for a time neck-deep, letting the water tug my cares and worries away. Evelyn might well have drowned, though that would have required reckless-ness and bad luck, both, as well as a serious lack of supervision on the part of her minders.

Where had Miss Oakes been when Evelyn had gone missing? I pondered that question, then recalled that Miss Oakes had been least in sight for a significant time that very afternoon. I would have a private discussion with the pretty governess early in the morning.

I longed to dunk myself thoroughly, to immerse myself in the river's pleasure, but darkness was fast approaching. If I did not leave the water soon, I would have to wait until moonrise to make my way through the woods.

I began to slog toward shore when a patch of darkness detached itself from the gloom of the woods. In that first instant, when I real-ized somebody had been watching me, panic hit me in a paralyzing deluge.

Would Bascomb do such a thing? Would Lord Pritchard make a jest of my predicament, sopping wet and truant from supper?

The shadow kept moving and became a man, who set a bundle on my blanket and then lowered himself beside it. "What exactly are ye trying to prove with this foolishness, Violet?"

"Sebastian."

"I begged off from the supper," he said. "Pleaded business with my tenants at the Ford, though Felix has them all eating out of his hand. I was simply..." Sebastian pulled off a boot and stared at the night sky. On the eastern horizon, stars were beginning to wink into view. "I was homesick."

For the past, apparently, rather than for Scotland. "Come on in, then. The water's lovely."

He pulled off a second boot. Jacket, waistcoat, stockings, sporran, *sgian dubh,* and shirt followed, until he was attired in only his kilt, and ye heavenly saints, he made a lovely picture in the gathering gloom.

He dove from a tree limb overhanging the river, cleanly cutting the water's surface and disappearing into the middle of the river. He could hold his breath for some time, and I was thus only a little worried when it took him a few moments to surface several yards from me.

"I have missed this," he said, whipping his head to sling his hair from his eyes. "I have missed this sorely." He struck off upstream, and I purely enjoyed the sight of him reveling in the water. Had Pamela Bonaventure ever seen him thus? Did she long to? She would never have the memories I shared with Sebastian of late-night swimming and long conversation overheard by only the crickets and forest creatures.

While Sebastian frolicked, I made my way to the riverbank and wrapped myself in my cloak. As a girl, I'd developed a sequence that involved shedding my wet chemise and then wiggling into a dry morning gown, all beneath the modesty of the cloak.

Undignified, but adequate for safeguarding my sensibilities. Rather than embark on that effort, I sat on the blanket with my cloak wrapped over my wet chemise and scanned the horizon for the glow that portended a rising moon.

Sebastian joined me ten minutes later, dark hair sleeked back, kilt dripping, like some northern kelpie gone astray. He sat on the blanket beside me, making no move to dry off or get dressed.

"Tell me of the summer cottage," I said. Had he found anything significant, he would have conveyed the news long since, but perhaps he'd noticed a peculiar detail or two.

"I am alone at moonrise with a lovely woman, and all she wants of me is a casualty report. You had a romantic nature once upon a time, Violet Marie." He bumped my shoulder good-naturedly, but his observation did not feel entirely like a jest.

"I had a foolish nature, and somebody married that and the

romance right out of me. I want to have a talk with Miss Oakes. She and Mr. Harkness are involved."

"Involved or co-conspirators?" Sebastian fished his sporran from the heap of his dry clothing. "I have something to show you."

He opened the sporran and extracted a scrap of white fabric. I could not see it clearly, though the moon would soon rise, so all was not pitch darkness.

"A handkerchief?" Linen, based on the texture, and thus meant to be serviceable rather than decorative. "It's stained."

"Not blood," Sebastian said, drawing his knees up and looping his arms around them. "I've seen enough blood-stained fabric to know. The stains aren't stiff like blood. They don't smell of blood. I'd say berry juice, and if you examine the embroidery in proper light, you'll see it's not very sophisticated."

I smoothed my fingers over the stitching, a simple pattern of leaves and flowers. "Evelyn's work?"

"Possibly. I found it at the summer cottage. I looked for footprints, too, but the surrounds are all grassy. Somebody has been there, though. An upper window was cracked open, and Lady Ellersby would never have allowed such an oversight in an unoccupied building."

A cracked window let in the damp, bugs, birds, rodents, trysting servants, village boys, vagrants... "Do you think Evelyn was held there?"

"Or she sheltered there on her own."

"But why? Why create all this drama?"

"I don't know. I do know that the moon is about to crest the horizon, and that is not a moment to waste fretting. We are doing all in our power to find the girl, Violet. Hush and enjoy the moonrise."

Were we doing *all* in our power? I remained beside Sebastian on the blanket as the great golden orb of the moon drifted up into the night sky. I hadn't enjoyed a moonrise in years, and certainly never with my husband. The experience imparted a sense of peace and wonder that was a balm to my soul.

Somewhere, I hoped, Evelyn was watching the same moonrise and looking forward to the day when she was once again the despair of her mother's aspirations and the terror of the nursery.

"I should go back to the Hall," I said as an owl hooted from the depths of the wood.

"I'll walk you to the edge of the trees."

I was glad for Sebastian's escort, but when I would have crossed the park to slip in a side door, he stopped me with a hand on my arm.

"If St. Sevier has developed doubts about marrying you now that you are willing to have him, I will gut him where he stands, Violet."

Sebastian had changed into dry breeches and held his damp kilt along with my bundled blanket. He could thus not defend himself when I kissed his cheek.

"I am more glad than you can know, Sebastian, that you are still my friend. St. Sevier has not developed doubts. No gutting will be needed."

I left my fierce friend in the shadows of the trees. Once back in my room, I donned a summer nightgown and stole down the balcony to find slumber in St. Sevier's bed, though I paused before going inside. There along the tree line, barely illuminated by moonlight, Sebastian remained, watching.

I slipped into St. Sevier's bedroom and went straight to his bed. When Hugh eventually joined me some hours later, I did not wait patiently or passively to see if he'd initiate lovemaking. I had my way with him, thoroughly, passionately, and more than once.

~

"You are quiet this morning," St. Sevier remarked as our horses walked up the Derwent Hall drive in the dawn sunshine. St. Sevier was once again on the grand chestnut gelding, and I wondered if he'd had the horse sent out from Town.

The beast looked too impressive—and too well suited to its rider —to be a guest horse from my father's herd.

"I am thinking," I replied, patting Aurora's sweaty neck. "I can attribute old bitterness to Bascomb on my account, but that makes a weak excuse for stealing a child. Mr. Botham is a disagreeable sort generally, though Lady Eutheria apparently enjoys his company, and that is no reason to take up kidnapping. Without a villainous motive, we are left to conclude Evelyn is being unforgivably dramatic, and that makes no sense either."

"Why not? Particularly if her mother is disporting with two different men at the same house party, the child might have reason to stage a tantrum."

St. Sevier had a point. After my mother's death, my father's various liaisons, with neighbors' wives, local widows, the occasional housekeeper—enthusiastically willing, I hoped—and God knew who in Town had vexed me exceedingly. Nobody had had to tell me what he was about. His foolishness was abundantly apparent to my adolescent eyes.

How dare he turn from my mother's memory so easily and so often? But then, I gathered from Mama's diaries that Papa had been far from faithful to her in life.

"Evelyn might well be upset," I said, "but I fear we must schedule a discussion with Mr. Botham. We've been so busy searching and interrogating villagers and tenants that we haven't made thorough inquiries of the guests, and they were under Papa's roof when Evelyn went missing."

Aurora plodded along. Without regular exercise, she wasn't in condition for much of a morning hack, a situation I would address with the grooms. Or perhaps I should inform Papa that Aurora was coming back to London with me, where I could oversee her care personally.

But no. If I were a horse, I'd much prefer a mostly idle existence among my life-long friends in the shires to the smoke and bustle of the capital.

And if I were a human...

"I have some inkling what's set your brothers against each other,"

St. Sevier said. "You recall the fencing exhibition right after we arrived?"

"The fencing exhibition that saw money changing hands in all directions and ladies plastering their noses to windows like forlorn puppies?"

"The fencing exhibition Pritchard won, though besting Hector took him a half-dozen rounds."

"What of it? I would hope the heat alone would deter his lordship from repeating that exercise." Though stripped down to only breeches in the shade of the oaks, perhaps that exertion had felt good?

"Hector wants a rematch."

"He is stubborn, a family trait."

St. Sevier let a few beats of clip-clopping hooves go by. "A family trait? I would never have noticed."

"Wretch." I swatted in his general direction with my whip, though of course I missed. The gelding danced away, another indication that the horse was no borrowed hack.

"Hector wants a rematch," St. Sevier went on, "and Ajax is trying to talk him out of it. They were overheard when the ladies withdrew last night. Ajax apparently lost a sum on his brother that he could ill afford to lose."

The stable came into view, and Aurora's walk acquired more purpose.

"What does Pritchard say about this?"

"He is more than willing to oblige Hector, apparently, and raise the stakes as well. Ajax has a litany of reasons why Hector must not take that bait."

"Perhaps because a child is missing, and we've neither explanation nor clues as to her whereabouts?"

The young, blond groom watched our approach, and I was again struck by the sense that I'd seen him somewhere before.

"Ajax did mention that a rematch would be bad form given the disappearance of a guest's child, but he also referred to Hector being too slow, too easily winded, and too hot-headed to prevail over the more strategic, stronger, and faster Lord Pritchard."

I drew Aurora to a halt. "Ajax *said that* to Hector where others could overhear him? Did Hector allow him to live?"

"Ellersby was present." St. Sevier's horse stopped as well. "Thus an exchange of blows was prevented for the nonce. I also became aware of something else you should know."

"I know I very much enjoyed sharing a bed with you last night, St. Sevier." I wanted to convey that sentiment to him before the worries of the day obscured my memories of the previous night. "You were impressive."

He'd been relentless and tender, and—unlike his usual lovemaking, which was peppered with whispered phrases in French, humorous asides, and the occasional request—he'd loved me in sweet, warm silence.

"I love you," St. Sevier said, regarding me very directly. "I could hide behind pretty French phrases or play games until we reach the altar, but I want you to know, Violet, that I love you dearly. I will never regret that."

He urged his horse forward at the trot while I wrestled with a welter of conflicting emotions.

Joy, because I had given my esteem to an abundantly worthy man, one secure enough in himself to declare his sentiments openly, without schemes or attempts to manipulate me through his attentions.

I also experienced confusion, because St. Sevier hadn't tarried long enough to allow me to make a reciprocal declaration, which he absolutely deserved to hear from me. Perhaps he wanted me to choose a quiet moment, as he had, to freely offer a testament of my feelings for him.

As Aurora mustered a trot in pursuit of St. Sevier's gelding, I also felt some bewilderment: What had St. Sevier meant about never *regretting* his love for me? Was I that difficult to love? Was he having second thoughts about offering for me?

And men claimed women were mercurial creatures...

He assisted me from my horse, his hands lingering only a moment at my waist. In our absence, the stable had swung into its morning routine. Stable lads led horses who'd spent the night at grass into stalls, while grooms prepared young stock for training sessions before the day's heat intensified.

The blond fellow was scrubbing out wooden buckets by the horse trough and watering beds of geraniums as he dumped each bucket.

Who is he? I was at the point of asking the head lad for an answer to that question when the boy himself smiled at me.

"Aurora is more her old self when milady comes to call," he said, tugging at the brim of his cap. "She's a dear old thing, and I do like to see her happy."

"She is a dear old thing." While this young groom was forward, if charmingly so. "Who might you be?"

"I'm Samuel, ma'am. I usually work at the smithy, but I'm on loan to the Hall at present. Got my start here, though you probably won't remember me. I've always been outdoor staff, first in the gardens, then in the stable."

"Samuel, back to work." The head lad, Fletcher, smiled at me. "Sorry, milady. Samuel is too sociable for his own good sometimes."

Samuel grinned and tossed the dregs of his bucket toward Fletcher's boots. "G'day, milady, and we will take the best care of Aurora for you."

He sauntered back into the barn, full of the cheeky good humor of the adolescent male.

"That one," Fletcher said, shaking his head. "Thinks because he was born at the Hall he's something special, though I must admit the horses like him. To be expected, I suppose." Fletcher bobbed a bow at me and followed Samuel into the barn.

To be expected? Why? An answer having to do with my father's love for horses and his periodic liaisons with his housekeepers came to mind, and I nearly marched into the barn to inspect Samuel for a resemblance to my brothers. Samuel was fair, while my siblings were dark-haired, but still...

St. Sevier left off conferring with a stable hand and propped his foot on a water trough to remove his spurs.

"Charlemagne disdains your hay here," St. Sevier said. "He prefers grass, which he doesn't get much of in London. The lads are worried he will gobble himself into a colic."

"Charlemagne is your chestnut gelding?"

St. Sevier passed me a spur. "I am his general factotum and tolerated rider. He does the same thing in Berkshire. Scythes the grass like a biblical plague, urinates on the hay, if I might be indelicate. But he has the heart of a lion and would jump the moon if I asked it of him. I am ready to do justice to breakfast, and I thank you for a lovely outing."

He removed the second spur, and I gave the first one back to him. I had not ridden with a spur, finding it unsporting when my mount was a pensioner.

He offered his arm, and we left the bustle and dust of the stable yard behind to take the path through the trees back to the Hall.

"St. Sevier?"

"Violet?"

"I love you too." What my declaration lacked in effusiveness, I hoped it made up for in sincerity. I owed Hugh St. Sevier so much, and I esteemed him greatly. To be able to do that—respect a man whole-heartedly—was wonderful.

He meandered along arm in arm with me, then paused beneath a stately maple—one that would provide us protection from prying eyes at the Hall—and kissed me.

"I hope we are always like this," I said, snuggling close. "Honest with each other and... affectionate."

He muttered something in French and stepped back. "If we are to arrive at the breakfast table in any sort of acceptable condition, my affectionate nature had best acquire some decorum. You were thinking to question Miss Oakes?"

St. Sevier doubtless did not mean to dash cold water on my declaration, but I felt as if I were a patch of geraniums and he a groom heedlessly wielding a bucket. Even so, St. Sevier was again being sensible: Evelyn was still missing, and we knew not why or where she'd gone.

"I will talk to Miss Oakes and to Mr. Harkness, and we should establish the whereabouts of the guests when Evelyn actually turned up missing. We've neglected that exercise."

"Because we do not want to be rude." St. Sevier patted my hand. "We should enlist Dunkeld's aid. A marquess will be seen as helpful when he asks incriminating questions."

"And he will get answers, not polite prevarications. Good thought. I will change out of this habit and see you at breakfast. I will also send a note over to MacHeath's Ford and inform his lordship—"

Lucy, my maid, came bustling down the path. "My lady, Monsieur," she panted, half bobbing a curtsey, "you are needed at the Hall."

"What's amiss?" I asked, for Lucy was difficult to upset.

"The nursery," she said. "We can't find Bella or Sylvie. They weren't in their beds this morning, and nobody knows where they are."

I gathered up the skirts of my riding habit and pelted for the Hall.

CHAPTER TWELVE

I did not intend to make the same mistake twice. "Take note of who was at breakfast," I said to St. Sevier as we entered the house through the conservatory. "I'm particularly interested in the whereabouts of Botham, Bascomb, and my brothers."

St. Sevier stopped me with a hand to my arm. "Miss Hewitt said only that the girls were missing from their beds this morning. They might have left the house at any point last night. The moon was nearly full, and these children know this estate."

"Evelyn does not know this estate."

"Evelyn's disappearance might well have inspired the younger girls to copy her mischief."

I wanted to smack St. Sevier for that bit of logic, because it *was* logic, particularly when applied to children.

"Sylvie and Bella have two loving parents. Uncles and aunties, a grandpapa who is occasionally doting, and... and... ponies. My nieces need not cause a fuss."

St. Sevier kissed my cheek. "We can debate motive later. Off to the nursery with you. I will also make inquiries at the stable and send word to MacHeath's Ford that we have another pair of disappearances."

I leaned into him, grateful for his cool head even as I knew the girls had not decided to make a breakfast call upon Uncle Felix. I knew something else too: The children had two devoted parents, but were those parents devoted to each other?

Had Sylvie and Bella come upon a tryst as I'd come upon Lady Eutheria and Mr. Botham? As I'd come upon my own father and his inamoratas from time to time growing up?

I pondered motives all the way to the nursery, which was a predictable scene of chaos and high emotion. Papa paced before the windows, discoursing generally on the vexatious nature of children, the incompetence of staff he paid well, and the need for his son and heir to take a firmer hand in the raising of a pair of willful hoydens.

Beneath all of this blaming, I detected an unusual thread of fear in the earl's bluster. Papa was literally lord of all he surveyed, most days, but three little girls had foiled his power handily—or their kidnapper had.

"Staff must sleep, my lord," I said, "and the children have apparently gone missing in the dead of night. Dottie, please take Henry and Stephen down to the classroom and set them to sketching." I would interview the boys later, when fuming and fretting adults were not on hand to stifle a child's candor.

I took the rocking chair before the hearth, much as my father often interrogated his factors and tenants from the seat behind his enormous estate desk.

"Hansom, when did you notice the children were missing?"

Hansom took two steps away from the door to the governess's bedchamber and ceased wringing her handkerchief.

"I didn't see nothin' amiss until the footman brung up the porridge, my lady. The boys were in here playing with the soldiers, and I thought the little girls overly tired from yesterday's outing. I went into the dormitory to rouse them for breakfast, and they were gone."

"Had their beds been slept in?"

"Aye, or made to look slept in."

Miss Oakes arrived, accompanied by Mr. Harkness, who appeared to have again neglected to apply a comb to his brown locks.

"The girls are gone?" Miss Oakes asked. "They are truly gone?"

"Had you reason to suspect they would be?" I countered.

A look passed between Miss Oakes and Mr. Harkness. *What to say? How honest to be?* I was growing heartily sick of couples and their looks.

"They did say they missed their ponies," Mr. Harkness replied. "For most of our nature walk, they were whingeing on about that. They wanted to walk over to the dower house stable to see the little beasts, but by then, the boys were tiring."

Papa ceased pacing. "I will shoot the damned ponies if they are the cause of this upheaval. My grandson is to be christened three days hence, and these hysterical female children and their pranks are not to be borne."

Hansom looked as if she might burst into tears.

"My lord," I said, "perhaps you'd best make sure your grandson is not among the missing children."

That suggestion had Papa striding from the nursery, precisely as I'd intended.

"They are not hysterical female children," Hansom said in the earl's absence. "They are good girls. Even Miss Evelyn. I would hate to think..." She descended into dabbing at her eyes with her handkerchief and sniffing.

"Please take a seat," I said, "all of you. We must put our heads together and decide how to proceed. It's possible the children are staging a prank, but as Hansom says, that is unlikely. They would face severe punishment, and deservedly so, if that were the case."

Hansom took the other rocking chair while Miss Oakes and Mr. Harkness sat indecorously close to each other on the toy chest.

"What else did the girls have to say on their nature walk?" I asked.

Nothing much of any consequence, apparently. They'd bickered with the boys about everything—English history, the names of plants, which trees would be easy to climb. The adults had mostly left them to it, only occasionally offering a botanical name for a shrub, or correcting the date of a battle.

"Sylvie and Bella were annoyed with Evelyn for disappearing from the nursery," Mr. Harkness said. "They felt she gave them an advantage of numbers over the boys, and now Mr. Bascomb's sons are rumored to be joining the gathering. Perhaps the ladies simply quit the field before superior forces arrived?" He posited that theory with a hopeful little smile.

"If the boys had disappeared, sir, would you similarly conclude they had quit the field? Is a nursery like the lists of a jousting tournament, a scene of battle, that girls must decamp on their own for parts unknown to find any peace?"

I spoke mildly, but I had been outnumbered by my brothers four to one. Just how formidable a nuisance did Mr. Harkness think small boys were to their female counterparts?

"The boys are sweet-natured little fellows," Miss Oakes said, twitching at her skirts. "The children actually get on fairly well, and Mrs. Hansom and I had discussed removing all three girls to the dower house if Mr. Bascomb's twins arrive."

The last thing this house party needed was more children underfoot. What on earth had Bascomb been thinking? I dreaded to ask him, but I would. His valet had left shortly after Evelyn's disappearance, after all.

"Did anybody look in on the children through the night?"

"I sleep in the governess's room," Hansom said, nodding in the direction of a door off the playroom. "The children were in the dormitory, of course, and I sleep with my door closed. They need a bit of privacy while they whisper and giggle themselves to sleep."

The dormitory opened off the opposite side of the playroom from Hansom's quarters and, like the governess's room, also had a door directly into the corridor.

"I have the bedchamber on the other side of the dormitory," Miss Oakes said. "My room shares the balcony with the dormitory and playroom, though I keep the connecting door to the dormitory locked. I could tell the children were talking back and forth as they settled into their beds, and nothing about their discussion struck me as unusual."

The nursery suite included several such bedrooms, for visiting governesses, companions, or poor relations. The accommodations on this floor were adequate, but modest.

"Could you hear what the children were saying?"

"I could not. I can tell you no voices were raised, no arguments undertaken."

Mr. Harkness patted Miss Oakes's hand. "There we have it, then. A prank to emulate Miss Evelyn's bad form. The girls simply left for some tree house or gamekeeper's cottage on a whim."

Hansom did not look convinced by that pronouncement, and neither was I. "Perhaps you are right, Mr. Harkness," I said, "but if so, we must still find our prodigals. You will all three want to break your fast, for the day will be long and trying."

They shuffled out of the nursery, leaving me to retrieve Dottie and the boys from the classroom. The boys went after some cinnamon buns left over from breakfast while I pulled Dottie aside.

"Let's have a look in the bureaus," I said, leading Dottie into the dormitory. "Can you tell me if the girls took any clothing with them?"

Dottie peered into drawers and rifled the contents. "Miss Bella took a spare dress, extra stockings, and her shawl. Miss Sylvie the same. Her bear is missing too, milady."

"Where do you think they've gone, Dottie?" She spent as much time with my nieces as anybody did, and in her way, she was quite observant.

"It's summertime, ma'am. They'll be fine wherever they are."

A commotion ensued in the playroom, and I returned there to find Lord Pritchard in riding attire, hair windblown, boots dusty.

"Lady Violet, what is this I hear about your nieces going missing?" He spoke quite sharply, no longer the charming rake. And now the children were *my nieces*, rather than Derwent's granddaughters. So much for a gentleman's innate gallantry.

Dottie hung back in the dormitory, and I did not blame her.

"What exactly have you heard?" I asked, striding up to him. "And from whom did you hear it?"

His countenance underwent a shift, from hauteur, to cool appraisal, to a faint smile. "Your father sent Ajax to the stable to organize a mounted patrol. I returned from a hack through the village to find pandemonium once again gripping the household."

"Not pandemonium, my lord. A search getting underway. My present objective is to talk to the boys, because they were the only people on hand when the girls either left the dormitory or were taken from it."

Lord Pritchard turned a severe eye on young Henry. "Well, lad, what have you to say?"

Henry examined at his half-eaten cinnamon bun. He stared at his little boots. He sent a miserable look in Stephen's direction.

"We slept on the balcony, my lord," Stephen said. "It's cooler out there, and the girls don't keep us awake with their chatter."

"You heard nothing?" I asked.

Henry shook his head, then blushed. "We heard giggling."

"From the girls?"

Now both boys were staring at the floor.

Pritchard regarded his son with interest. "From Miss Oakes's room?"

Henry nodded.

Oh dear. "Could the little girls have been in Miss Oakes's room?" And why had Pritchard noted the sleeping arrangements of a mere governess?

Stephen took to gazing past my shoulder. "I don't think the girls were in Miss Oakes's room, milady. Miss Oakes laughs like she's trying not to laugh. Ha-ha. Ha-ha. She won't just let go with a good laugh. We heard Miss Oakes, not the girls."

Ye gods, with her balcony door wide open and four children in the very next room. "Thank you for your honesty, Stephen. You and Henry have been very helpful."

"Mind you don't disappear," Pritchard said, mussing his son's hair. "I would miss you, scoundrel that you are." Pritchard beamed at the boy, and Henry grinned up at his father.

"My lord, shall we repair to the breakfast parlor?" I asked. "If you can tell me where you rode this morning, that will narrow the area to be searched."

Pritchard left the nursery with me and offered his arm. I took it, though his belated manners would gain him little ground with me.

"I had a good hard gallop yesterday," he said. "Today's outing was just to take the air and get my horse moving. I started on the path through the home wood, crossed to MacHeath's Ford, cantered the drive, and spent most of my time daundering along the village green. The inn wasn't serving yet, of course, but the village is peaceful at dawn. I dismounted and for some time strolled about, simply enjoying the quiet." He tilted his head and smiled. "Perhaps tomorrow, you'd like to ride out with me?"

Not if he were the last escort remaining in England. "Thank you for that kind invitation, but let's see what today brings before we decide whether tomorrow will lend itself to lazy hacks on the village green."

"You are so formidable," he said as we approached the breakfast parlor. "I usually lack patience with formidable women—I prefer the biddable and agreeable sorts—but I must say, you do command my attention, Lady Violet."

"What a shame," I replied, dropping his arm. "For the biddable and agreeable sort of gentleman holds little interest for me. I much prefer the formidable sort. Perhaps you'd best choose another lady to accompany you on your *ride*, for I doubt—given my preferences—we'd be good company."

I curtseyed and strode off, not exactly pleased with myself for having insulted a guest, but determined to get out of my habit and don cooler attire. I was in my shift and sponging off the effects of my morning's exertion before it occurred to me that Pritchard had been lying.

St. Sevier and I had taken the same route Pritchard had described —through the cool of the woods, down the shady drive at MacHeath's Ford, and on to a leisurely circuit of the village. If his lordship had truly *daundered along the green* and tarried for some time on foot, I would have spotted him on his travels.

His dusty boots confirmed that he'd been out and about somewhere, if only to the stable yard, but he'd not been honest with me about the specifics. Was he protecting a lady's good name, or hiding some more unsavory behavior, such as checking on the welfare of his captives?

~

"A search of the dower house makes sense, Ellersby." If anything would sway my oldest brother's thinking, sense ought to do it.

Still, Mitchell remained by the window in my father's office, looking remote and severe. "I will not have our home upended by a lot of Derwent's gossip-grubbing sycophants."

Did he include St. Sevier, who stood by the door, among that number? The Marquess of Dunkeld, who was directing a renewed search of the local tenant properties?

"Then only family will conduct the search. Felix, Ajax, and Hector will aid you, as will I."

"Ellersby," said the man's wife, "I agree with Lady Violet. Where else would the girls go?"

He turned toward us, which was some consolation. A gentleman did not give a lady his back, much less conduct a conversation from that posture.

"They have thousands of acres where they might go. They have a river they might have fallen into. Tree houses where they may be stuck. Hog wallows where they've met a terrible fate. I hardly know where they could have gone, because I hardly know my own daughters, but I can tell you that Violet ran away twice as a girl."

Now he cited facts, if only ancient, irrelevant facts. "I was mortally vexed with my brothers both times. Bella and Sylvie are blessedly free of such annoyances."

"Through no fault of mine."

Ellersby's nasty, honest comment was proof that, contrary to appearances, he was nearly hysterical with worry.

"I'm sorry," he said. "Annabelle, I'm sorry. I didn't mean... I am sorry. I am beside myself with awful possibilities, and I don't know what to do. I have not been this upset since..."

Lady Ellersby's gaze was impassive. "Since?"

His expression acquired a diffident quality. Were he a small boy, he might have stared at his boots. "Since Bella was born."

This apparently had significance to Lady Ellersby, because her lips curved in a faint smile. "Lady Violet, Monsieur, would you allow my husband and me some privacy?"

"A question first, Ellersby," I said. "What exactly is Lady Eutheria to our father?"

Ellersby glanced at St. Sevier and both of them probably thought the question irrelevant. "An old friend and a former close associate of our mother."

That was a prevarication worthy of the earl himself. "We will speak later, my lord. I have more questions for you."

St. Sevier and I withdrew. I would have preferred to linger outside the door to eavesdrop, but Lord and Lady Ellersby were unlikely to oblige me with raised voices.

"Did you have any breakfast?" St. Sevier asked.

"I did not, and now that you remind me of my oversight, I am famished." Also a little queasy. A more delicate lady would have been too upset to eat. I was no longer that delicate, or that melancholic, and an unsettled stomach was sometimes soothed by nourishment.

Perhaps my digestion was troubled because Derwent Hall had taken on the qualities of a house anticipating a death. The servants went about their duties in silence, a tension hung in the air, a quality of waiting for anxiety to resolve into heartbreak.

Three little girls, gone. "Where and why?" I muttered as St. Sevier and I reached the breakfast parlor. Mr. Botham was at the table, his attire sporting its usual exquisite punctilio despite the humid morning. By noon, his neckcloth would be a mass of wrinkles, and the starched lace at his cuffs would droop like willow boughs.

He half rose and one-quarter bowed. "My lady, Monsieur. Good day."

I curtseyed, but nobody was up to making small talk. St. Sevier silently passed me the teapot when I'd taken my place at the table. The eggs were cold, the ham as well. I buttered my toast—also cold—and added raspberry jam.

"I've decided that Stephen and I will depart this morning," Botham said. "I understand Derwent wants the christening to go forward as planned, but I must put the welfare of my child before other considerations."

I grasped Botham's point, but did not care for the notion that he was slinking off before we'd answered the pressing questions—where were the girls, and why were they gone?

"Might not Lady Eutheria benefit from the support of a friend?" I asked.

Botham stirred his tea. He folded his table napkin beside his plate. "You believe me to be a particular friend of her ladyship?"

"I believe I saw you emerging from the fishing cottage with her several days past." And a good time had been had by all, clearly.

"You could not have." He aimed a scowl at the open door. "The only person to see us, after we'd regained the path, was that dratted child. Evelyn is at a difficult age, I know, but I also know how nasty girls can be—boys, too, for that matter—and..."

St. Sevier had gone alert while pretending to placidly sip his tea.

"And so," I said, "when the opportunity presented itself, you shoved 'that dratted child' into the priest hole to teach her a lesson about the harm that comes to snoops and eavesdroppers."

Botham scowled at the pot of pink roses sitting in the center of the table. "Don't be absurd."

"Choose your words carefully, Botham," St. Sevier said mildly. "Lady Violet can smell a lie from twenty paces upwind. Do not compound abusing a child with abusing a lady's sensibilities."

The mantel clock ticked a half-dozen times while St. Sevier set down his tea cup and folded his arms. I, too, was prepared to wait all morning for Botham's excuses, for he surely had them to offer.

"I would have let her out," he said. "She was lurking in a damned tree of all places, like a gargoyle, spying on her mother. I didn't get a good look, but I saw white skirts and a pale hand. I knew who it was. A complete hoyden, well deserving of some severe discipline. But then a great uproar ensued, and Lady Eutheria will see me ruined if she learns what I did."

"As well she should."

"The girl was completely out of line," Botham said, drawing in his breath as if winding up for a peroration on the need to keep girls *in line* at all times. "Hiding in a blasted tree, spying on what should remain private. The nerve. I told Eutheria that a severe finishing school would be well advised for a daughter at that age. Bread and water, Scripture, long walks in the countryside. The girl is incorrigible."

Poor Stephen, though having had the good sense to be a boy, his fate was likely rosier. "Mr. Botham, you have been completely *out of line*. Evelyn was nowhere near that tree. She was not spying, while you *were* trysting in a building that Lady Ellersby had decided to leave open to all guests. Evelyn is no hoyden, and I fear you are no gentleman."

That great insult had him on his feet. "You know not of what you speak, my lady. I will attribute your ungoverned speech to the heat and the upheaval of the day. I am not proud of what I did, but somebody needs to take that girl in hand, witness her further behavior."

St. Sevier took up a butter knife and dabbed at his toast. "Sit. Down. Now."

Botham looked as if a potted palm had started issuing directions. "I beg your pardon."

"You will beg Miss Evelyn's pardon, once she is found," St. Sevier said. "Your frolicking in a near-public location was observed by Lady Violet, who—having been raised on this estate—knows all the best climbing trees. You behaved with unspeakable cruelty to a mere girl, and despite the child going missing—perhaps because she fears more such assaults from you—you have withheld the particulars of your stupidity."

Botham subsided into his seat like a leaky balloon sinking to earth. "*Lady Violet* was in that tree? But ladies don't... That is to say, a real lady would never... I can't..." He swallowed audibly. "Oh God. Derwent will kill me."

And not a word of apology for what Evelyn had gone through. "No need for hysterics, Mr. Botham," I said. "If Derwent didn't kill you for trysting with Lady Eutheria where any might come upon you, he's not likely to kill you for mistreating Evelyn—though I might."

"Happy to serve as your second, my lady," St. Sevier said, saluting with his toast. "Do we now entertain the possibility that Evelyn recognized Botham as the man who assaulted her and took herself somewhere safe?"

I perused the elegant knot in Botham's cravat and the starched lace brushing his knuckles. "We must consider such a theory."

"She could not have recognized me," Botham retorted. "The room was dark, and she faced away from me."

"She smelled the starch you have so liberally applied to your clothing," St. Sevier said. "And on your way down to dinner, you would have been quite nicely turned out, would you not?"

Botham touched his neckcloth. "Every man with any pretensions to style has his cravats starched."

"Did you say anything to Evelyn as you were shoving her into a terrifying darkness?" I asked pleasantly. "'Take that'? 'In you go'? 'That'll teach you to spy?'"

Botham patted his cravat, which cascaded just so from his throat. "Perhaps. 'Little beast.' 'Rotten girl.' Something along those lines."

I did not know what to feel at these disclosures. On the one hand, we'd solved a small, sad puzzle, but on the other, Botham exhibited no remorse. He was worried over what my father—a party wronged only indirectly in that his hospitality had been disrespected—would think of him.

"Here, from Evelyn's perspective, is what happened," I said. "She was bored witless in the company of younger children and worried because her mother was acting like a flirt and a fool, as some adult women will in company with adult men. Evelyn did what she could to learn more of what the adults around her were getting up to. She meant to listen through the flue to what was going on in the parlor below. With no warning or explanation, she was rudely shoved into a dank hole by one of those adults."

"I know what happened," Botham snapped. "You need not lecture me."

"*Silence, imbécile,*" St. Sevier said quietly. "Her ladyship has not finished."

"Evelyn's mother might have had some inkling who was responsible for mistreating the girl and thus began immediately casting the incident as a servant's prank. Evelyn knew her mother would not admit that you were at fault, so now Evelyn is off somewhere, hiding from a *rotten beast* of a man, whom her mother finds inexplicably alluring. Sylvie and Bella might well have joined Evelyn in solidarity with her display of independence. If I have the right of it, Mr. Botham, you have precipitated a grievous harm. You will not slink away with your son in tow, spouting inanities about what a concerned father you are when you might help us locate the very children you've put in harm's way. When we find Evelyn, you will apologize to her in her mother's hearing."

Botham's mouth worked. He picked up his table napkin and set it down again. I let him struggle with the radical notion that he was to be held accountable for his bullying. He'd appointed himself victim, judge, jury, and jailer all on the strength of his own arrogance.

Given enough time, perhaps he'd work out the syllogism any schoolboy should be able to follow: *I am a gentleman; therefore, when I err, I take responsibility, apologize, and effect reparation for the wrong I have done.*

I rose before St. Sevier could assist me with my chair. "Monsieur, I find I have lost my appetite. You will excuse me."

St. Sevier stood and bowed, his gaze conveying a touch of humor and perhaps even some admiration.

"I will consult with Ajax to see if I might be of use to the searchers," he said. "Charlemagne is certainly up to another outing, and I hazard that your ladyship will want some solitude in which to consider various puzzles."

"You hazard correctly. I will draw a map of the estate and stare at it for a time. Somewhere on my father's acreage, three little girls are in hiding."

St. Sevier bowed over my hand and held his peace. Perhaps the children were in hiding, but equally likely, somebody else was hiding them—and those were the least-distressing possibilities.

CHAPTER THIRTEEN

"They aren't here." Ellersby perched like a battle-weary soldier on the toy box. "We've been through the whole dower house, and they aren't here."

"We will find them, Mitchell." I used his name advisedly, because right now, he was not lord of anything. He was simply my brother, who'd spent a long, miserable afternoon searching in vain for his children.

I had used the balance of my morning to consult my maps—to no avail—and when Hector, Felix, and Ajax had come in for a noon meal, I'd dragooned them into a search of the dower house.

"I cannot help but think," Mitchell said, letting his head fall back against the window, "that if I'd been a better father, a kinder father, Sylvie and Bella would not be lost now."

The girls had been kidnapped, or they had run off. I hoped they yet bided in the corner of England they knew as their only home, the one place they would never be lost. The only place, in a sense, where I had not been lost.

"Lord Ellersby is being fanciful," I said, dropping to the cool stones of the raised hearth. "Somebody should notify the radical press."

He sighed and sat forward. In deference to the heat, he'd removed his jacket, and I had to admit that Mitchell Deerfield was an excellent figure of a man. Taller and leaner than the earl and more dignified than his brothers. All in all, an impressive specimen.

With whom Annabelle, apparently, was at her wits' end.

"I am not fanciful, Violet. I am guilty. Derwent thrives on intrigue and drama, while I thrive on order. When he provokes chaos —which is twice a day if Parliament is sitting—I withdraw into the ledgers, the tenant squabbles, the steward's problems, and the committee reports. The work available to distract me from the earl's histrionics is endless."

Mitchell had always been the serious, detached eldest among the five siblings. He was the heir, a status to be envied, a boy set apart. For the first time, it occurred to me that he'd been terribly lonely, consigned to the unrelenting scrutiny of a father he did not seek to emulate.

Perhaps he was lonely still.

"And in distracting yourself from Papa's nonsense, you became distracted from your family?" I surmised.

He scrubbed a hand over a tired face. "Something like that. The whole business is complicated. Annabelle had a hard time bringing Bella into this world. We were in the country, and her sister could not attend her. I was thrust into a role during the birthing that Annabelle herself would doubtless have spared me, and, Violet..." His gaze went to the ceiling fresco, where cupids cavorted amid fluffy clouds. "I should not be telling you these things."

He should not be keeping these things to himself. "I lost a child at six months along, Mitchell. I labored as if the pregnancy had run its course. I am familiar with the process."

And with the utter collapse of body and soul that followed when *the process* did not result in a happy, healthy baby.

He sighed again, somehow conveying sadness and bewilderment.

"Annabelle labored *all afternoon,* and I could do nothing. She was in such pain, hour after hour. I nearly hated Bella by the time she arrived that evening. An awful thing to say. And now... I want my daughters home, safe, and annoying the hell out of me. Please, God... Grant me this one boon and I will never again complain about their noise, their high spirits, their lack of decorum in church. I have been such an ass."

He bowed forward, his head in his hands, and I left the hearth to take the place beside him.

"Mitchell, you love them."

"Of course I love them." He sat back, a touch of his typical hauteur returning. "But I told myself I would not be the blustering, meddling, bumptious sort of father you and I have. I would be steady and calm, the pattern card of probity. Now the girls have run off, and I have no idea where their secret hiding places are. Every child has secret hiding places. I knew how to get you out of the priest hole because I would read in there by the hour."

He had? By the hour? *What* had he read by the hour? Certainly not sermons and Latin texts. "I never thanked you for showing me the mechanism."

"I was loath to give up the only place I had privacy from our brothers, but you were... traumatized. I could not bear to see the hurt and fear in your eyes, and Derwent was clearly out of his depth with the whole situation."

And this man thought himself an awful father? "Promise me something."

"If I can."

Always cautious. He was *nothing* like our father. "Promise me that when we have retrieved my nieces from whatever folly or cow byre they are biding in, you will take Dr. St. Sevier aside and ask him about the normal course of a labor and delivery. He has brought many children into the world, Mitchell, and he can tell you that for a child to arrive after less than twelve hours' travail is shorter than usual. He can assure you that your presence was a comfort to your wife, and that in lesser households all over the realm, women cling to their husbands' hands as children make their way into the world."

Though I had not clung to Freddie's hand, and damn him for all eternity for absenting himself from the ordeal and from our house. I could forgive him much, but not that.

"Do you truly think the girls are hiding?"

"Your promise, Ellersby."

"I hope my daughters have one-half your fierceness, Violet."

"And one-half Annabelle's patience. An interesting combination. Will you talk to St. Sevier?"

He gave me a wan smile. "Yes, my lady."

Though a chat with the good doctor would not heal the entire breach between Lord and Lady Ellersby. Something larger had gone awry between them, but I had the sense that Bella's birth was at the root of it. Perhaps St. Sevier could sort them out.

"Where do we search next?" Mitchell asked. "I confess that when I try to apply logic to the situation, my mind refuses to function. I have failed my daughters, and... I can think of nothing else."

"Think of not failing your wife, sir. She is beside herself with worry. Bad enough if the girls have run off, but Evelyn is missing, too, and that suggests something other than your imperfect parenting is at work here."

My logic apparently reached where my sympathy could not. "What does Lady Eutheria have to say about the child's disappearance?" Mitchell asked.

I explained Botham's role in Evelyn's earlier mishap, though I had yet to determine how to broach the subject with Lady Eutheria herself.

"Trysting with Botham," Ellersby said. "Fast work on somebody's part, but then, her ladyship has always been a lively sort of widow."

The playroom, despite several open windows, was quite warm this late in the day. The westering sun slanted directly into the room, and fatigue pulled at me. I had done justice to neither breakfast nor lunch, having been too preoccupied with the events of the day.

I was hungry, but so far gone with it that the feeling was more one of lethargy and a foggy mind than the pangs of an empty belly.

"Why quarter a lively widow in the family wing, Ellersby, if she's not directing her liveliness at Derwent or one of our brothers?" Lady Eutheria was at least a decade older than either Ajax or Hector, but that was no deterrent to a couple who fancied themselves smitten.

Ellersby rose, braced his hands on his back, and stretched. "You truly don't know?"

"Don't know what?"

"Lady Eutheria is Mama's younger half-sister. Grandpapa was old-school, meaning more than his eye wandered, and Lady Eutheria is the result."

I was glad I had remained seated. "She is our *aunt*?"

"I have always known, as do our brothers. I'm sorry. Somebody should have alerted you, but it's hardly a secret. Derwent is sufficiently indifferent to any old gossip that he houses her ladyship in the family wing when she visits here."

"So... Bella and Sylvie and Evelyn are cousins of some sort?"

"At a remove. Young Evelyn is actually our cousin—yours and mine. Boggles the mind. Do you think the girls have simply run off?"

The sun was hot against my back, and I was hungry, tired, and thirsty, but Ellersby's question deserved an honest, considered answer.

"They have no motive strong enough to keep them away from the house overnight, Ellersby, but it's possible, having achieved that feat of courage, they are now too fearful of the consequences to come back to us." From a young girl's perspective, that theory made a certain sense. The loss of ponies, being sent away to school, even a stern and loving parent's articulately conveyed disappointment... punishments more awful than death in the imagination of a fanciful child.

"You believe they remain in hiding," Ellersby said, "fearful of their father's wrath?"

He was nothing if not consistent. "Do you beat them? Do you allow Miss Oakes to beat them?"

"Never."

"Does their mother force them to stand with their hands behind their backs and their heads down for hours on end?"

"What an awful, diabolical..." He frowned at me. "Finishing school?"

"Several different finishing schools." And, I suspected, the origins of my megrims. "Do you force them to write out entire books of the Bible for the grave offense of humming?"

"Annabelle hums when she's happy. I would never... Violet. I'm sorry."

"I hate the Pauline letters, if Vicar should ever ask. My point is, you are a good father. Conscientious and caring, if not exactly a font of affection. Your daughters love you, and we will find them. The sad fact is, they might not have run off. All three girls might be imprisoned somewhere for reasons known at this point only to their captor."

"Felix has posted footmen to guard his nursery, and I suspect Pritchard and Botham will ask Derwent to do likewise. Children are too easy to pick up and cart off. Let's get back to the Hall, shall we? Annabelle believes in serving meals promptly, and I must change for dinner."

Mitchell would focus on proper attire and punctual meals when his heart was breaking. The whole situation was awful, and yet, to have found some sympathy for and understanding of my oldest brother surely counted as a silver lining.

I popped off the toy chest, resigned to the march back to the Hall. I was too...

My vision went dim around the edges, and I heard a roaring in my ears.

"Violet?" Ellersby's voice had a distant quality, though he'd come to my side. "Violet, maybe you should sit down."

I did not sit so much as I half fell back onto the toy chest. "I stood up too quickly, and I am famished."

"And you are likely sleeping as poorly as the rest of us in this damnable heat. I will search for my daughters until the last trumpet shall sound, but I also want this to be *over*, however awful the resolution. Shall I have the gig brought around, Violet?"

I would rather spend more time consulting the maps I'd drawn of Papa's estate than trudging along the paths between dower house and Hall.

"Please. I can drive myself if you'd rather go on foot."

He treated me to a brooding perusal. "I tell myself that if I troop through the wood often enough, if I have a look through MacHeath's Ford's outbuildings just one more time, Bella and Sylvie will jump out from behind some patch of hollyhocks... but they won't. I'll drive you."

I rose more carefully, noting the uncharacteristic tidiness of the playroom. With no children on the premises, every book was shelved, every toy soldier was at attention on the mantel. No smear of jam marred the windowsill. No forgotten bear perched atop a throw pillow.

"If the children were kidnapped," I observed, "the kidnapper knew enough to gather up Bella's bear, Charles. That suggests somebody who knows children, a parent, or an attentive grandparent."

Ellersby escorted me from the nursery, his pace uncharacteristically slow. "I don't know as I would have thought to bring along her bear. Annabelle would have. Bella brings the damned thing to church."

His voice caught, though we proceeded through the house with his lordship's usual decorum.

"Three of Derwent's guests are familiar with the nursery staff and routine, Ellersby. Mr. Botham, Lord Pritchard, and Lady Eutheria."

"As is Annabelle," he said thoughtfully, "and she has every reason to be upset of late."

Annabelle? The poised and gracious Lady Ellersby, with her exquisite and unusual needlework and her apparent inability to bear a son?

Annabelle? My goodness. A wife overcome with wrath at her

husband, one furious at having to host a christening party for a nephew rather than a son, might remove daughters from such a gathering to make a point.

That motivation was both obscure and diabolically effective, for the whole company was now fixated on the missing girls and not on Derwent's grandson. But would Annabelle indulge in such a grand, henwitted, gesture, and if she had, how would her marriage ever come right again?

~

"We have focused along the waterways," Sebastian said. "But children are warned from infancy to be careful around water."

His lordship and I were taking our evening meal on a bench in the garden. Supper, by decree of Lady Ellersby, was a buffet on the terrace. This arrangement allowed for less effort on the part of the kitchen and less enforced socializing among the guests.

Mr. Botham had attached himself to Lady Rowbottom, while Lady Eutheria was partnered with Ajax. Mr. Bascomb was nowhere in evidence, much to my relief, while Lord Pritchard entertained a group of young ladies beneath the laburnum alley. The golden blooms had faded, though the alley still afforded shade by day and privacy at all hours.

"Children are warned to be careful of everything," I replied. "The laburnum is poisonous, especially the seeds. Roses have thorns. One can choke on porridge. Ponies kick. Dogs bite." Husbands strayed. Children went missing...

"You are frustrated because you have not solved this puzzle. Eat something." Sebastian passed me a roll of thinly sliced ham wrapped around a bite of melon.

At that precise moment, smoked ham with cool melon loomed as nectar of the goddesses. I took the treat and washed it down with a sip of champagne.

"Where are they, Dunkeld? If they aren't near the water, they aren't in the outbuildings, they aren't biding with a tenant..."

He put another roll of ham and melon on my plate. "We haven't searched the village, and Sylvie and Bella, at least, know it well."

Evelyn did not, and yet, the children might have coordinated their exits, a juvenile rendition of Haydn's Farewell Symphony, where each musician left the stage in turn until only two violinists remained. Then those two had departed, in hopes that the prince would finally allow his loyal orchestra to go home to their families.

"We will search the village tomorrow." Ellersby and I had agreed on that. "When you were a boy, if your sister Clementine had taken it into her head to punish adults for some slight or insult, would you have joined her rebellion?"

Sebastian held out his plate to me. I took the remaining slices of ham and melon.

"You are asking," he said, setting aside his empty plate, "why the little boys are still in their aerie, while the girls are gone. If what you've told me about Lady Eutheria is correct, the girls are all related, while the boys are not family to them."

A Scotsman would see that. "But do the girls know they are related? I found out only today." I'd been surreptitiously studying Lady Eutheria for a resemblance to Mama ever since. "Is there some-place girls can hide that boys cannot? If the objective is ransom, Pritchard would pay dearly to keep his boy safe and has significant wealth. Botham isn't poor."

"If I were a kidnapper," Sebastian replied, "which I am not, lest you get to speculating, I would steal the baby."

His words gave me a chill, despite the close evening air. "Felix has posted guards at his nursery."

"*I* posted guards at his nursery door. He was too busy explaining to darling Katie why the christening must still wait until Friday. Derwent's plans cannot be disturbed merely because children are in peril."

The food, or Sebastian's company, was easing a bothered quality the day had acquired early in the morning.

"You have a point." I wrapped a pale slice of cheese around the next portion of ham and melon. "The baby is in line for the title, vulnerable, and a Deerfield. Why snatch noisy, troublesome little girls when a future earl is on hand? Except that Felix's nursery is a quiet place these days, while the Derwent Hall nursery resembles Piccadilly at noon."

Then too, babies were delicate. Little girls were far sturdier than many adults believed. How was that misconception possible when half of all adults had *been* little girls?

Sebastian stretched out long legs and crossed them at the ankle. "This all weighs in favor of the theory that the girls ran away rather than that they were kidnapped. Shall I fetch you another plate, Violet?"

"No, thank you. This will be enough." And more to the point, I'd eaten food that agreed with me. Substantial and flavorful, but not too heavy or spicy. "I argued with Derwent earlier today."

"When the Deerfields gather, somebody is routinely embroiled in an argument with the earl."

"If the girls are staying hidden out of some sort of pique, or perhaps fear of consequences for a wrong we haven't uncovered yet, then the sooner the gathering ends, the sooner they will come out of hiding. I wanted Derwent to move up the christening."

Sebastian took a sip of champagne, the evening light catching the crystal in his hand and the red highlights in his dark hair. He would age splendidly. I hoped Mrs. Bonaventure appreciated that about him. Lord Dunkeld would turn heads even in later life, and the lady on his arm would be envied her handsome spouse.

Sebastian was not attractive in the refined, blond, aristocratic mold English girls were taught to prize, but he was striking, with his aquiline nose, piercing blue eyes, and imposing physique. He was also honorable to his toes and proud without being arrogant.

"Let me guess," he said. "Derwent argued that once the guests disperse, the kidnapper could well leave, and the girls will never be found?"

"Precisely. He said we must manage the situation with the worst case in mind, and for once, I had to defer to his logic."

"Or to Lady Eutheria's logic. The earl and her ladyship seem close."

I thought back to Lady Eutheria's many uses of Papa's first name. "With Papa, one does not speculate. He is a titled rascal, and she is a link to my mother. In his way, Papa did love Mama." Of that I was sure and more certain still that Papa missed the wife he'd treated so cavalierly.

How much easier to resent him if he had not missed her.

"Shall I escort you back inside, Violet? You look to me to be in need of an early bedtime."

"I am tired, but I will wander for a bit before going upstairs. Have you seen St. Sevier?"

Something flickered across Sebastian's expression, not quite impatience, but a faltering of the demeanor of family friend. He was tired, too, and likely as frustrated as I was by the whole situation.

"I have not, but then, St. Sevier rode over half the shire today, inquiring after the girls. If he ever wants to sell that magnificent chestnut gelding, please let me know. The horse has bottom to spare."

Sebastian rose, bowed, and strode off, his kilt swinging in a manner that the twits simpering around Lord Pritchard would have goggled at. Rather than goggle, I bestirred myself to visit the stable.

No place on earth was as peaceful as a well-kept stable on a summer evening. Aurora was put out to grass at night, owing to the heat and her age, and I wanted to confer with her as I had in girlhood. She never betrayed a confidence, never reproved me for throwing my arms around her neck and holding on tightly.

She was a symbol of benevolence that I perhaps associated with my mother, who had still been alive when Aurora had been given to me. Had Mama chosen her for me? Tried out her paces before allowing Derwent to purchase her?

So much I did not know. I wandered through the conservatory and down through the towering trees to the stable, the chatter of guests fading behind me to the calm of a summer night. Crickets chorused, and from the direction of the home farm, a cow lowed.

I found Aurora in the mare's paddock, peacefully munching grass. When I clambered onto the fence, she came over to greet me, nibbling a lump of sugar from my outstretched palm.

"We haven't found them," I said. "We still haven't found them, and I dread to go to sleep tonight for fear another child will be missing tomorrow."

Not the baby. Please, heaven, not the baby. Not him, not Henry, not Stephen... What kind of fiend would steal children, or entice them from the safety of the nursery?

I scratched Aurora's ears, then her chin, in a routine we'd developed fifteen years earlier. She ambled away when it became apparent I had brought only the one lump of sugar, but I promised to come back on the morrow with more.

My dear old friend was aging. Her back dipped more deeply with each passing year, and I was not on hand to provide her the exercise she needed to slow that process. On that melancholy thought, I wandered back toward the stable, thinking I might find St. Sevier consulting with his Charlemagne.

An enormous long-haired cat sprinted across the path, and my first thought was that all that fur must be stifling in this heat. Then I realized I'd seen the cat before, or seen his likeness in Evelyn's sketchbook. He scampered off down the path that led to the home farm, and I wished him good hunting.

A big fellow like that would need plenty of mice to maintain his manly—tom-ly?—physique.

A voice drifted to me from inside the barn, a man speaking in low, persuasive tones. No hint of a French accent reached my ears. I told myself to turn about and repair to the house, lest I come upon a tryst.

I recognized the voice. Lord Pritchard had apparently extricated himself from his harem, and he was intent on wheedling something out of somebody. He did not strike me as the wheedling type. He was more the kiss-first-and-wait-for-thanks-later type.

In a few years, he could well fall into the aging roué category, but for now, he still carried off a sense of sophisticated élan. He didn't sound very sophisticated now. He sounded desperate and importuning.

I turned to leave, but my hems brushed a muck fork leaning against the outside of the barn. The fork clattered to the ground, and both Pritchard and the blond stable boy, Samuel, came to the end of the aisle.

"My lady." Pritchard bowed. Samuel swiped off his cap, and both fellows wore expressions of equal caution.

Exactly *what* had I interrupted? "My lord, Samuel. A lovely evening, is it not?"

"Very pretty," Pritchard said, perusing me with what I knew to be deliberate flirtation. "I was just asking Samuel to have my horse ready for a gallop tomorrow morning, first thing. Perhaps your ladyship would like to accompany me?"

By rights, Samuel should have withdrawn. At the least, his countenance should have been sporting the carefully blank expression every person in service knows to keep handy. The boy was instead shamelessly listening and clearly amused.

"Thank you for the invitation, my lord, but no. My mare is too venerable to enjoy any more gallops, and my day will be spent on other pursuits." Finding the girls, I hoped, though where else could they be?

"Then perhaps you will allow me to accompany you back to the Hall?" Pritchard said, offering me his signature handsome-cavalier smile.

What a lot of perishing twaddle. I had a handsome cavalier—a chevalier, no less—and right at that moment, I missed him. Where had St. Sevier got off to, and how soon could we climb into the same bed?

"No need for that, my lord. I can find my way to the Hall without benefit of an escort."

If Lord Pritchard thought to impose his company on me, he was thwarted not only by my demurral, but by Hector and Ajax saun-tering into the stable yard. Ajax carried two foils and some towels.

My dinner nearly threatened to make a reappearance.

"No duels." I marched up to my brothers. "I don't care who insulted whom, who cast a slur on which lady's name, or who spoke treason. No damned duels, do you hear me? Children have gone missing, and petty displays of masculine stupidity could not be more ill-timed."

"Teach her to fence," Pritchard drawled, "and there won't be a man standing."

"Her tongue is her weapon," Ajax replied. "We all bear the scars."

I wrested the foils from him, and his grin died aborning. "My wits are my weapons, you jackanapes, and you cannot engage in this fool-ishness if I take your swords. Try to take them back, and I will scream so loudly the London constables will hear me."

"She means it," Hector observed, "but as usual, Violet, you are indulging in dramatics before apprising yourself of the facts. Pritchard's swordsmanship exceeds my own—his literal swordsman-ship, in any case. I sought to spar, no spectators, for the sake of improving my craft and working up a good sweat. Please don't begrudge us the pleasure of exertion when exercise is a sorely needed boon."

I wanted to flounce off, nose in the air, swords in hand, but Hector—for his countless, myriad, innumerable, egregious faults—was not a liar.

I thrust the weapons at him. "A cut will fester in this heat. Tip the damned foils. We have enough to worry about without watching one of you slowly rot to death."

They let me have the last word, which was prudent of them. Ajax bowed, Hector saluted with his blade, while Pritchard and Samuel grinned at me, the same idiot grin flashed by naughty boys since the much-lamented invention thereof.

CHAPTER FOURTEEN

I lay awake for a long time, letting the night breezes coming through the open balcony of St. Sevier's bedroom cool my body. My mind was another matter.

I pondered, I considered, I conjectured, and I speculated, all to no avail. The suspects were few, the motives weak, and yet, the children were still missing.

The dignified and poised Lady Ellersby, possibly staging a tantrum.

The little girls, indulging in a childish scheme gone very far awry.

Mr. Bascomb, preparing to rescue his own captives in an effort to gain Derwent's esteem.

Who else, and why on earth commit a triple felony—for kidnapping carried the death penalty—for the sake of some obscure point of pride?

When St. Sevier came into the room, the hour was well past midnight, judging from the angle of the moonlight. He lit no candles and undressed and washed in silence, probably thinking—or hoping—that I was asleep.

When he climbed into the bed, I rolled to his side. "I've missed you, sir."

He wrapped me in a gentle embrace, his skin cool from his ablutions. "I was asking questions in the village, to the extent a Frenchman in an English pub can ask questions. Dunkeld showed up, and tongues loosened somewhat."

"They know him from his boyhood, and he can be charming." And how interesting that both Sebastian and St. Sevier had thought to go for a casual pint with the same intent.

St. Sevier arranged himself over me, crouching on all fours so that we did not touch. "Your marquess watches me. If I were ever to play you false, you would not have to fillet me. Dunkeld would have me drawn and quartered before I could murmur a prayer for my eternal soul."

"You will never play me false." I kissed him, vaguely disturbed by the topic. Sebastian was protective of family, and I was nearly family to him. Or I had been once.

"I will never willingly betray you." St. Sevier kissed me, a slow, sweet prelude to mutual seduction. Because of the heat, we moved languidly with each other, and because I had missed St. Sevier terribly, and I was frightened for the girls, and the hour was late, and my defenses at low ebb, the loving for me became deeply emotional.

How I treasured this man, for his mind, his heart, his honor, his delightfully healthy body... Had I met Hugh St. Sevier earlier in life, I would not have appreciated him. He was the answer to many an unvoiced prayer on my part, and I cherished him with my carnal enthusiasms to the limit of my ability.

We lay spent, side by side, some half hour later, hands entwined.

"I want you to promise me something, Violet."

"I want a promise from you too, St. Sevier. Promise me you will not go off alone again. We know not what has become of the children, and I would hate to see harm befall you."

"I can make that promise. Please assure me, though, that if

anything happens to me, and you cannot seek my aid, you will turn to Dunkeld."

I rolled to my side, the better to study him, but the light was inadequate to illuminate St. Sevier's features. His voice, though, conveyed utter seriousness.

"You speak as if you are returning to war."

"I am French. When in England, I will always have detractors, if not enemies. Dunkeld loves you. He will keep you safe if ever I cannot, but you must not be too proud to seek his protection."

What on earth was this about? "I have four brothers, not to mention a titled father. I should be able to turn to them, shouldn't I?"

He faced me, his hand cradling my cheek. "I recall a certain widow at the end of her mourning. Her family did not visit her on any reliable schedule. She hadn't seen her oldest brother for months. They did not write to her. They did not invite her to come to the family seat for a respite. They might drop by for a cup of tea unannounced out of guilt, but this woman was suffering greatly, and her family could not see that."

His honesty brought a lump to my throat. "They did not want to see it." I had not wanted them meddling, either. Papa and my brothers were, somehow, part of the problem I'd faced making the transition out of mourning. The one truth I'd known then was that I could not and would not resume my place as the sheltered, *ignored* Deerfield family ornament whom they'd married off with such relief.

"Dunkeld *sees* you," St. Sevier said. "He will always see you, and he will never deny you aid should you need it."

At various points in the day—studying my maps, talking with Mitchell, petting Aurora—I'd been plagued by the urge to weep. I had walked through the day with a sense of the old passing away, perhaps because I contemplated a new life with St. Sevier, perhaps because reading Mama's journal always made me miss her.

Or perhaps because I was mad with worry for three missing girls.

"Are you trying not to cry, St. Sevier? For I certainly am."

He drew me into his arms, and despite the heat, I bundled close. I

fell asleep in his embrace, feeling absolutely safe and—more signifi-
cantly—deeply loved.

"You will make an inspection of the nursery?" St. Sevier asked.

He was once again in riding finery, looking spruce and gorgeous in
the early morning sunlight. I poured him a cup of tea and gestured to
the seat beside me on the balcony. Something sweet and ineffable had
passed between us in the night. Something that could not be taken back,
no matter how brisk we were with each other in the muggy light of day.

"I feel like a shepherd," I replied, watching steam curl up from
his cup. "I want to count the flock at the start and finish of every day."
Before yesterday's supper I had apprised St. Sevier of the day's developments. He thus knew of my connection to Lady Eutheria and of
my unusual discussion with Ellersby when the search of the dower
house proved futile.

"I will find a moment with his lordship today," St. Sevier said,
sipping his tea. "He will hear from me about the realities of childbirth
whether he wishes to or not. I assume you plan to assist with a search
of the village?"

"I know the village. I was allowed to wander there freely as a girl,
and watching the stagecoaches arrive and depart was considered
good fun in my childhood." Watching the men at the forge had been
more interesting still. I'd even whiled away pleasant hours keeping
the sexton company as he'd dug graves.

He'd patiently explained to me that the fossor's job had art to it,
that the dirt must be returned to the grave in the reverse sequence in
which it was removed so that the lives of plants and small burrowing
creatures were disturbed as little as possible by the burial.

"I suspect your middle brothers are up to something," St. Sevier
said, finishing his tea. "I know not exactly what, but mention of them
merited awkward silences and knowing glances in the pub."

"They are always up to something. More tea?"

"No, thank you. I feel an urgency to be in the saddle before the heat builds. You will eat breakfast, please. A proper meal."

"Said the physician haring off without his own proper meal. I came upon Hector and Lord Pritchard preparing to spar last evening. Ajax was on hand too."

St. Sevier rose, and I was reminded of all that lean, magnificent male pulchritude sharing a bed with me.

"Where was this impromptu sparring session?"

"At the stable. I came upon Pritchard conferring with the groom Samuel, and Hector and Ajax interrupted."

St. Sevier turned, bracing his backside against the balustrade so he faced me. "What would Pritchard have to say to a stableboy at that hour?"

"His lordship claimed he wanted his horse readied first thing in the day."

"A communication usually made to the head lad, not some young fellow on loan from the forge."

True, though I was reluctant to admit it. "I did not overhear Pritchard's words, St. Sevier, but I overheard his tone. He was pleading with the boy. Why would a self-indulgent lord take the risk of importuning a youthful stable hand when my brothers were expected at any moment?"

St. Sevier looked thoughtful. "Bascomb came into the pub fairly late last evening. He made a nuisance of himself to the tavern maid, and she could not have been more than fifteen. He's not a lord, but he's certainly capable of dissolution. Dunkeld and I were in the snug, and Bascomb did not see us."

To a man of Bascomb's nature, a tavern maid of fifteen would have been fair game. "What happened?"

"The girl's father sent her back to the kitchen, and Bascomb had sense enough not to antagonize the man. Pritchard, by contrast, is at least tolerated by the locals. He's generous with vails, treats his cattle well, and, in the opinion of the alewife, has grown into a proper hand-some lord."

I should not have been surprised that the alewife would make such a remark.

Just as Pritchard's own son was a guest of the Derwent Hall nursery, the aristocracy sent their young people a-visiting between households. If Pritchard's papa had dragged him about to house parties, the staff at Derwent Hall and, by extension, their relatives in the village would have encountered Pritchard as an adolescent. Lady Eutheria had characterized Pritchard as having a lot of growing up to do, implying that she'd known him as a youth as well.

"Pritchard is not a proper lord," I retorted. "Not if he's seeking an assignation with Samuel."

"We don't know what he was up to with Samuel. Perhaps I'll have a word with the lad before I ride out."

"A private word."

"I will be the soul of discretion." St. Sevier kissed me on the mouth, a tea-flavored indulgence that stirred delightful memories.

I did not want to let him go, though go, he must. "Let's be married this autumn, St. Sevier. A quiet ceremony, a few witnesses, and a honey month at your Berkshire property."

He straightened slowly, his expression stunned. "You are certain, *mon coeur?*"

If I had harbored even a scintilla of doubt, last night had loved it right out of me. "I am certain. I love you as I have never loved another, and I would like to spend the rest of my life as Madame St. Sevier."

The declaration left me a little shaky, though I'd spoken the absolute truth. The old was passing away, and to become Madame St. Sevier was my heart's desire, though that luscious future was full of unknowns.

St. Sevier sank back into the seat next to me and took my hand. "You honor me, Violet. You honor me profoundly..." He stared off into the distance, and for once, I wished he'd lapse into French effusions.

Was he pleased? Shocked? Bewildered? Did he think I'd been leading him a dance?

"In the autumn, then, my lady. It shall be as you wish."

I liked those words. I hoped they presaged good things for our union. "We will tell my family only when the details have been confirmed. Nary a word, for now." I need not explain to him that finding the girls took precedence over all else.

"Not a word." He kissed me again, on the cheek. "But you have made me the happiest of men. I will not fail you, Violet."

He strode off, leaving me to my cooling tea. I was still pondering that final assertion—*I will not fail you, Violet*—when I made my way down to the breakfast parlor. Fail me at what? St. Sevier was my friend, my prospective spouse, my lover... In what way could he possibly fail me?

I walked into the breakfast parlor, my mind a-whirl while my gaze settled on Lord Pritchard. He was seated beside Lady Eutheria, leaning toward her, clearly having entertained her with his witticisms for the duration of their shared meal.

And he was not attired for riding.

Both boys were present and accounted for in the nursery, as were Dottie, Miss Oakes, and Mr. Harkness. Hansom was off somewhere "putting her feet up," but with a tutor, governess, and maid on hand, a nanny would have been superfluous.

"What will you boys do today?" I asked as the footman came around to collect the children's breakfast dishes.

"We should pick berries." Dottie had spoken out of turn, as she was wont to do. "Enough for another pie before they are all gone. We'll get a storm, and they'll go to rot on the vine."

"We need rain," Miss Oakes said. "If the heat doesn't break soon,

I won't answer for the consequences. It's too hot to sleep." She exchanged a glance with Mr. Harkness, and Stephen looked disgusted.

"I like berries," Henry said, taking a box of soldiers, horses, and artillery to the carpet. "They make good cannonballs. Where's the dragon?"

I fetched the requisite reptile from the mantel and set her upon the carpet, taking a position cross-legged on the battlefield.

"Perhaps you fellows would be up for another nature walk before it gets too hot, or perhaps Mr. Harkness could take you into the village. We'll be looking for the little girls there today."

"We could play hide-and-seek," Henry said, setting out soldiers in a line.

"Not like that, Henry." Stephen joined us on the carpet. "Infantrymen fight in squares, and old Boney's men flee in terror."

I expected Mr. Harkness to explain how most of Europe had been vanquished by old Boney's Grande Armée, but the resident scholar was engaged in looking pensively out the window.

"I should help with the search," he said. "The sooner we find those girls, the sooner we can return to a semblance of much-needed routine."

"I'm sure your assistance would be appreciated." I set up a square of lobsterbacks behind the dragon. "Dottie and Miss Oakes are certainly capable of managing the boys for a day."

"Go, Darrell," Miss Oakes said. "Lend your aid where it's most needed. The boys and I will be fine."

Darrell appeared rent to his soul over whether to impress the fair Miss Oakes with his fearless gallantry in the wilds of the far-off hostile village, or to spend the day ogling her hems in the nursery.

"We need another dragon," Stephen said, "so the battle will be fair."

Excellent suggestion. "Perhaps Mr. Harkness can find another dragon in the sundries store among the toys. For a small village shop, Mrs. Canary stocks a broad inventory."

Mr. Harkness took that bait—a token for a lady might be found at a well-stocked sundries shop—and bowed his farewell to us.

"I never met a tutor who did so little teaching and so much sighing," Dottie remarked, using a pillow to get her artillery onto high ground.

"In summer, less teaching is expected." I ignored Stephen's naughty grin and Miss Oakes's blush. "Will you boys make an outing to the berry patch this morning?"

The battle lines were taking shape, and if the children thought it odd that Dottie would play soldiers with them, they were too gentlemanly to remark it. She set up cannon on opposing pillows, spread her cavalry out on the battlefield's perimeter, and showed herself to be a seasoned veteran of carpet warfare.

"We could go wading," Stephen said, "at the ford. Lord Dunkeld said the ford is shallow."

"No wading," Miss Oakes said. "If you fell in, I could not pluck you out."

"I could," Dottie said. "I know how to swim. It's easy."

"No wading," Miss Oakes said more firmly. "A nature walk will suit once breakfast has settled."

"We could play hide-and-seek in the woods," Henry suggested. "We need a stream or a river for our battlefield. Armies always cross rivers, and horses get swept downstream." He whinnied like a terrified charger. "We should take our soldiers to the river—"

"No wading." Stephen's tone was martyred. "Besides, we play hide-and-seek every day, and you always win." Clearly, this bothered Stephen, who as the older boy was entitled by the laws of nature to win every game.

"Miss Dottie told me the secret to winning," Henry said, using the dragon to attack a cannon and making fierce, growly noises. "You hide where you can watch the searcher, and when they aren't looking, you change hiding places and sneak into a place they've already looked."

"That's cheating," Stephen retorted, looking aghast. "You have to pick the best hiding place and wait until the searchers give up. When they give up, you win."

"What if they never give up?" Dottie asked, firing an opposing cannon at the dragon. "What if they don't know how to tell time, so they just look and look and look until the dinner bell, and there you are, under the porch with a lot of spiders, your pinny all dirty, and everybody is mad at you for hiding so well?"

The sequence of events flummoxed young Stephen, and I wondered if Dottie was reciting ancient history or being fanciful. I had certainly never hidden under any spider-laden porches.

"Perhaps," Miss Oakes said, "we can observe a cease-fire to collect the wounded while we take our walk? The morning will be quite warm, and we'd do well to get an early start."

Did she hope to chart a course for the village on that nature walk? What about breakfast needing to settle?

"Half the fun is setting up the army," Henry said. "We can put them away and take them out again. I still think we should go wading. It's ever so hot, and we could look for the girls at the ford."

I was seized with a longing for the sensation of cool water rippling across my bare toes. "How do you know where the ford is, Henry?"

"We saw it on our other nature walk. The river is broad and shallow there, with stones on the bottom. Carts used to cross, which is why it's called a ford. Then some old lord or baron had the cart bridge built between Derwent Hall and MacHeath's Ford, and nobody uses the ford anymore, except maybe badgers and deer and such."

"Or poachers," Stephen said.

Dottie rose to return the dragon to the mantel while Henry and Stephen took up firing soldiers into the box like missiles.

I sat on the carpet and mentally reviewed my maps of Derwent Hall's policies. The children's first nature walk would have taken them directly past the ford, one I had crossed barefoot on many a summer day as a girl.

On the opposite bank lay pensioners' cottages, some vacant, some occupied. Staff from both MacHeath's Ford and Derwent Hall bided there, though I hadn't visited the cottages for some time. The cottages were visible from the Derwent Hall side of the river, and Bella and Sylvie would have known of them.

I wished the children good berry picking, abandoned my plan to assist with the search in the village, and instead made my way through the woods toward the river. I crossed not by wading the ford —no time for that indulgence—but by using the cart bridge.

I encountered my brother Felix in the MacHeath Ford stable yard and dragooned him into accompanying me on my errand.

Because the day was hot and fair, most of the pensioners were sitting outside their abodes in the shade of their porches. Mrs. Beekins, a former housekeeper at Derwent Hall, sat on her front stoop shelling peas, no doubt saving the hulls for her sow.

Mr. Hammersmith, a retired first footman, occupied a rocking chair on Mrs. Beekins's porch and smoked a pipe. A small boy—somebody's great-nephew or grandchild—played with a pine cone adorned with wool and decorated to resemble a sheep.

Or possibly a hedgehog, rat, or badger.

"You've heard about the commotion at the Hall," Felix said when greetings had been exchanged, the weather had been lamented, and the great height to which Felix had grown had been remarked at length. For me, there were condolences on my bereavement from Mrs. Beekins, though my spouse had died nearly three years past.

They'd kept track of me, in other words. These former retainers knew the gossip from every hall and manor in the shire. Perhaps they also knew where the girls had got off to.

"We've heard," Mr. Hammersmith said, digging at the bowl of his pipe with a square nail and tapping the pipe against the sole of his boot. "Bad business when young ladies turn up missing. Ellersby must be beside hisself."

An accurate observation. I perched beside Mrs. Beekins and took up shelling the peas with her. "We honestly don't know if the girls are playing a naughty prank, or if somebody has hidden them away and wishes them ill."

"Either way," Mrs. Beekins said, "bodes ill. Children think themselves indestructible, but we none of us are."

"None of us except you, old woman," Mr. Hammersmith replied. "Your granny lived to be a hundred and three, and you will put her in the shade. Our Mrs. Beekins was on hand when the oak at the vicarage was struck by lightning, an eyewitness to the event itself."

As exciting as a recitation of *the event itself* would have been, I felt an urgency to get on with our inquiries.

"The loudest crack of thunder you ever heard," Mrs. Beekins began, her gaze going to the far bank of the river. "Made my ears ring, 'twas so loud. I was sure the sky was about to shatter in pieces on the ground. I was just a girl, mind you, and I'd never heard anything so loud. Fair to split the heavens."

"Artillery is like that," Felix said. "I hate storms for that reason."

"Aye." Mrs. Beekins paused in her pea shelling. "A good rain is one thing, but God's wrath in wind and hail is another. As the thunder rolled away, I felt my heart beat twice, and then—"

"God missed," Mr. Hammersmith said, the cold pipe between his teeth. "He aimed His thunderbolt at the naughty little besom in the churchyard, but hit the tree instead. Your granny must have stayed His hand."

"My granny weren't dead yet, you nasty old man. The tree made a noise, like a crack and a moan at once-t, and the air smelled odd. Electric and sulfurous and awful. I wanted to run, but my little legs was froze in place. Then the tree burst into flames at the top, like a great, huge candle, despite the pouring rain. The whole thing went up, and all I could do was watch and pray to the angels it didn't fall upon me."

"Woulda served you right," Mr. Hammersmith said. "You had no business being out in the rain all by yourself, Maudie Beekins."

They had doubtless been having this exchange for decades, and I had heard a version of the lightning story at many points in my upbringing. A tale to stop children from playing outside during thunderstorms, though with my brothers, its effectiveness had been limited.

"When this weather breaks," Mrs. Beekins said, resuming her shelling, "them girls will be out in it, and we're due for a storm, Matthew Hammersmith. We're due for a turrible storm."

Across the river, Miss Oakes and her charges emerged from the path through the woods and onto the trail by the stream. Dottie brought up the rear, bearing a bucket.

"Good picking this year," Mr. Hammersmith observed. "Wouldn't mind a pie, if somebody was considerate enough to send one our way."

"I'll have Mrs. Deerfield see to it," Felix said, "assuming the children leave us any fruit."

The little group stopped at the berry patch and began to fill the bucket.

"I don't suppose you've observed other berry pickers across the river?" I asked.

"Of course we have," Mrs. Beekins retorted. "Too hot to stay in the house. Miss Dottie stops on her way to and from the dower house. Dunkeld helps himself when he's crossing from the Ford to the Hall. The pretty governess and her swain pretend to pluck berries, though they're more interested in forbidden fruit."

"Maudie, mind your tongue," Mr. Hammersmith said. "Young people have few enough pleasures in life."

She threw a pea at him. "Old women have fewer, thanks to the likes of useless old men."

Felix turned away to indulge in a coughing fit while Mr. Hammersmith ate the pea that had fallen to his lap.

"What about a child alone?" I asked. "Did you see a girl or boy without any adult supervision the day before yesterday?"

"A girl," Mrs. Beekins replied. "Was carrying a bundled-up shawl, her bonnet down her back. Not a care in the world. She put me in mind of you, my lady, out for a ramble on a summer day. I didn't think nothing of it because Hammersmith said the Hall was missing three girls, not just the one, and I would know Miss Sylvie and Miss Bella."

This was not proof positive that Evelyn had been at the berry patch—Mrs. Beekins could have spotted a village girl tarrying by the raspberries—but it was encouraging.

"She wasn't in any hurry?" I asked. "Not looking over her shoulder?"

"No, my lady. She ate a fair number of berries, then went on down the path."

Felix pushed away from the porch post. "Which direction?"

"Toward the Hall and just sauntering along. She turned off the trail before she reached the path to the Hall, though. I lost sight of her then."

An odd feeling came over me, a chill despite the heat, a silent bodily thunderclap. "Felix, will you come with me to the fishing cottage?"

CHAPTER FIFTEEN

"I could carry you across the ford," Felix said, an eye on the sky.

"And drop me in the middle of the stream? No, thank you." I was nearly certain the fishing cottage hadn't been searched, but then, Lady Ellersby had locked it, the better to discourage trysting couples.

We made our way back to the cart bridge, and just walking in the sultry air had me sweating. "Felix, what do you know of the trouble between Ellersby and his wife?"

"What has that to do with three girls gone missing?"

We trooped onto the raised wooden bridge, which was wide enough for foot traffic or a single dog cart, but insufficient for wagons. I stopped in the middle of the bridge to catch a wisp of a breeze and to get some answers from my brother.

"Lady Ellersby is hosting an enormous celebration of the christening of *your son*. James could well become her husband's heir. How do you suppose that makes her feel, when apparently, Ellersby and her ladyship haven't been intimate for some time?"

Felix peeled out of his jacket, braced his elbows on the bridge railing, and peered into the water flowing below. He was a fine figure of a man, as the saying went, and having undertaken a business raising and training horses, he'd acquired some quality of adult masculinity previously lacking.

He'd matured, both physically and otherwise, or perhaps marriage and fatherhood had gilded the lily of his manliness.

He busied himself turning back his cuffs and slipping his sleeve buttons into a pocket. "I thought Ellersby had effected a rapprochement of sorts with Annabelle when James was born."

"Or did Ellersby assume a rapprochement would follow, or try to negotiate one unsuccessfully?"

"God knows. I wish to hell it would rain."

Near the horizon, the sky was a leaden white that boded well for Felix's wish, though not in the immediate future.

"Even if that means a storm?" I hadn't been aware of Felix's problem with loud noises, but then, many soldiers returned from battle with hidden wounds.

"I go to the nursery when the weather's bad. James can sleep through anything, unless his teeth are bothering him."

The thread of reverence, of awe, in Felix's voice was new. "You love that boy."

"I would die for him or for Katie, would kill for them, would curse the king and damn the angels, Violet. My whole soul is devoted to my family's welfare in a way I never devoted myself to anything, even when soldiering."

As the water burbled along, and the breeze teased at my hair, the urge to cry came over me again. "I know, Felix. I know."

He kept his gaze on the water flowing so placidly beneath the bridge. "Belmaine said it was awful when you lost the second baby. He said the first was a blow, but the second... I've never seen a man so quietly distraught, Vi. And he asked me—me, a complete gudgeon—what to do for you."

But for a few days of subdued conversation at meals and a few weeks of avoiding my bed, Freddie had appeared to do what Englishmen were bred and born to do—he *carried on*. With business, and also with his mistresses, his friends, his clubs, and his sporting entertainments.

"I told him to leave you in peace," Felix said. "When we were growing up, if you had been done some insult by a governess, or Hector accidentally dropped your favorite book of poetry into the pond, we all knew to leave you to sort yourself out. Sometimes, it took days, and when Mama died... but Papa said to cease pestering you and jollying you, and you would sort yourself out."

A tear trickled down my cheek, and I did not even know why I cried. "And that's the reason you abandoned me in mourning? Because I always sort myself out if given enough solitude?"

Felix passed me a handkerchief with an exquisitely embroidered border of roses. "We weren't to hover, not that we'd know how. Papa said you were like Mama, and hovering was never a good idea with her. Not when she was angry and not when she was sad."

I was both. I was furious with my menfolk for having so badly mishandled my bereavements and so very sad that I hadn't known how to gainsay my father's apparently good intentions.

"Promise me something, Felix. Promise me, if you and Katie should ever suffer disappointments, if she is overwhelmed and sad or at her wits' end with some domestic drama, don't leave her alone unless she tells you that's what she wants. Be with her. Listen to her before you march off and ignore your impulse to comfort her."

Felix wrapped an arm around my shoulders and gave me a squeeze. "Katie and I aren't like that. We talk about everything. I never knew... well, suffice it to say, she is my greatest comfort, and I aspire to be hers."

He patted my arm awkwardly and stepped back. "Off to search the fishing cottage?"

"Tell me about Lord and Lady Ellersby."

He tromped across the bridge, and I followed him.

"I only know what Hec and Ajax have passed along," he said, "though their intelligence is usually reliable. Lady Ellersby had a rough time of it in childbed with Bella, and thinking to spare his wife needless suffering, Ellersby set up a second household in Town."

"He took a mistress." Men of Ellersby's station were almost expected to seek extramarital pleasure. "He told himself he was sparing his wife the risk of childbed."

"He was on hand when Bella was born, Violet." Felix glanced up the path in the direction of the berry patch, where the children were making a considerable racket. "I gather the experience upended his notions of genteel childbirth. Katie's mama had told me some of what to expect. Katie asked me to wait in the library for the first part, but I was with her when James came into the world. Papa waited with me, told me not to get drunk or use profanity in the birthing room, no matter how terrified I was. When Katie summoned me... Papa's advice turned out to be useful."

Don't get drunk. Don't hover. My father lacked for a certain type of wisdom, but I could no longer attribute to him quite the degree of obliviousness that made staying angry at him easy. Apparently he did notice when his family was in distress, but knew not what to do about it.

"You and Katie will decide how to go on should James acquire siblings. I gather Lady Ellersby was insulted by her husband's show of consideration?"

"Ellersby has a by-blow, Violet. A little boy. A son he acknowledges and supports. The lad is barely out of leading strings, and he's Ellersby to the life."

And as marital wedges went, that illegitimate child would serve nicely. He proved that Ellersby was blameless in the lack-of-heirs department, leaving Lady Ellersby to shoulder that burden on her own. No wonder Annabelle was distant, and no wonder Ellersby was bowed down by guilt.

"You have seen this child?"

Felix held back a branch so I could precede him up the path to the fishing cottage. "His name is Michael. He's a very bright lad, and Ellersby sees that he wants for nothing."

Except legitimacy.

Except a father's loving presence.

Except a place here at Derwent Hall when the Deerfield family gathered.

"Is Ellersby still involved with the boy's mother?"

"I gather that arrangement was brief."

The air was cooler in the woods, though the very trees seemed to — wait for the weather to relent.

"Ellersby is not suited to sophisticated sinning," I said. "He meant his wedding vows, though he and Lady Ellersby were not a love match."

"The hell they weren't."

"Explain yourself." Lady Ellersby had said, very clearly, that she and Mitchell were not a love match.

"Derwent had a list of young ladies Mitchell was to consider, ranked in order of political usefulness, fortune, and I know not what else. Papa was determined that Mitchell make an advantageous match."

"Annabelle was not on the list?"

"They had a very great row about it. Mitchell shouted Papa down, an occasion for the history books. Said he'd have Annabelle or no one, and Papa apparently believed him."

Good gracious. Mitchell, the pattern card of probity, had gone to war over his choice of bride. "Do you know who else was on the list?"

Felix rattled off a half-dozen names. That he'd recall them after all these years suggested the argument between Mitchell and Papa had been spectacular—or that Felix had lost some bet associated with its outcome.

"Mitchell did us all a favor," Felix said as we reached the porch of the fishing cottage. "He told Derwent that meddling in our lives was one thing, but interfering with our marital choices was another. We boys were to marry where we saw fit, and Derwent was not to interfere, lest we end up in the sort of mess Mama endured with Papa. It's the only time I've heard Mitchell slam a door."

The "boys" were to marry where they saw fit, while I was married where Papa saw an advantage to himself. I could not be furious with Papa, but I could certainly feel entitled to a grudge.

The fishing cottage sat beneath the oaks, dwarfed by their grandeur, for all the cottage would have made four of the pensioners' dwellings put together. I took the key from above the lintel and opened the door.

"If the place was locked," Felix said as I replaced the key, "how would the girls get in? They are too small to reach that high."

"Evelyn might be tall enough to reach the key, or she might have found a loose window. Let's have a look, shall we?"

Felix's question troubled me, because the porch had no handy bench or sturdy flower pot upon which Evelyn might have stood. The logical conclusion was that only an adult could have unlocked the door.

The cottage was tidy, if a bit dusty. We poked around the parlor, which betrayed no sign of recent habitation. The bedrooms upstairs were inconclusive—one bed had been hastily made, which I attributed to Lady Eutheria and Mr. Botham's assignation—while another was stripped, with sheets and blankets folded up on the exposed mattress.

"The kitchen will tell the tale," Felix said, leading the way to the back of the cottage. "Children haven't the knack of tidying up a kitchen. Mrs. Beekins always knew when we'd raided the larder, because we left..."

His voice trailed off as we reached the spacious area devoted to storing and preparation of food.

"We always left crumbs on the counter," I said, peering at the evidence. "But from what? The pantry will hold only staples, and those will be under lock and key."

I sank onto a hard chair at the plank table that did double duty as a place to work and eat. "If the girls were here, somebody let them in, and somebody brought them provisions." And that same somebody had perhaps locked the children in here as well.

Why, why, why?

Felix swept the crumbs into his palm and dumped them into the dustbin. "The children aren't here now, if they ever were. Maybe the searchers in the village have had more luck."

Weariness hit me like a blow to the middle, and yet, I rose. "I will return to the Hall, and I thank you for your assistance."

We parted by the river, and to my great surprise, we parted with a hug. A hug I had very much needed and hadn't known to ask for.

I took a solitary luncheon in the conservatory, my maps spread out before me on a low table.

"It hasn't changed, has it?" Sebastian said, coming down beside me and setting his plate atop my maps. "A hundred years from now, it will still be Derwent Hall, with the same farm lanes and hedges, the same boundaries and pastures."

"I hope so. How goes the search in the village?"

"Pointless, but we had to try. None of those people would hide Derwent's own grandchildren from him, nor would they take a notion to indulge in a triple kidnapping. How was your morning?"

I appreciated his brisk honesty. "Not quite pointless. Evelyn or somebody like her was seen at the berry patch carrying a bundle and enjoying the bounty of the land. Mrs. Beekins still has keen eyesight."

Sebastian popped a strawberry into his mouth, and the sight had me longing for strawberries. They'd been available in abundance from the buffet in the gallery, and I had passed over them.

"Help yourself," he said, picking up his plate and holding it out to me. "Mrs. Beekins was three housekeepers ago."

"Possibly four. She has no children apparently, and thus she bides here." Would I have children with St. Sevier? The odds were poor, but still... I wasn't *that* old. I had proved that I could conceive. We were enthusiastic about conjugal intimacies.

Very enthusiastic, though thus far, St. Sevier had taken measures to reduce the possibility of children. I looked forward to the time when we could discard those measures.

"Katie keeps an eye on the pensioners," Sebastian said when I'd plucked a half-dozen berries from his plate. "She's a good woman. Felix chose well, and MacHeath's Ford has benefited."

"Felix and I searched the fishing cottage. Somebody left crumbs in the kitchen, but who? If the children were there, how did they get in when they could not have reached the key, assuming they know where it's kept?"

Sebastian took one of the berries from my plate and held it up to my mouth. "Eat. You will fret yourself to a shadow. Perhaps Botham and his trysting partners left the crumbs. Hector and Ajax aren't speaking to one another."

I munched a succulent berry and knew that if heaven lived up to its reputation, ripe, fresh strawberries would feature prominently on the celestial menu.

"Hec and Ajax quarrel as frequently as they conspire." Though they hadn't reached the silent-stalemate phase of disagreement for several years. "Usually over a lady, sometimes over a wager."

Sebastian fashioned himself a sandwich of buttered bread, ham, and some sort of pale cheese speckled with caraway seeds.

"Today's display was a public row outside the posting inn. Every man present heard Ajax pronounce Hector's scheme to open a fencing studio hopelessly misguided."

Sebastian passed me the sandwich. Good of him, because the scent of caraway had tickled my fancy.

"Hector's scheme is far from hopelessly misguided. Only a few of the sprigs lounging about Town can afford Angelo's, and Hector is very skilled with a blade. He's patient, he's analytical by nature, and he can put up with Ajax. He must do something with himself, else Papa will force him to stand for the hustings along with Ajax."

"Perhaps Ajax is jealous because Hector has devised a plan for escaping Derwent's control."

That didn't make sense either. "Ajax isn't the jealous sort. He's a good egg." The brother most likely to tease me out of my sulks, despite Papa's apparent decrees to the contrary. The brother who'd told me that I didn't have to marry Belmaine if I didn't want to, though Ajax hadn't been forthcoming about why I might be unenthusiastic about Freddie's suit.

Besides, I had wanted to marry Freddie, or so I'd assured myself.

"Pritchard and Bascomb overheard the altercation, as did half the village. St. Sevier was taken captive by the local apothecary, who apparently hasn't had anybody to discuss herbs and tisanes with since William popped over from Normandy."

The sandwich was scrumptious and fortifying, and I washed it down with cool lavender-flavored lemonade.

"You didn't think to rescue St. Sevier?" The apothecary, Mr. Basil, was a gentleman of African extraction who could have talked the Conqueror himself into submission. One asked for Mr. Basil's medical advice only if one could bear to stand upright for the next two hours enduring a barrage of Latin plant names and arcane recipes.

Though Mr. Basil's lore was almost always helpful, unlike the local physician's efforts.

"Violet, St. Sevier delights in all things medical. He gave as good as he got, and I suspect he will be fondly remembered in the village for generations, thanks to one conversation with a loquacious shopkeeper. Basil will quote him in three languages and toast the good doctor's health for decades to come."

Sebastian made himself a sandwich, though one sandwich was barely a snack to a man of his robust physique.

"Where haven't we searched, Sebastian?"

"Someplace that will be obvious in hindsight, unless Bascomb's valet has the girls secreted at a location of Bascomb's choosing. But then, why would a coxcomb like Bascomb steal children?"

Not children, *little girls*. "St. Sevier said Bascomb was pestering a young serving maid last night."

Sebastian grimaced. "Had his hands on her where a gentleman

ought not. I was about to put my hands on him, but mine host summoned the girl to the kitchen. St. Sevier was growling in French."

St. Sevier could also purr in French. Where *was* my darling Hugh when a lady contemplated an afternoon nap? My longing wasn't particularly carnal. I simply wanted to be in his embrace.

"We are missing something, Sebastian. Something to do with the children."

"Not for lack of trying to find them, Violet." He rose, towering over me, and I realized he had not been intent on having his own lunch so much as he'd been focused on making sure I ate something. "St. Sevier and Basil conducted much of their discussion in French."

"And?"

"And I could not be certain because my French is rusty, but I thought I heard St. Sevier asking Basil about a female with red hair. *Fille rousse.* The missing children aren't redheads."

"You obviously misheard, which is what you deserve for eavesdropping. Did you know Ellersby has a son?"

Sebastian stretched, like a great cat upon arising from a nap. "I'd heard something to this effect. No details. It happens, though I gather Lady Ellersby somehow found out and was not best pleased."

I rose, then sat back down. "Damn this heat."

"Violet, are you well?"

"A touch of light-headedness. More lemonade is in order." And perhaps another sandwich? I was far from full, and I hadn't had much breakfast.

Sebastian had a scowl that could curdle milk. A flat, damning stare that would make a sainted martyr reexamine her conscience. I was far from a sainted martyr. I sipped my lemonade and held the glass against my cheek.

"We will stop by the library," Sebastian said, sounding quite severe. "You will select a book. A lighthearted play, some foolish poetry. Then I will walk you down to the stable. You can read in the gazebo and forget all about missing little girls for an hour. When you have restored your energies and rested your eyes, you shall summon

Katie to the Hall to confer with you regarding the details of the christening. I will hold the boy, lest you drop him. You need only repeat a few phrases, and the ceremony will be over before you know it."

This time when I rose, I did so with Sebastian's assistance. "I hadn't really thought much about the actual christening."

"You are dreading it." He picked up my drink and offered his arm. "Put your mind at ease, Violet. I'll be with you, and everybody will fuss over the baby."

"And fuss over you in your fancy kilt."

He did not so much as crack a smile.

"Sebastian, do you think of having children with Mrs. Bonaventure?"

"The heat has made you daft." We processed to the library at the speed of inebriated dowagers, and it occurred to me that I'd frightened Sebastian with a simple case of lightheadedness.

"You will tell Dr. St. Sevier that you nearly fainted, Violet."

Or I will. The words hung in the air, along with the scent of scythed grass and beeswax. Every window in the Hall was open, and not a breeze to be found. I chose Wordsworth's pastoral verses and let Sebastian toddle with me to the gazebo near the stable. He seated me and turned to leave—I hoped—but stopped at the steps.

"Pamela Bonaventure is in every way a lovely woman," he said, "but she does not seek to remarry at this time." His posture, militarily correct, suggested the admission had cost him.

"You asked her?"

"None of your damned business, woman, but no, I did not, nor will I." He stalked off, kilt swinging.

"She's an idiot," I called after him. "A fool. A buffle-headed, hen-witted, noddy-peaked dizzard."

And yet, I was relieved that Sebastian had not made her an offer —or she hadn't allowed matters to progress in that direction. He deserved more than a practical union. Even my brothers deserved more than that.

I was embarrassed to say that Mr. Wordsworth's brilliance had a soporific effect. I made it through three or four poems before nodding off, the book in my lap. When I awoke, Lord Pritchard was sitting beside me, his gaze on my mouth.

"Try to kiss me," I said, "and I will slam this book into a part of your person you hold ridiculously dear."

He sat up straight. "Good day to you too, Lady Violet. I thought perhaps I'd offer you some answers, though if you'd rather be kissed, I am happy to oblige."

I set aside Mr. Wordsworth's *Daffodils*. "Who is Samuel to you, and why were you pestering him?"

~

"I am accounted a very skilled kisser," Lord Pritchard replied.

"As legions of women will doubtless testify?" And very likely a few men too. I hoped boys had not made his list... or young girls. "Great experience does not necessarily make for great skill, particularly when it comes to a vain and powerful man's amatory abilities."

"You think me powerful?"

His sense of *amour propre* was nearly as oppressive as the heat. "You are titled. You have significant wealth. You sit in the House of Lords and determine how many are to starve so your fellow landowners can sell their grain at premium rates, when cheap Baltic wheat would prevent those deaths."

"Good gracious, you spout politics, but then, you are Derwent's daughter. Does he know he's spawned a radical among his brood?"

"I am not radical, but how much exploitation are the common folk to put up with in the name of thwarting revolution while you, my father, and his kind raise rents, raise food prices, and drop wages in the manufactories? People are forced from their villages by enclosures and have nowhere to live in the cities, so we arrest them for vagrancy. We toss them into the poorhouses, where disease is certain to kill them off, and yet, we call ourselves a Christian nation."

I had no patience with violence of the French variety, but successive Tory governments would back John Bull into one too many corners if present policies continued unchecked. Freddie had kept out of politics, but he'd been a keen observer of mercantile realities, and his ability to predict Parliament's behavior had made him wealthy.

"Lord Byron agrees with you and said as much on the floor of Parliament. You will notice he's no longer underfoot to serve as the conscience of his peers."

His lordship was off in Italy somewhere, already graying though barely thirty years old, and growing somewhat stout, if the rumors were to be believed.

"He's writing poetry that serves the same purpose. Tell me about Samuel."

Pritchard scrubbed a hand over his face, a countenance that would go prematurely soft beneath the chin if he did not moderate his vices.

"Samuel is my son. I want him to come live with me, want to send him to university for a proper education when the time comes. I can understand why public school has no appeal, and it's grown a bit late for that anyway, but he deserves better than to sweat his life away at a village forge."

I thought back to the matching, naughty-boy smiles, to the tone of Pritchard's conversation with the boy. There was a resemblance, but that still did not feel like the entire explanation for why Samuel seemed familiar to me.

"He's your son?"

"My firstborn son, as it happens. As youthful follies go, he'll do. I intend to leave him his own property and enough to live quite comfortably, but if he's never experienced anything beyond darts night at the local pub and walking milkmaids home from Sunday services, he won't know how to go on with means greater than his wages."

"He's young. He might change his mind." Though the work at the forge seemed to *go on* happily, in an atmosphere of bonhomie and democracy. Any man, regardless of station, could be an expert on whether a horse was sound, lame, or simply stiff behind. The forge was the village green gentlemen's club that admitted all and sundry fellows on equal footing.

"The problem is Derwent," Pritchard said, crossing his boots at the ankle. "He's left the decision to Samuel, which of course inspires Samuel's undying loyalty toward the earl, and thus I will never have the pleasure of my son's company."

Of all the solutions to the conundrum of Pritchard and Samuel, I had not foreseen this one. "What of the boy's mother? If he's close to her, he would not want to leave her."

"She has never known want, and it's not as if Samuel need cut off all contact with her. Nobody even told me I had a son, but then I noticed Samuel a few years ago at Derwent's Yuletide open house. The boy laughs exactly like my youngest brother did, he walks like Tom, he winks—with his right eye—as Tom did. I started asking questions, and Samuel's paternity became obvious."

"Does Samuel know you're his father?"

"Of course, and as far as he's concerned, I might be a great lord, wealthy, and on joking terms with the Regent, but that's nothing compared to jollying a nervous colt through his first shoeing."

Samuel had ambition, in other words, but not the sort of ambition Lord Pritchard understood. My father, by contrast, would grasp the pride the boy took in a potentially dangerous job well done.

"Does your situation with Samuel have anything do to with three little girls going missing?"

Pritchard leaned his head back against a post supporting the gazebo's roof. "I can't see that it does. I have no use for other people's children, and my child has no use for me."

"You have Henry."

"And Henry and Samuel are brothers, but they've never met. You might think me a dissolute blight on the backside of humanity, Lady Violet, but I believe brothers should be friends. Tom and I certainly were, and nobody dared mention that he'd been born on the wrong side of the blanket. My father saw to that, and my mother agreed with him."

"Then I suppose you will have to visit Derwent Hall more frequently," I said. "Make the effort to get to know your older son without taking possession of him as if he's a hunter you admired at Tatts. You must bring Henry to the stable to meet Samuel and see that they hack out together when Henry is off the lead line."

"You are telling me I will have to work at being a father."

"At being a good father. Samuel is young, and you might have missed most of his boyhood, but family lasts well beyond childhood, if we're lucky."

Pritchard sent me a pensive glance. "You aren't preparing to lecture me about the wages of sin and being no better than I should be?"

Pritchard had been a heedless youth when Samuel had been conceived, a failing his lordship was finally trying to outgrow.

"Lecturing most men merely amuses them, such is their hubris. I have better things to do with my energy. If it's any consolation, Samuel seems to be a good lad. Well-liked, hardworking, competent. He's a son to be proud of, and may God help him, he's inherited your devilish good looks."

I had surprised Lord Pritchard. I, who had no children to be proud of. "Thank you, my lady. Not being free to openly acknowledge the boy has vexed me sorely."

"So acknowledge him. Ask his opinion about your coach horses when others are on hand. Call him son in private so he gets used to the notion. Tell your familiars you're off to Derwent Hall to look in on your oldest boy. Your father apparently raised a by-blow. Nobody will think anything of it that you also have illegitimate offspring."

Though times in this regard were changing, and not for the more tolerant.

"You make it sound easy."

"My lord, you can sit upon your handsome fundament and lament the consequences *to you* of your own reckless behavior, or you can make a start at repairing the damage caused to others. Samuel is doubtless literate—my mother insisted on that much for all of the Hall's staff—and you can drop him a note along with a coin or two for a young man's unforeseen expenses."

I should not have to explain such simple measures to Pritchard, but he was listening, so I continued. "Write to him of your properties and the horses thereon. He might well be enticed by a post as stable master on your estate five years hence, provided he has the skills. Offer to take him to Newmarket for the race meet. Open every possible door and let him decide if he wants to walk through any of them."

Pritchard was quiet for a moment, and I hoped he was considering my suggestions. Family should not be parted, but Samuel was too young to realize that, and besides, for all I knew, he had six siblings in the village, a mother, step-father, and two grannies who doted upon him... Except I had not heard of any such connections, and I generally knew the village families.

"Your menfolk," Pritchard said, rising, "claim you are not to be trifled with. I used the word 'formidable' to describe you."

"I took it as a compliment." Though at the time, he'd not meant it as such.

"I neglected to add, Lady Violet, that you are also surprisingly kind." He bowed over my hand. "Thank you for that. Thank you very much for your kindness. If ever you need a friend, for any reason, please do call upon me. I insist upon it."

He strode off in the direction of the stable, where I hoped he and his son could make a better start on being family than they had so far.

I collected Mr. Wordsworth and steeled myself for my discussion with Katie, though I did wonder who Samuel's mama was.

CHAPTER SIXTEEN

"I'd best be going," Katie said, finishing her tea. "The sky promises rain, and I don't like to be too far from James for any length of time. Felix says Mrs. Beekins spotted the Anderson girl by the berry patch a day or two ago."

Katie was a quiet, pretty woman, made beautiful by her love for her family. She and Felix gazed upon each other with nothing short of naked devotion. A year ago, I would have called them daft, besotted, or worse.

Now, I sought the same regard from St. Sevier, and when we were not in company, I lavished it upon him. He had offered to ride to Bascomb's estate and make inquiries of Bascomb's valet. Bascomb —who had decided *not* to add his children to the gathering after all— had consented to that indignity, because the alternative was doubtless to incur my father's wrath.

The christening of Papa's first *legitimate* grandson was being overshadowed by a lot of drama, and the earl's temper was growing short.

"I told Felix that being James's godmother might be hard for you,"

Katie said as I walked her to the Hall's front door. "You must not feel obligated to dote upon the boy or visit us, if that would be painful."

It would be painful, also sweet. I passed Katie her bonnet and parasol. "I will try not to hover or spoil him, but a young fellow needs somebody to take his part unconditionally, and my mother isn't on hand to fulfill that office."

"You are so practical," Katie said, grabbing me in a swift hug. "So brave. I told Felix we needed to pension Geddes, Violet, and she will pay an extended visit to her sister once the christening is behind us. I had put off that discussion, but I knew you would have faced the matter squarely. I hope you know I admire you very much. Felix does, too, though he's too shy to tell you that."

Felix, shy? Some marvel of marital optimism was at work if Katie saw Felix as shy, though perhaps with her, the love of his life, he was shy. And thank heavens Geddes was being allowed to step back from her duties.

"Dunkeld says you've brought MacHeath's Ford back to life, Katie Deerfield. That is no small accomplishment."

She beamed at me. "I love that my name is Katie Deerfield. I am Mrs. Felix Deerfield, and I thank God for that blessing every day."

I passed her gloves to her. "I hazard that you thank the Almighty for your marital state after dark on occasion as well."

Katie was a mother and married lady, but she blushed like a schoolgirl. "I've told Felix I want a large family."

Perhaps St. Sevier needed to have a talk with Katie as well as Ellersby. "You want a well-spaced family, Katie. James should be at least a year old and weaned before you try for a sibling."

"Felix says the same thing. He can be very stubborn."

Thank God for stubborn Deerfields. I accompanied Katie down the front steps. The afternoon air had progressed from stifling to sullen. A gusty breeze unsettled the canopy of the woods bordering the park, and the sky had acquired a blanket of pewter clouds.

"Take the cart bridge, Katie. Don't travel home through the village. When the weather breaks, we will be inundated."

"Right," Katie said, not bothering to open her parasol. "I will see you at the christening, Violet." She bustled off, a dear, sweet woman and, much to my surprise, an ally. I had neglected to cultivate the friendship of my sisters-in-law, but I promised myself I would remedy that oversight.

I was no longer in mourning, by God, and was, in fact, anticipating remarriage. On that thought, I gathered up my own shawl and bonnet and, despite the rising wind, made my way to the stable. I missed St. Sevier, and was hungry for the sight and feel of him.

Bascomb's property was a good seven miles distant, but St. Sevier had been gone long enough that he had to return soon.

Unless, of course, he'd been set upon by brigands.

Or kidnapped.

Or that enormous chestnut gelding had taken a fright at a rabbit and tossed his rider.

"Stop it," I muttered, passing beneath the tress on the path to the stable. "Stop fretting and breathe." St. Sevier had taught me that. Taught me to stop my anxious, racing thoughts by dint of mental discipline and to focus on something else.

"Clean your weaponry," he'd said. "Soldiers clean their weapons the night before a battle, not because the weapons need cleaning, but because the soldiers need a distraction from their own thoughts."

As if cleaning anything had ever precluded thinking at the same time. Soldiers should be housekeepers if that were the case.

The ginger cat darted out of the gazebo and bolted down the path to the home farm. The stable boys were bringing horses in from the paddocks with the sort of controlled haste characteristic of sailors battening down the hatches before a looming storm.

I stared in vain down the drive, hoping to see my beloved returning.

"What the hell are you doing outside?" Sebastian stood in the doorway to the barn, the wind plucking at the hem of his kilt.

"Taking the air. What of you?"

"Hannibal threw a shoe this morning. I wanted to make sure the lads had soaked his foot."

A raindrop hit my cheek with stinging force.

"Get back to the house, Violet. We're in for a deluge."

This was what came of allowing Sebastian his little display of dictatorial masculinity in the conservatory. Permit a man to give one order, and he was soon incapable of speaking in anything but imperatives.

"I shall wait here for St. Sevier."

"Then at least wait inside the damned barn." He looked like he was ready to toss me over his shoulder, so I marched past him for the open barn door. At the opposite end of the barn aisle, stable boys had already dragged the doors closed, and Samuel was extinguishing all the lamps in the barn save one, in the center, secured to a beam.

"Sebastian, have we searched the stables? Really searched them?"

"Of course. We started with the home farm and then looked here. The tenant properties and outbuildings were next. Why?"

The ginger cat would not leave my mind, even as distant thunder rumbled, and a gust of wind knocked over a rake propped against the wall.

"Leave the barn door open," I called as Samuel hustled past me. "St. Sevier is due back any moment."

"You don't know that," Sebastian said. "If St. Sevier has any sense, he's biding in the village rather than dashing the last mile."

Hugh would come back to me if he could. Of that I was certain. He'd come back to report on Bascomb's valet and to be with me as I fretted and fumed over the missing girls. A hard report of raindrops spattered against the barn roof, and a horse in the nearest stall startled.

St. Sevier's gelding was surefooted, but was he sane in a storm? Was any horse?

I stood by the open barn door, arms wrapped about my middle. The temperature was rapidly dropping, and the sky had gone greenish gray.

"I hate to think of the girls out in this," I said, for Sebastian loomed at my elbow, "or weathering the storm on their own. They will long for the safety of the nursery, for a good carpet battle, a game of hide-and-seek..."

The darkening sky shuddered with lightning. Five heartbeats later, thunder rumbled again.

"Getting closer," Sebastian muttered, taking off his coat and draping it around my shoulders. "You'll catch your death, and your damned Frenchman will blame me."

A wooden pail bounced and rolled through the stable yard, and more horses shifted restlessly behind us. They were safe in their stalls, while the children...

As if my mind had been illuminated by lightning, insight struck. "I know where the children are."

Henry had said that winning hide-and-seek was a matter of hiding in a place that had already been searched. Had he known where the girls were? Had his father told him?

"They will be wishing themselves in France—"

"Sebastian, they are at the home farm. The first place we searched. The damned cat tried to tell me..." I marched out into the stable yard, making straight for the path through the hedge.

"Violet, get back here! For God's sake..." Sebastian hurried after me, but I would not be stopped. Bella was afraid of storms, as I had been in early childhood. The girls had been hiding for days, and if they weren't cold and hungry, they soon would be.

Also frightened. I did not care who had taken them or why, or if the children were playing the stupidest prank in the history of stupid pranks. They would not weather this storm on their own.

"Violet!"

The voice was not Sebastian's, but rather, St. Sevier's. He sat atop his horse, whose coat was dusty, and the beast was dancing sideways across the stable yard.

"I know where the girls are!" I shouted. "We must get to the home farm." I took off at a jog, Sebastian beside me.

"We searched there," he snapped, jogging at my side. "They aren't there."

"You win by cheating, by switching your hiding place." I picked up my pace until the gate across the path came into view. The majestic edifice of the home farm's venerable hipped barn loomed a hundred yards past the gate, silhouetted against a black sky.

"You will never make it," Sebastian said as St. Sevier trotted up behind us on horseback. "You'll get soaked, and—"

His words were drowned out by a ferocious spate of rain. I slogged onward on the slick path, with St. Sevier shouting something unintelligible from the rear. I would get to that barn, I would find the girls, and they would be well, if unnerved.

"Violet," St. Sevier bellowed. "Look!" He pointed in the direction of the barn, and from his higher vantage point atop the horse, he'd seen what I had not yet discerned.

Two children stood holding hands in the barnyard. Evelyn and Sylvie. They had no bonnets, only summer cloaks, and the wind played havoc with their hems. Sylvie was gesturing toward the barn, but I could not make out her words.

"Hurry!" I yelled, nearly losing my footing on the path. "Oh God, hurry." There should be three girls, three upset, contrite...

The rain turned to hail just as an ear-splitting crack of thunder shook the very earth. St. Sevier's horse reared, and at the same time, the barn's thatched roof erupted in flames.

Evelyn shook free of Sylvie's grasp, cupped both hands around her mouth, and hollered something in the direction of the barn.

I saw then a sight that will haunt me for the rest of my days. Like most barns, this one was designed to store hay on the upper floor, while animals sheltered below. To facilitate moving that hay from the lofts down to the barnyard, the front wall of the barn was pierced by a door that now flapped open in the ferocious wind.

Bella stood in the doorway, clutching something small and brown to her middle. She was eerily still as the barn roof gusted into flames, and hail pinged up from the grass.

"Violet, move aside!" St. Sevier's words penetrated the roar of the storm, but I could not move. Sebastian pulled me off the path as St. Sevier circled his horse and made for the gate at a dead gallop.

"Don't look," Sebastian said, adding some prayer or curse in Gaelic and pulling me into his arms.

I *did* look as St. Sevier on his great beast pounded through the mud toward a gate at least five feet in height. On the other side, Sylvie and Evelyn were screaming at Bella to jump, but a leap of fifteen feet onto slick cobbles would surely kill her.

Half the barn roof was on fire, despite the hail, and my heart beat so hard it hurt.

St. Sevier's gelding gathered speed as it neared the fence, and in sloppy footing, that was surely not wise. I wanted to look away, but could not so much as blink as the horse soared aloft in one great bound.

"He made it," Sebastian said. "Thank whatever God looks after French madmen, the bloody fool made it. Come on." He half dragged, half carried me down the path as St. Sevier galloped on ahead of us. I climbed the gate, slipped in the mud on the other side, and would have gone down but for Sebastian's quick reflexes.

"He cannot go into that barn, Sebastian. He will die if he goes into that barn..."

And Bella would die if he didn't. St. Sevier loved children. He wanted to become a doctor for children, and that he would be denied that dream enraged me. I ran on, lungs afire, as St. Sevier gained the stable yard.

"Mind the girls," Sebastian said, bolting ahead of me.

Bella was no longer in the open door. She was nowhere to be seen. Good God, she'd retreated into the burning barn, but how far could she get with cinders falling from the roof onto dry hay?

St. Sevier brought his horse to a halt beneath where Bella had stood. He called Bella's name, and still she did not appear.

Sebastian added his voice to St. Sevier's, and as the scent of smoke tainted the air, Bella reappeared in the barn doorway, clutching her bedraggled bear. St. Sevier leaped from his horse and dashed for the side of the barn.

"Not that way!" Sebastian yelled. "Hold the damned horse!"

I had no idea what Sebastian planned, but St. Sevier seemed to grasp the plan. He took the reins, and Sebastian yanked off his boots and climbed into the saddle. The horse, winded by his exertions, or perhaps recalling some battlefield maneuver, remained still, sides heaving.

Sebastian stood on the horse's croup, arms upraised. "Jump, Bella. A wee hop. I'll catch you."

He sounded as if he were teasing, not perched on a horse in a pelting storm, shirt plastered to his skin.

"I'm scared."

A portion of the barn roof gave way on a crash, sending up a shower of sparks and black smoke and causing the horse to startle.

"I'll catch you," Sebastian said, somehow keeping his balance. "No need to fret, but Charlemagne might like to see his stall sooner rather than later, so let's be about it."

So calm. So utterly focused. I wrapped my arms around Sylvie and Evelyn, both of whom were shivering.

"Come, darling Bella," St. Sevier said, all brisk dispatch. "If Dunkeld says he'll catch you, you are as good as caught. You can trust him, and if you cannot trust him, then you will land on him, and even he is a good deal softer than the cobblestones." St. Sevier raised a hand, waggled his fingers, and smiled as if he'd never enjoyed such a fanciful lark. "*Vite, vite, petite lapine!*"

Bella did not leap like a little bunny so much as she hugged her bear tightly and plummeted like a shot grouse just as another great slab of burning roof collapsed. Evelyn and Sylvie buried their faces against me while I prayed without words.

Sebastian caught Bella easily, and her momentum carried him off the horse. He somehow landed on his feet, as nimble as a cat, just as Charlemagne tried to bolt from St. Sevier's grasp.

Sebastian passed Bella to me, and we ladies shamelessly clung to one another. I heard shouting as men came running to get animals and equipment out of the barn before the fire could reach the lower level.

I moved with the girls under the overhang of the nearby spring-house, draping Sebastian's coat around Bella.

"She went back for Charles," Sylvie said. "She almost forgot him."

"Charles is your bear?"

Bella nodded even as she remained barnacled to me, arms around my neck. "I could not leave Charles."

"I know," I said, kissing her cold cheek. "My darling girl, I know."

The rain and hail roared on, leaving a smoking skeleton where an ancient barn had been. Papa would be angry at the expense of the repairs, but the girls would have a story to tell well into old age.

I used a corner of Sebastian's coat to wipe my eyes and waited for the storm to pass.

～

The first person to spot our bedraggled little cavalcade returning from the home farm was Ellersby. I had never seen my oldest brother move that quickly. He came at us across the lawn at a dead run while Sylvie and Bella each clutched one of my hands.

"Papa will be angry," Sylvie whispered.

"Will he take Charles away?" Bella asked.

"He would not dare. I would disown him for thinking of it."

Ellersby stopped two yards away, sank to his knees in the wet grass, and held out his arms. "You're safe. Thank a merciful God, you are safe."

Bella went to him first, followed a little more hesitantly by Sylvie. He hugged his daughters with gentle ferocity, his face buried against Sylvie's bony little shoulder.

"I missed you so," he said, "more than you can know. Your mama did too. She will rejoice to see you." Still, he clung to his children while Evelyn slipped her hand into mine.

St. Sevier, leading his now calm horse, came up to my side. "The children should be dry and warm as soon as possible, and they are likely hungry."

Ellersby rose, holding each child by a hand. "I'll see to it. They will have the best of care." He got about three steps in the direction of the house before scooping a daughter onto each hip. They would soon be too big and dignified for that type of display, but they hugged their papa close now.

"Ellersby!" I called. "No interrogations. Not yet. The explanations can wait."

He nodded without breaking stride.

"You know why we did this?" Evelyn asked.

"I have some ideas about how you were convinced to do it," I replied, "but there's time for that later. Your mother needs to know you are well and whole, and, Evelyn, no matter how upset she is, no matter what nonsense she spouts, know that she loves you. She might disappoint you from time to time, but that's part of being a family."

Sebastian draped an arm around Evelyn's shoulders. "Come along, ye wee besom. We'll find your mother, and I will convince her you're old enough to have your first sip of a toddy. And, Violet, I will tell Lady Eutheria there's to be no inquisition until you convene one. Will the library do?"

"If the fires have been built up. The children need to dry off and eat something first."

"Right," Sebastian said. "No toddies on an empty belly. St. Sevier, that was fine riding."

"Charlemagne is a good horse. He makes up in courage what he lacks in steadiness."

Sebastian gave St. Sevier a shove and shepherded Evelyn toward the house. I continued with St. Sevier toward the stable.

"You should get warm and dry too, Violet. I will follow directly, but I wanted..."

I wrapped my arms around him, needing to know that he was safe too. "I saw you gallop for that gate, Hugh St. Sevier, and I have never prayed so hard in my life."

"Nor have I." He held me loosely as rain dripped from the leaves, and the sound of the barn door being rolled back scraped against the afternoon air. "If anything had happened to that child..."

"But it didn't. She saw that help was coming. She listened when you called her name. She trusted Dunkeld because you reassured her."

He propped his chin on my crown, apparently in no mood to let me go. The horse began to crop grass, and still, St. Sevier and I embraced.

"After a battle," he said, "one does not know what to feel. Relief to be alive, sorrow for fallen comrades, determination to restore order and carry on, or simply a great hollowness where horror will soon be. I want to make love with you, Violet. While parents are fussing, and children are wolfing down steaming bowls of porridge with butter and honey, I want to make love with you."

He passed the horse off to a groom, and we walked up to the Hall, our arms entwined.

I waved Lucy off and indulged in the very great pleasure of having St. Sevier serve as my lady's maid. We lingered over the details—he brushed out my hair, I assisted with his ablutions and tied the sash of his banyan for him. Though the afternoon had turned fresh and relatively cool, I drew the drapes over the windows in St. Sevier's bedroom.

"I knew you'd come home to me," I said, climbing under the covers. "I knew you'd beat the storm."

He peeled out of his robe and prowled to the bed, wearing not one stitch. "I did not beat the storm, but I knew you would fret."

We said nothing more with words for a good long while, but with touch and silence, we spoke volumes. The pleasure became a holy thing, a golden, luminous connection such as I had never known with my husband. St. Sevier's caresses were at once reverent and unbearably evocative, weaving an intimate tapestry of desire and caring.

Without using either French or English, St. Sevier promised me that he would always weather the storm to reach my side, and I vowed to him that I would be waiting for his safe arrival. I slept in his embrace, more deeply at peace than I could recall ever being.

When I awoke, he was dressed but for his coat, sitting cross-legged at the foot of the bed, watching me.

"I am tempted to get you right back out of those clothes, Monsieur."

"I am tempted to get right back under those covers, my lady, but the children will need your assistance to tell their tale. The estimable Lucy slipped a note under the door. Derwent has declared a family gathering in the library, a drink before supper to celebrate the children's safe return."

"To lecture them, you mean." I sat up. "Nobody can deliver a scold like Derwent can, but the situation is more complicated than children being naughty." I had worked that out more or less in my sleep.

"One suspected as much. Arise, and I will put you to rights. You will check Derwent's ire and see the truth revealed, but you should also eat something, Violet."

"Ever the physician." I would speak with Hugh about that, about my urgency for him to resume his medical practice as he longed to do. No more haring about the realm for weddings, christenings, or house parties. We would settle down wherever he deemed it most advantageous to his professional ambitions.

If that meant inuring myself to life in London, well, I had inured myself to life in London before.

Lucy brought me a cold collation along with a pot of hot tea, St. Sevier chose a soft, blue velvet afternoon dress for me, and I was soon as much on my mettle as ever I would be.

"To the library," I said. "And, Lucy, would you please have the nursery staff join us?"

Lucy nodded, though her expression conveyed surprise. I gave her a few other instructions, and her surprise faded to puzzlement.

"I thought as much," St. Sevier said. "Let's be about it, shall we?"

As we made our way through the house, we encountered smiling footmen and humming maids. Lord and Lady Rowbottom wished us a very good day on their way to take the garden air, and the house-keeper was replacing the flowers on the landings.

The staff, in their way, was rejoicing, but St. Sevier and I heard Papa shouting before we were within six yards of the closed library door.

CHAPTER SEVENTEEN

"My lord." I curtseyed to my father, intending that gesture as a reproach for his unmannerliness. "A glass of sherry would be appreciated."

I was not in the mood for sherry, but Derwent was the host for this gathering, my father, and a gentleman, and he apparently needed a reminder on every one of those points.

The three girls sat on the sofa, their hair neatly combed, their pinafores spotless. Ellersby stood behind Bella and Sylvie, Lady Ellersby at his side. Lady Eutheria perched on the arm of the sofa nearest Evelyn, and to my eye, both mother and daughter appeared pale.

"I have asked the nursery staff to join us," I said, accepting my glass of sherry from a footman. "The girls would like to explain why they went missing—"

"Why they ran off," Papa interjected. "Why they completely upended what should have been a pleasant gathering celebrating a happy family occasion. They will explain why, in the fashion of hysterical females from time immemorial, they—"

"My lord, hush." I spoke gently, for shouting at Papa only

inspired him to shout back. "Nobody can explain anything if you insist on displaying your oratorical skills at such length. Consider what we know." I took the place at the head of the reading table, St. Sevier performing the courtesy of holding my chair.

Sebastian stood by the fireplace, one elbow propped on the mantel. He was already attired for supper, looking splendid in his formal kilt.

"We know three young ladies deserve a sound thrashing," Derwent retorted.

"Nobody thrashes my daughters," Ellersby said as Lady Ellersby moved closer to her husband. "Nobody."

"Nor mine," Lady Eutheria added.

"I commend you, Violet." Papa lifted a glass of brandy in my direction. "You have fomented insurrection under my very roof, and it took you less than a fortnight."

"Guard your tongue, my lord." St. Sevier had also spoken mildly, but I saw Ajax and Hector, lurking by the comedies and plays, exchange a look. A bet had been decided by St. Sevier's warning, one that apparently transcended whatever spat separated my brothers for the nonce. I would have a word with them about their unseemly wagering.

"Perhaps my nieces and Evelyn might enjoy a tea party in the family parlor," I said.

As the children shuffled out under a footman's watchful eye, Miss Oakes, Mr. Harkness, Hansom, and Dottie were admitted, along with Mr. Botham and Lord Pritchard.

Papa set his drink aside. "Will we be joined by a company of strolling players next, Violet?"

I had considered adding Samuel to the gathering, but did not know the boy well enough to gauge whether he would have appreciated the invitation.

"If a troupe of strolling players held the answers to our questions, I would have added them gladly, my lord. As it is, I believe we must start with Dottie. Hansom, if you would like to preside over the girls' tea party, I'm sure they would appreciate your presence."

Hansom peered at me in some confusion until Miss Oakes touched her arm. "Tea party with Bella and Sylvie in the family parlor." Miss Oakes had raised her voice, and now she pointed toward the door. Hansom bobbed a curtsey and scurried off.

St. Sevier remained standing, though near enough to my chair that his presence was a palpable comfort. Dottie, meanwhile, was trying to impersonate a potted palm, lurking behind Miss Oakes and Mr. Harkness.

"'Tweren't nothing to do with me, Lady Violet," Dottie mumbled, "I swear."

"Dottie," Pritchard said, a cajoling note in his voice, "you must be honest with us. Did you help the girls run away?"

Her expression turned mulish, while my father had apparently been inspired into a sudden vow of silence.

"Somebody was mean to Miss Evelyn," Dottie said, aiming a glower at Pritchard. "That's how it starts. They tease you first, then they dare you to let them kiss you. I am not quick, but I'm not stupid either. Miss Evelyn was scared, and nobody would listen to her. I know all about house parties and what gentlemen get up to."

"What is she going on about?" Papa muttered.

"Sylvanus, let her speak." Lady Eutheria's tone was surprisingly stern. "Evelyn was sorely mistreated and the culprit never found."

"Dottie isn't talking about shoving a girl into the priest hole," I said. "Or not just about that. Lord Pritchard, you seem very familiar with our Dottie for a man who has brought his young son to the Hall for the first time." I'd noticed his friendliness with the nursery staff and thought it an excess of charm at the time.

But he referred to Dottie by her first name. I recalled as well that Dottie had hung back in the dormitory when his lordship and I had had sharp words in the playroom. She had not been exercising a domestic's discretion so much as she'd been avoiding Pritchard altogether.

Or sparing herself the sight of Samuel's father. I recalled as well my sense of having met Samuel on some previous occasion, when, in fact, I was noticing a resemblance between Samuel *and his mother.*

"Perhaps," Pritchard said, trying that cajoling note on me, the fool, "now is not the time to air this old business."

"Then I will address my question to Dottie," I said. "Dottie, did you first meet Lord Pritchard at a long-ago house party here at Derwent Hall?"

She nodded tersely. "He were handsome then too. And friendly. But he wants his way in all things."

We look after our own, Ellersby had said, but apparently *our* vigilance had seriously lapsed in Dottie's case.

"Were you forced?" I had to know, not that any consequences would flow to Pritchard if he'd committed rape.

Dottie shook her head. "He were all sweet and tender. But I didn't realize... Mrs. Beekins had to explain it to me. The earl said it weren't no matter, that I could stay on when the baby came, seein' as I was not yet of age myself, but it mattered to me. There I am with a child, and me barely able to manage my letters."

This recitation was greeted with silence, though surely Dottie was owed an apology.

"I thought Dottie was merely shy," Pritchard said. "A little backward, but delectably coy. I had just gone up to university and was in my way nearly as ignorant as she."

I wanted to dismiss his explanation as self-serving tripe, but he was being honest. He had genuinely been too inexperienced to know hesitant demurral from a complete lack of understanding. Or—more likely—Dottie had been enthusiastic about the intimacies without grasping the consequences of those pleasures.

And Pritchard, young dunderhead without compare, had likely assumed that Dottie, as a female in domestic service, knew not only the mechanics of conception but also how to prevent it.

Samuel's parents had been two very young people, one aspiring to comport himself like a worldly rake, the other doubtless shocked and flattered to have the notice of a youthful Adonis. A crime had been committed, but Pritchard was not the only party responsible.

Society, in its neglect of female education, in its failure to instill honor—much less discernment—in young men, bore much of the blame.

"Evelyn is pretty," Pritchard said. "Did you think to protect her from me, Dottie?"

Dottie bit her lip, and my admiration for her nearly brought tears to my eyes. She was in a room full of people who no doubt thought themselves her superior, intellectually and morally, but several people—my father among them—had sorely failed her and were failing her still.

"You are still handsome," Dottie said. "You still flirt *all the time*. You're like a boy with a sweet tooth. You can't help yourself, except it isn't you ends up with the bellyache. Evelyn is pretty."

"Dottie," Pritchard said, "Evelyn is still a child. She's just a girl. No gentleman would ever..."

Dottie stared at him, hard. "I were just a girl. I was a good girl too. But stupid. Somebody started in teasing Miss Evelyn, and I wasn't going to let her be stupid too."

"Not stupid," I said. "Innocent. Your innocence was disrespected, Dottie, but you are a good mother to Samuel, aren't you?"

"Aye. I love my Sammie, and now this one,"—she jerked her chin toward Lord Pritchard—"thinks to take my boy away from me. Why would I let my boy go off and learn to be wicked like his papa? That doesn't make any sense."

Well, no, it did not. Not from the perspective of a protective mother who knew what a heedless bounder that papa had been.

"Dottie," I said, "you are Samuel's legal custodian." My husband's many peccadillos had given me reason to know the law where illegitimate children were concerned. "Because you and Lord Pritchard were not married when Samuel was born, Lord Pritchard has no legal authority over the boy. He cannot take Samuel from you." Not legally. Practically speaking, Pritchard could kidnap the child, and Dottie would be powerless to seek justice.

"Lady Violet is right," Pritchard said. "I have no authority over the boy. I did not acknowledge him at birth, I have not contributed to his support, and I understand why you think I would be a bad influence, but, Dottie..."

"Don't wheedle," Dottie snapped. "Wheedling men are up to no good, and wheedling lords are a plague on the nation. Mrs. Beekins told me that, and I know it to be true. She helped me raise my Sam, and she never lied to me."

Sebastian found it necessary to study the carpet. I did not know if he was amused by Dottie's pronouncement, chagrined, or both.

"Miss Dottie," St. Sevier said, "you spirited Evelyn away to keep her safe, did you not?"

"I said as much. I know how to get into the fishing cottage and the summer cottage—all the cottages. Evelyn was scared, and that wasn't right. She shouldn't have to be scared, and no house party lasts forever." Dottie's tone implied that was a dear consolation, and I had to agree with her.

"What of Bella and Sylvie?" St. Sevier asked. "Did you fear for them too?"

Dottie shook her head. "They heard me and Evelyn making plans. Hansom is nigh deaf, and the little girls just decided they weren't happy sharing the nursery with the little boys. They wouldn't listen when I told them they could not run away. They piked off as soon as it started getting light and showed up at the fishing cottage."

That recitation filled in a few gaps. The little girls had told me that they had unpacked their own valises, and yet, Dottie had known exactly what was missing from their bureau drawers. Without examining the toy chests, she'd known that Bella had taken her little bear as well.

And the handkerchief Felix and I had found had belonged to Dottie rather than Evelyn, which I should have guessed based on St. Sevier's recollection that Dottie's fingers had been berry stained.

"The little girls were already in trouble by the time you learned they'd run away," I said, "and Evelyn wanted company. You brought them food from the dower house kitchens, I take it?" Why else would Dottie have continued to travel daily between the Hall and the dower house, when only the little boys remained in the nursery?

"Aye. Food and books. The girls were having a grand time, but I knew Lord and Lady Ellersby were frettin' something awful. They do love those girls powerful fierce. I shoulda made them two go back to the Hall, but Evelyn told them they might be bullied next, and they wouldn't listen to me. Nobody listens to me."

Sebastian spoke up from his place near the hearth. "We're listening to ye now, lass."

A tear trickled down Dottie's cheek. "But you won't. When his lordship promises my Sam his own horse, or tutors, or whatever Sam's heart desires, off he'll go, my only boy. Three girls go missing, and the whole Hall is turned upside down for days. Everybody searching, everybody overset. Pritchard can take my boy, and I'm supposed to go pick raspberries or daisies..."

She began weeping openly. Sebastian passed her his handkerchief while the sound of a heart breaking filled the library.

"I have nothing but a few pence in wages," Dottie went on. "I am dull-witted. I know that, but that's how God made me, so it can't be a bad thing. I love my boy. He's all I have to love, and he loves me. I don't want to lose my b-boy."

She wept on Sebastian's shoulder with the noisy grief of an inconsolable child, and yet, her sorrow had dignity too. No loving parent should be unwillingly parted from a child, and if Pritchard was suffering some heartache for want of Samuel's company now, that was a small measure of justice long overdue.

"Sit ye doon," Sebastian said, guiding Dottie to the sofa. "Nobody will take your lad away until he's ready to go. Even then, he'll come back around, wanting to see his ma and boasting to her of his manly accomplishments."

He went on in that vein, offering simple, honest reassurances. St.

Sevier poured Dottie a finger of cordial, which she accepted with all the condescension of a dowager duchess.

Papa refreshed his own drink. "Is this where I pretend I have forgiven my naughty granddaughters and declare all's well that ends well?"

Lady Eutheria speared him with a pensive look. "I still don't know who treated Evelyn so unkindly, Sylvanus. To frighten a young girl is vile behavior, and Evelyn is owed an apology."

Mr. Botham stepped forward from the alcove that held an outdated globe. "I am to blame. A misunderstanding. I will offer my apologies to the wronged party."

"You?" Lady Eutheria might have been addressing a spot of manure on her best pair of slippers.

"Evelyn is in the family parlor," I said. "The other children should hear how a gentleman apologizes, Mr. Botham. I'm sure your efforts will be heartfelt and impressive."

Lady Eutheria took him by the arm. "They had better be." They left on a fulminating silence, Miss Oakes and Mr. Harkness in their wake.

"Mr. Botham shoved Evelyn into the priest hole?" Dottie asked, sipping her cordial. "The quality is daft. Mrs. Beekins says that too."

"Are we finished here?" Papa asked, setting his glass aside. "I, for one, would like to change for dinner and put this whole miserable exercise from my mind. If that makes me daft, so be it."

"You are free to leave, my lord," I replied, "but Lord Pritchard and Dottie have matters to discuss. Lord Pritchard would like to get to know Sam better, Dottie. Not steal him away, but not be a stranger either. He might like to take Sam to a race meet, for example, which Sam would enjoy. He can't know what Sam would like, though, unless somebody tells him how to go on with the boy."

"Do I have to?" Such reluctance laced Dottie's tone.

"No," St. Sevier said, "but it would be kind of you."

"Merciful," Sebastian added. "Pritchard would be in your debt."

Dottie clearly liked the sound of that. "Come with me to the nursery, my lord. And keep your hands to yourself."

Pritchard rose. "Yes, ma'am." He offered his arm. She gave him a measuring look, then accepted his courtesy and left with him.

St. Sevier, Sebastian, Ajax, and Hector followed them—everybody was in a tearing hurry to change for supper, apparently—and Lord and Lady Ellersby professed a desire to look in on the tea party.

I was left alone in the library with my father, who looked rather old and weary.

"You have a scold left for me, I trust," he said. "You will explain how this whole contretemps is my fault."

"Am I really so bad as all that?"

He saluted with his brandy. "You are your mother's daughter, and that woman harangued old George himself on occasion. They used to compare notes about whose sons were naughtier. I'd say George's lot has won that competition handily. Pity your mother did not live to see our defeat."

"I think the girls had another motive for running off beside just keeping Evelyn company, Papa."

"Ellersby and his lady are not cordial. They hide it well, but their differences have gone on too long not to be noticeable. Children remark these matters in the most inconvenient ways, though I must say, I saw Annabelle take Ellersby's hand by the time I'd finished rattling my lordly swords."

He did notice. He did care. "You will please explain to Lady Ellersby how hard Mitchell fought for *her* hand, how many estimable alternatives he batted aside to meet Annabelle at the altar."

"The boy was ready to disown me," Papa said, smiling at his drink. "He'd have done it too."

"And," I added, "you will explain to her ladyship that for Mitchell to take a mistress in Town was *your idea* and intended to spare Annabelle from too many birthings in close succession."

Papa sighed, though in his vast lexicon of sighs, this one was merely resigned. "If I must."

I patted his arm. "You must, Papa. For the sake of your unborn grandchildren, you truly must."

I left him among his books, portraits, and decanters, but as I left the library, I thought I heard him mutter, "Just like your mother..."

And he sounded patently admiring.

Dottie and the children had visited upon me an overdue insight: Children were not chattel any more than wives were chattel, regardless of whatever imbecilic pronouncements the law made to the contrary. The heart was above the law, and it was my heart that had ached so sorely over the missing children.

A handsome young son was not a prize to be exhibited at the race meets, or a consolation for a lost brother.

A young girl awkwardly approaching womanhood was not a social nuisance to be endured. She was a very young lady, thorns and all, and deserving of utmost protection and respect.

And as for Sylvie and Bella... They had apparently had a stern talk with their parents, about loyalty to those who matter to us, about the importance of picnics and apologies. If my eyes did not deceive me, both Lord and Lady Ellersby had listened.

My frame of mind on the day of the christening was thus such that I intended to hold baby James as much as his parents would allow me to. We took the coaches for the short trip into the village, the baby traveling with his parents, and St. Sevier and I joining Sebastian in his elegant traveling vehicle.

"Will you return to Scotland next?" I asked Sebastian.

He and St. Sevier sat with their backs to the horses, while I perched in solitary splendor on the forward-facing seat. I did not often have a chance to compare these two fellows side by side, which was fortunate. They were almost too magnificent for one mortal female to contemplate.

Sebastian tended more to brawn and St. Sevier to elegance.

Sebastian's features bore a hint of the Romanesque, while St. Sevier leaned in an ascetic direction. They were both keenly intelligent, relentlessly honorable, and pragmatic, as both soldiers and physicians must be.

I loved St. Sevier passionately—I could admit that now—but I would also miss Sebastian terribly when he returned to his castle in the north.

"The grouse moors will soon be teeming with Englishmen," Sebastian said. "I might bide here in the south for a bit, give Felix a hand with his beasts."

"You should go up to London for the little Season," I said as the coach rolled around the village green. "It's not nearly as busy as the spring madness, and the weather can be quite pleasant." Besides, Mrs. Bonaventure might need her handy escort back, and now that I knew she had no chance to become Sebastian's marchioness, I could compliment her good taste.

St. Sevier watched the green roll by, though I had the sense I'd amused him. Well, fine. I hoped to frequently amuse him in the years to come.

"The church will be crowded," Sebastian said. "Many a pint will be raised to the health of young Jamie Deerfield."

St. Sevier swiveled his gaze to Sebastian. "Jamie?"

"We're no' calling him Jacques," Sebastian retorted. "I'm his godfather. I get to bestow the nickname. It's an old Scottish tradition."

"Thirty seconds old," I said. "But a fine tradition nonetheless." I was in charity with the world, and if Sebastian wanted to bestow nicknames, no matter. Better Sebastian's choice than the names cousins or siblings could come up with.

A christening in high summer was a lovely occasion. The cool water trickled over James's forehead provoked him to smiling and kicking, and the church was festooned with fragrant roses. Vicar's sermon was short and full of admonitions to Felix and Katie about seizing the joy of raising a child on every possible occasion.

He invited the congregation to participate in that joy. A fortnight earlier, I might have heard his invitation with resentment. I had my disappointments to cling to, after all, and they were real and bitter disappointments.

But I had children to love too. Nieces who needed an aunt possessed of the disinterested caring of the nonparent. Nieces, who appreciated being taken wading, or my cousin Evelyn, who needed somebody to show her how to put up her hair purely to pass the time. A nephew I held in my arms, and a nephew in Town whom I had yet to meet.

I had taken Henry and Stephen into the village to choose their own dragons from the shelf in the sundries shop, and I had seen both boys stand a little taller when I'd thanked them for not contributing to the general mayhem by also running away.

I held James for most of the ceremony, which was fortunate, because Katie was busy sniffling into Felix's handkerchief, and Felix was busy patting Katie's shoulder. Sebastian blinked rather a lot, while St. Sevier's smile was both tender and wistful.

Derwent Hall was open to guests after the service, and no expense had been spared on the planned celebration. The assemblage preceded the carriages from the churchyard, lest they eat the dust of the coaches rattling up the drive.

After the ceremony, I lingered on the church steps next to St. Sevier, feeling pleased with myself for my deportment during the services and looking forward to our upcoming journey to Berkshire. I was tempted to slip my hand into Hugh's and suggest we announce our engagement once the crowd had gathered at the Hall.

I hesitated for a moment, content to enjoy the day. The weather was perfect, the occasion lovely, the man beside me lovelier still and so dear.

"I love you," I said quietly—I had not taken complete leave of my senses.

"*Je t'aime aussi, mon coeur.*"

Derwent's coach rolled up to the curb as the last of the village stragglers toddled off in the direction of the Hall. A woman stood across the street on the green, holding a child by the hand. Both woman and girl had flaming-red hair, and the lady was peering directly at St. Sevier.

"Do you know her?" I asked, nodding in her direction. She was staring intently, but I had the sense she did not mean to be rude. She simply could not look away.

St. Sevier's gaze went to the woman and her child, and it was as if all the sunshine drained from the day. His countenance became unreadable, his bearing glacially remote.

"Is there a problem?" Sebastian asked, jogging up the church steps. "She looks familiar, and she seems to know you, St. Sevier."

I knew.

I knew before anybody said another word. Seeing lightning cleave the heavens and hearing thunder split the sky had been a mere novelty compared to the sensation that coursed through me. I became a pillar of cold, a monument to shock. I understood then why women fainted upon hearing tragic news, because all that held me upright in that moment was a stubborn refusal to yield to the fiendish vagaries of fate.

"If I am not mistaken," I said, "that is St. Sevier's long-dead wife, and apparently, she has a daughter." I spoke calmly, just as I'd been calm when I'd thanked one of Freddie's friends for bringing me news of his death. The mind rolls along, like a carriage whose coachman has fallen from the bench, while the heart dies.

A trick of the morning light allowed me to see what had not been obvious earlier. The woman was crying. She neither shuddered nor sniffed, but stood in the gorgeous summer sun, tears coursing down her cheeks.

Perhaps she and I were equally shocked, equally numb, and equally upset.

"That cannot be." St. Sevier stared at the woman. "Ann is dead. My commanding officer said there were no survivors. That woman cannot be my wife."

The coach pulled away, leaving only the five of us—four adults and a child—gaping across the empty street as dust drifted in the air. The little girl was not crying. She was regarding us with solemn curiosity, doubtless taking in every word and glance.

"There is a child," I said, unable to overlook that fact as much I might long to. "She is small, blameless, and her mother is upset. Civilities are in order."

St. Sevier seemed unable to move. "Dunkeld, if you would be so kind..." He gestured in the direction of the street.

Sebastian moved off to the green. The girl watched him coming closer and shrank against her mother's skirts. Quiet words were exchanged, and the woman stood straighter. She walked across the street, the little girl at her side.

"Come," I said, taking St. Sevier by the arm and leading him down the steps. "This must be dealt with." A tempest of emotions boiled up inside me. St. Sevier had not deceived me—he would never have deceived me on so serious a matter—but my reality had shifted in the past two minutes, and in a terrible way.

Grief swirled among the sentiments ricocheting around in my heart, as well as rage, sorrow, disbelief, weariness... *Not again. Not more bereavement. Please, no...*

And yet, as much as I was consumed with dread, what must St. Sevier be feeling? What dashed hopes, what fury, what sorrow, or what renewed hopes? He needed me now, and I would not fail him. A last gesture between parting lovers, or perhaps the desperate loyalty of battlefield comrades, but my support in this shocking moment was all I had to offer him.

St. Sevier descended to the churchyard with me while Sebastian remained beside the red-haired woman and her child.

A silence ensued, the only sound the ringing of the blacksmith's hammer against the forge across the green.

"Hugh." The red-haired lady curtseyed. "You are alive."

He bowed. "As are you, Ann."

"You're sure she's your Ann?" Sebastian asked.

St. Sevier gently pushed russet locks back from the lady's temple to reveal a crescent of puckered flesh. "I cleaned that wound. She fell against the laundry wagon in bad footing. We behold Madame Ann St. Sevier."

He had kissed that scar in all likelihood, traced its contours with gentle fingers... I would go mad if I allowed my mind to dwell on such matters.

"You look well," Ann said. "Very well. I was told you'd fallen at Bidassoa."

"Wounded, not seriously. I was told your party was ambushed with no survivors."

"I survived. I pled my grandmother's Catholic faith, and the good Romish bandits spared me. I did not know when I left the British camp that Fiona was on the way. I would never have... done what I did had I known that."

Another silence stretched, painful in a whole new way. St. Sevier, who loved children, who longed for children, had a daughter, a gorgeous, solemn little girl with her mother's hair and her father's intelligent brown eyes.

I studied the girl, seeing Hugh's chin, his brows. Seeing all the children I would never have.

Sebastian's coachman had kept the MacHeath's Ford team waiting a dozen yards down the street. One of the horses stomped a hoof, making the harness jingle.

"Let us repair to MacHeath's Ford," Sebastian said. "The manor will be deserted, thanks to the festivities at Derwent Hall, and the rest of this discussion should not take place in the churchyard."

Hugh and Ann continued to stare at each other.

"*Maman*," the girl whispered, "*J'ai faim*."

"She speaks French?" Hugh asked.

"Aye, and the Gaelic, thanks to my granny and cousins. English, of necessity. The French was for you."

Sebastian signaled to his coachman, who moved the team up.

"The child is hungry," I said. "Somebody should find her some sustenance. I can walk to the Hall." I was unable to watch any more of this rapprochement and most especially unable to watch Hugh become captivated by his small daughter.

"Violet." His regard for me was solemn. "I would take it as a kindness if you would accompany us to MacHeath's Ford. Dunkeld is correct—there is a discussion to be undertaken, and you are part of it."

No, I was not, but neither would I refuse Hugh's request. "I must put in an appearance at the Hall at some point, as must Sebastian. We are the godparents."

"You will not be missed for some time, and we have need of you. I have need of you."

He said that with Sebastian, Ann, and the child looking on.

I stalked over to the coach and endured the short ride to the Ford with Ann sitting beside me, Fiona on her lap. St. Sevier could not take his eyes off the child, nor could Ann take her eyes off St. Sevier. I felt as if I traveled in a funeral coach toward the interment of my own dreams.

Sebastian got out first and assisted me to alight. I did not recall how it came to pass that we ended up in Katie Deerfield's formal parlor, a tea service on a tray before me, but Sebastian must have managed it.

He poured out as well, though I suspect nobody tasted the tea we drank. I appreciated the display of civility, though, because if nothing else, we all needed time to recover from what had been a grievous shock.

I suspected I would be recovering for a good long while, possibly for the rest of my life.

CHAPTER EIGHTEEN

After Fiona had partaken of some sandwiches, a footman was found to take her to see Felix's foals. She had delightful manners for such a small child, and when St. Sevier had addressed her in French, she'd assayed a bashful smile.

His own bashful smile turned upon him, one of a vocabulary of smiles, each of which I held dear.

"Tell me what happened," St. Sevier said. "When I came home to an empty tent, I surmised that you'd had your fill of regimental life and of marriage to me." His tone was that of the physician beginning an interview with a patient whose illness he had not yet diagnosed. To the casual observer, he was politely curious, but I felt the tension in him, the temper, and the dismay.

"I was homesick," Ann said. "I was so homesick and grieving. I should not have remarried so quickly, but the colonel told me quite plainly that passage home was out of the question. I was to make myself useful to the regiment, and I'd be permitted rations."

The commanding officer, gallant soul that he'd been, had commended a young widow to whoring for her meager bread.

"You chose me instead," St. Sevier replied. "At the time, I was flattered."

Ann speared him with a look. "At the time, you were young, chivalrous, and lonely. Those English bastards worked you to death, and you had no woman to do for you. I needed rescuing, Hugh, but so did you."

"So why abandon me?" St. Sevier asked, still sounding all but unconcerned about the answer.

I knew better. I knew the guilt and bewilderment that had haunted him and given him nightmares.

"I was growing too fond of you. If we stayed together long enough to conceive a child, I knew I would never see home again. Never hear my granny's voice again, never put flowers on my mother's grave again. I could not bear that. I was not thinking clearly, and I'm sorry for the hurt I did you, but I was trying to look after myself for a change."

Sebastian had absented himself so far as to stand by the window that looked out over the back gardens. The scent of honeysuckle graced the room, and I suspected in future, that fragrance, reminiscent of Hugh himself, would always carry difficult memories for me.

"We were *married*," St. Sevier rejoined flatly. "There are no options when a wife runs off, Ann. I could not have remarried, and neither—legally—could you."

She looked at her hands, and I felt an unwelcome stab of pity for her. As a new widow, I had not always thought clearly. Even when I'd made sound decisions, I'd doubted myself, failed to implement my decisions, and forgotten entirely why I had chosen as I had.

And I had been of mature years, with means and family nearby. Ann had been all of eighteen, living from battlefield to battlefield. She'd remarried to a near stranger rather than be forced into prostitution.

"Do not blame Ann," I said, "for the fact that Wellington's glorious army would have cheerfully raped a widow for their own pleasure while the commanding officers considered her fate a mere exigency of war."

Ann looked at me as if I'd sprouted horns and a scaly tail.

"You were never there, Hugh," she said tiredly. "You were always off at the infirmary or examining a battlefield for what the mortal wounds told you about anatomy. I thought you ghoulish, and the smell of blood was always on your clothes. Then too, there were those who believed that marrying a Frenchman didn't put me as off-limits as I'd hoped."

"You said nothing to me about that."

"When was I to say anything? We fumbled around beneath the covers in the dead of night and never spoke more than necessary to pass the salt or find your mended stockings. I was not whoring for the whole regiment—and I thank you for that—but I was dying inside, and the war was never going to end."

In my imagination, Ann St. Sevier had been a pathetic young widow, flighty, unsettled, self-centered. The picture that emerged from her recounting was very different, and more substantial, than the one I'd drawn in my head.

She had fought her own war and been married to a young man too fascinated with his calling to notice that he'd been a terrible husband to a grieving woman. Perhaps in the intervening years, Hugh had realized some of his shortcomings, and the insights had honed him into a man capable of reaching me when my own bereavement had become so complicated.

I was not prepared to admit that I owed Ann St. Sevier anything, but neither could I hate her—a disappointment for the ages.

"You left," Hugh said, "but you did not die. How did you find me?"

Sebastian had taken up a perch on the piano bench, and I was glad for his presence. When my composure failed—as I was sure it must, and soon—Sebastian would put me back in the coach with directions that I was to be let off in the stable yard, from there to slink into the Hall through a side entrance.

"I nearly didn't find you. An army can march ten leagues a day, but I wasn't able to travel at nearly that rate. The local ruffians came upon me in the company of a patrol I'd been shadowing and did what ruffians do in a starving countryside tired of meddlesome armies. I had by then realized that I was carrying. I was considering a return to camp, though the coast was closer. The leader of the mob that killed the patrol took me to a convent to await a prisoner exchange."

She poured herself a cup of tea, which I took for a measure needed to aid her composure.

"More time passed," she went on. "I was traded between various warring factions until I ended up in France with a Scottish regiment. I was visibly expecting by then, and the commander knew my uncle. He gave me passage home and also informed me that you'd been on the casualty list from Bidassoa. He showed me the list. I never once thought to doubt him."

St. Sevier scrubbed a hand over his face. "I was on the first list, but not the corrected list that followed. A horse reared, and I caught a hoof on the back of the head. A stupid mishap."

"And that would have been the end of it," Ann said, "but then I saw a man in Perth this spring who resembled you to the life. I made inquiries and learned that he had your French accent, though he was of course older than my Hugh had been and far from France or London. I told myself it could not be you, but then I saw a wedding announcement in the local paper, and Monsieur Hugh St. Sevier, physician, was listed among the guests."

Sebastian, from the piano bench, asked the logical question. "Why not leave well enough alone? Why travel the length and breadth of England to disrupt lives that took a long time to settle?"

"Her, in part." Ann aimed a glower tempered with humor at me. "If Lady Violet was traveling with Hugh and attending weddings with him, then he might be thinking of offering for her. Imagine how an earl's daughter would be treated when it became known her marriage is bigamous. Lady Violet is a widow. Widows deserve to know the truth, as do all women, come to that. And then there is wee Fiona."

Fiona. The argument I could not gainsay, no matter how badly I wanted to.

"She asked about her papa," Ann went on, "and the more I put her off, the more she asked. She has Hugh's chin, his way of pausing to think before asking a question, and while my family has seen to it that she lacks for nothing, she lacked for a father. I had no inclination to remarry—twice was enough for me—but neither could I deprive Fiona of a father who is, in his way, one of the most decent men I've known."

No bedamned argument there.

"I thought I saw you in Perth," St. Sevier said softly, "but told myself of course I had not. Scotland is full of red-haired women, and surely after all this time, you could not be alive. Then it happened again, earlier this week in the village. Fatigue, I told myself, a trick of the mind. Memories stirring because of the heat. Anything but the truth my eyes told me."

And he'd kept those worries and fears to himself, while making desperately tender love with me.

"I can go back to Scotland," Ann said. "I'll take Fiona with me, and we need not trouble you again, but I wanted you to see for yourself that you have a wife and daughter. I wanted to see for myself that you were real."

"I am real," St. Sevier said. "About as substantial as fairy dust at the moment, but real."

He was real, and he was her husband and Fiona's father. Ann had done me a substantial service, too, in preventing a bigamous marriage. I would thank her for that in a hundred years or so.

Maybe.

"Is there someplace I can freshen up?" Ann asked.

Sebastian directed her to a guest room and rejoined St. Sevier and me in the parlor. "The marriage cannot be easily annulled, St. Sevier. You'd render the child illegitimate if you pulled it off. Army weddings are well documented, and as a widow, Ann's young age would have been no barrier to valid consent on her part."

"Dunkeld," I said, rising, "would you excuse us for a moment?"

He considered me for the span of three heartbeats, nodded, and stalked for the door. "I will be within hailing distance, and I'll keep Ann from barging in on you."

He closed the door firmly in his wake, leaving me alone with St. Sevier for what would very likely be the last time.

"Violet, I am so sorry." St. Sevier had risen as well, but he seemed to know to keep his distance from me.

"You have nothing to apologize for. This is not your doing, and you and I are not who matter here." How calm I sounded, how rational.

"And neither is Ann. She thought only of herself when she left the camp, though I don't blame her for it, and now she's landed us all in a contretemps."

"The problem," I said gently, "is Fiona. You have a child, St. Sevier, a little girl who deserves her father's love."

He looked away, and I knew he might protest, he might demur, he might even offer to try to have his marriage annulled, but he was desperately hoping I would not ask him to visit illegitimacy on his only child.

"Violet, I love you. I love you as I have never loved another woman."

"And I love you, which means—much to my consternation—that I do not get to treat you like my favorite carved wooden dragon, to be trotted onto the battlefields of my choice or left on my bedside table while I dream."

"I have no idea what you are talking about. I have been more of a husband to you, a partner in all the ways that matter, than I ever was to Ann."

His voice shook, and I realized that as upset as I was, as bewildered and resentful, Hugh had been thrown into a complete muddle. Ann's reappearance likely stirred all manner of horrid memories, a Pandora's box of nightmares and regrets that he'd believed tamed and locked away.

"You are honorable," I said, putting the sofa between us for my sake more than his. "You are kind and decent. You would not inflict illegitimacy on your only daughter simply for the pleasure of marriage to me. And say you did manage to have your first marriage annulled, though given that the nuptials occurred in Spain, you are French, and Ann is Scottish, that process could take years."

St. Sevier stared at me as if I spoke some dead language, but I knew he was listening, so I plowed onward.

"At some point, when Fiona is not accepted at your choice of finishing school, when she begins socializing, when her marital prospects are limited by her bastardy, you will resent the wife you took on out of guilt, St. Sevier. You believe you owe me marriage, but you don't. We became lovers without any expectation of a legal union on my part."

"But I had hoped..." He closed his eyes. "I prayed. I bargained with the Almighty. I schooled myself to such patience that Job was a fidgety schoolboy by comparison, and my patience was at long last rewarded."

"It was, and I have no regrets, St. Sevier. I will always be glad that we did not fuss about waiting for vows to be spoken, that we seized opportunity when it was before us. I'm proud of myself for that, in fact. But I do not want my happiness to come at the expense of your honor or Fiona's prospects."

I had another argument in reserve: St. Sevier had conceived a child with Ann, and in very short order. He wanted children, wanted a family, and with Ann, he could have that. He already had that, in fact.

"My honor." He came around the sofa, and I held my ground. "I hate my honor at this moment. I do not want to lose you, Violet."

"You either lose me as your prospective wife, or you lose the respect you are owed as Fiona's father. You cannot have both."

"And that," he said, scowling down at me, "is why I love you."

I did not reprove him for his admission, because he spoke the truth, and I needed—and deserved—to hear the words from him. If our paths crossed again, and he insisted on the same declarations after publicly acknowledging Ann as his wife, I would protest.

But not today. Not on this beautiful, awful summer day.

"Where does this leave us?" he asked.

Apart, of course. Forever and always apart. "I will have to face down some talk. I traveled with you, and taking another woman's husband as my escort is not quite the done thing, even for a widow. You were apparently visiting your family in Scotland, though, and I am hardly an object of interest to the gossips anymore. By this time next year, you will have a thriving medical practice in London or Edinburgh, and I will be doting upon various nieces and nephews."

"Will you remain in London?"

"That is none of your business, St. Sevier."

Voices drifted in from the corridor. Sebastian's baritone, Ann's lilting brogue.

"Violet, I respect that you are trying to apply clear thinking to our situation, and I esteem you for it, but I need to know that you are well."

He was not being the detached physician now. He was being a dear man, whom I would always miss.

"You gave me the tools I need to weather losses, Hugh St. Sevier. You gave me courage, common sense, affection, and, most of all, hope. I will never again suffer as I did with Freddie's death. I will know that, somewhere in the world, I have at least one friend thinking well of me, and whose door will always be open to me."

The voices in the corridor rose, or Ann's did. Sebastian was apparently trying to charm her, though I suspected with that lady, charm would get him nowhere. And with Sebastian, Ann's histrionics would be utterly unavailing.

"And what of me, Violet?" St. Sevier said. "Will I always have one friend, somewhere in the world, thinking well of me? Will her door always be open to me?"

"Yes. Depend upon it." Though my bedroom door would be closed to him. His bleak expression said he knew that.

"Ann has a temper," St. Sevier said as the voices in the corridor rose. "That clearly has not changed."

"I have a few words for your wife, and I don't much care who overhears them."

"I have no idea what to say to my wife, but right now, much profanity comes to mind." He went to the door and opened it. "Dunkeld, accompany me to the stable, please. We will retrieve Fiona from her peregrinations."

He marched past Sebastian and a gaping Ann. She turned to me, eyes narrowed.

"Don't start," I said. "Don't even think about starting with me, *madame*. You are married to the most estimable of men, who will provide generously for you and Fiona. He will never turn his back on that child, and he will eventually reconcile himself to being your husband. Get in here, and I will tell you how to hasten that process."

"I don't need an earl's daughter to tell me how to behave."

"You need somebody's help, because from what I can see, you've made a complete hash of most everything you've undertaken. *So have I*. We can either gratify our respective tempers or negotiate a cease-fire."

One side of her mouth tipped up, and I knew why a younger Hugh had stepped in to preserve this woman from infamy. Ann St. Sevier was winsome. Not only pretty, but also accepting of human foibles. She had humor and resilience, and a very sweet smile.

She crossed the threshold to rejoin me in the parlor. "What is it you think I need to know about my own husband?"

The husband she'd run from years ago...

"The war left him with more of a medical vocation than he took with him to Spain, and his heart's desire is to focus his practice on children and expectant mothers. You help him make that dream come true, and you will earn his devotion. London is full of children who need medical care, and he's well respected by the émigré community. Start there."

Ann wandered over to the tray and helped herself to another piece of shortbread. "What else?"

"He doesn't boast of it, but he's an excellent horseman. He is skilled at treating the bereaved, and he still has terrible nightmares."

She munched her shortbread. "I'm to pity you because you know that about him and now must give him up?"

I wanted to smack the shortbread from her grasp, but I knew bravado when I saw it, and in her life, Ann St. Sevier had probably had to rely on bravado far too much.

"You are to thank God in all His almighty mercy that you will have the privilege of comforting St. Sevier in the night, if your husband allows you that honor. If you scorn him in any regard, I will delight in seeing to it that you regret your stupidity."

Ann sank onto the sofa and dusted her hands over the tray. "I like you. I don't want to, but Hugh has ever had good taste in the company he keeps. My mother was a midwife. Hugh and I delivered some babies together, back in the day. He was good at it. The women trusted him. The men respected him."

"I don't like you," I said, "and that doesn't matter. If you regain Hugh's esteem, I will be content."

"I had his esteem once, and his liking," she said, staring at the porcelain teapot. "I was a fool. I thought long and hard before coming south, my lady. Hugh tried his best with me in Spain, but nobody could have reached me. He did try, though, and I owe him worlds for his kindness. I owed him the truth, too, but beyond that... I still owe him."

That confession was all I needed or deserved to hear.

Ann and I were very civilly discussing mutual acquaintances among Perthshire society when Dunkeld and St. Sevier rejoined us.

Fiona was perched on her father's hip, the sight at once endearing and devastating.

I asked Sebastian to see me back to the Hall while arrangements were made for St. Sevier and his... his family to bide at MacHeath's Ford.

I parted from St. Sevier on the front steps, a bow-and-curtsey farce that nonetheless got us through the moment. I would take a more permanent farewell from him when the house party disbanded in two days' time, unless I slunk away in the dead of night before that.

"The coach or the woods?" Sebastian asked as we stood alone on the drive.

"The woods."

We walked in silence over the cart bridge, though both of us were doubtless thinking of St. Sevier and Ann taking their first steps toward resuming a marriage that had been built on wartime quicksand.

"They'll muddle through," Sebastian said as we descended onto the path through the woods.

"I know."

"Will you, Violet?"

"I always do." Though I had needed St. Sevier's help to muddle through my grief and a few other obstacles. "I wish them well."

"Liar."

"I want to wish them well." Fifty yards farther on, we'd reach the park below the Derwent Hall gardens. I would smile, make small talk, endure Katie and Felix beaming at each other, and notice Ajax and Hector off in corners, exchanging portentous looks or bets. Papa would be the jovial paterfamilias, and children would dart among the crowd in the ballroom, making a ruckus.

"Will you make my excuses, Sebastian? I am not up to more play-acting at the moment."

"Of course. I can accompany you back to London tomorrow if you like."

"Not necessary, but thank you." I could feel a blanket of composure settling around me, though I would not allow myself its comfort for long. That blanket could become a shroud and composure an excuse to stop living.

The way forward was hard, but I knew what must come next. I parted from Sebastian at the side door to the Hall and made my way up to my apartment. I traversed the balcony to St. Sevier's bedroom and rummaged in his wardrobe until I found the blue banyan he'd worn the last time we'd made love.

I shed all of my clothes, wrapped myself in Hugh's scent, curled up on his bed, and wept as if my heart was breaking.

Because, once again, it was.

"She is curious," St. Sevier said as he and I ambled down the laburnum alley. "Fiona reminds me of you. Thoughtful, not given to outward displays. One must earn her trust."

He'd known his daughter two days. He was already enthralled with her. That was good for all concerned.

"You will take her to Berkshire?"

St. Sevier and I did not touch. We had not touched since he'd bowed over my hand on the steps of MacHeath's Ford while his wife had pretended to admire Katie's potted salvia lining the drive. In an hour's time, he would depart with his family in Sebastian's coach, and perhaps depart from my life as well.

If so, I could not bear to face that now. I could bear only to wish him safe journey, as if he and I could expect to meet in a week's time on some shady London bridle path.

"Not Berkshire. Kent. I have never bided there and it strikes me as..." He waved an elegant hand. *"Territoire neutre.* We have all had a shock, and some rural peace and quiet is on order. I prefer the Berkshire property, but the staff was alerted to expect..." He muttered some French profanity, then smiled at me. "This is difficult, *non?"*

A vast understatement. "Let's sit." I took the nearest bench, which was not visible from the house or the conservatory. St. Sevier came down beside me, observing a few inches of distance that cut me to the quick.

"I wish you joy, St. Sevier. I hope you know that. I truly want you to be happy."

"And I long to see you happy as well, Violet, but in your case, I have some hope that my wish will come true."

Intimacy came in many forms, and I only in that moment realized that former lovers still had a sort of intimacy—affection, familiarity, shared memories, and shared regrets.

"Listen to me," I said, "and don't think to retreat in Gallic philosophizing. At one time, you risked your future for Ann's sake. She made bad choices as your bride, but she never meant to hurt you. She is trying to do the right thing now, and you owe it to yourself to meet her halfway."

"Hush." He nudged me gently with his shoulder. "I tell myself the same things. We were young. There was a war that, as Ann said, felt endless. Men desert in battle all the time, brave men who woke up that morning prepared to die for their country. Ann loves our daughter, and for that alone, I must respect her."

Our daughter. Another cut.

"Don't merely esteem her, Hugh. Look for ways to like her, to *let her in.* She said she had delivered some babies with you, that her mother was a midwife. I dread the thought of attending a birth, but Ann can share that with you. Must I draw you a map?"

He looped an arm around my shoulders. "Stop it," he said, his tone both harsh and tender. "Stop taking care of me, and Ann, and Fiona, when I long to take care of you, but no longer have that right."

I was comforted to know of his frustration, to know that fatherhood had not infatuated him out of all sorrow at our parting.

"I want you to be happy," I murmured, burrowing close as the damned, wretched, stupid tears started. "I want you to be happy, so I lecture you. I don't know what else to do."

He, wise man, simply held me while I indulged in the pure

misery of a loss I shared only with him. When I'd made a fool of myself at some length, I sat back, my inherent impatience with futility making a belated appearance.

I had cried enough, for now.

"I don't want to leave you," St. Sevier said, "but honor requires that of me. If you need me for any reason, Violet, do not be too proud to ask for my aid. I am still a competent physician, and..."

I glowered at him. "And a dunderhead. If I need a tisane for swollen ankles, I will find somebody else to prescribe it."

"If you need a friend, then. A good, true friend. Propriety must come between us, but pride need not."

"Will you make me the same promise, St. Sevier? To not stand on pride where I am concerned?"

"Yes. I can make you that promise. I make it gladly, in fact."

I rose, and Hugh came to his feet as well. "Then I will wish you farewell and expect to hear wonderful things regarding your London practice some fine day."

He linked my arm through his, and we started down the path to the sunnier parts of the garden. "You are dismissing me."

"But not abandoning you. There is a material difference." I was not the wife who had willingly left his side.

"I will miss you terribly."

"Good. I would not want to be the only one lingering over wonderful memories."

"Ah, Violet." We were six steps from the end of the alley, six steps away from public view. He bent and kissed me on the mouth, then on the forehead, then stepped back. "*Au revoir*, as we say in France."

"Until we meet again, my friend."

He smiled, I tried to, and then he was walking away. His stride never faltered as he marched down through the garden, out into the park, disappearing into the trees without a backward glance.

I returned to the bench where I'd so unceremoniously lost my composure and inventoried what feelings I could name.

Anger, of course. Hugh and I should never have been parted. Fate had been deucedly unkind. Again.

Relief, because the parting was done, and the next steps, burdened by grief and resentment, could be faced.

Good wishes for Hugh and his family. Those were necessary to my pride, also genuine. He deserved to be happy, by God, and the children of London—or Edinburgh or Kent—would thrive in his care.

Bewilderment, an old foe. A widow faced bewilderment. What was she to *do*, who was she to *be*, when there was no longer a husband to substantiate her marital status?

Except, I had found much to do since putting off mourning, and I had found more of myself after Freddie's death than I'd ever possessed prior to his passing. Steps on the gravel warned me that my solitude was at an end, though I had much to ponder.

Hector ambled along, Ajax nowhere to be seen.

"You've been crying," he said, passing me his handkerchief. "Ajax said to leave you alone, but I thought you might want to know that we've ruined John Bascomb."

"Hector, at this precise moment, I do not care if Bascomb has been clapped in irons and transported to Botany Bay."

"Botany Bay is a stretch, but debtors' prison is a real possibility, if you want it to be. Dunkeld said we must leave it to you to choose."

I was fresh out of mental momentum. No matter how I tried to make sense of my brother's words, I could not. "Explain yourself, please, preferably using small words and speaking slowly."

Hector glanced down the alley. "Bad luck, about St. Sevier's missus."

"When people believed dead are instead discovered to be hale and whole, one cannot regard the luck as bad."

Hector snorted. "You are worse than Derwent, which is saying something. Ajax and I hatched a scheme to raise some blunt. It worked."

The words he'd used were not that large, but I was still unsure of his meaning. "Does this have to do with your rematch against

Pritchard?" The final event of the gathering before last evening's supper had been another fencing match. Hector had trounced Pritchard, despite most of the guests betting against him.

"Ajax spent all week muttering that I wasn't up to Pritchard's weight, that a rematch would be my ruin, that only fraternal loyalty stopped him from pronouncing me a complete gudgeon. By the time the betting began, everybody felt sorry for Ajax, because he was compelled by brotherly duty to put his money on me, though I was doomed to lose."

Not quite working a rig, but close to it. "Did Pritchard know?"

"He might have suspected, but he certainly gave a good account of himself anyway."

So nobody would challenge the win—or the winner.

"Bascomb is ruined?"

"He's has a gambler's arrogance, always thinks luck is on his side, but luck doesn't work like that. Dunkeld said Bascomb had treated you poorly years ago, and the wrong had never been addressed. He suggested we might be in a position to administer a little justice, and made a substantial bet with Bascomb. Do you want Bascomb in debtors' prison, Violet?"

"You are ruthless." And for once, I found something in Hector to appreciate.

"Debts of honor are to be paid quickly. If Ajax and Dunkeld insist on collecting from Bascomb, there won't be much left over for the kind of debts that courts take notice of. The trades will see him declared bankrupt."

A robin fluttered down from the greenery shading the alley. He cocked his head at me, twitched his wings, then flew off. As I watched him flutter away, I realized that Hector and Ajax were offering me what comfort they could for the turn of events with St. Sevier.

A bit of justice, and to my surprise, their gesture was a profound consolation. "Bascomb has children, Hector. We must consider them."

"Must we? Must we not consider that they need a responsible example of adult masculinity in their father rather than a bloviating arsewipe?"

"Yes, which is why I will buy most of Bascomb's vowels from Ajax and Dunkeld and pay for them immediately. You will use that money to open your fencing school, if that's what you wish. I could use some family in London, family that isn't preoccupied with perishing Parliament and politics."

"Buy Bascomb's vowels? He cannot redeem them, Violet. He's close to rolled up."

"I know that. I am counting on it."

"Ruthless," Hector said. "I like that. You will manage in Town until we can get up there to look in on you?"

"I will manage." That much, I knew, and not in any shaky, despairing, stiff-upper-lip way. I would manage, despite some bad days, and more than that, I would find a way to thrive.

"Then I'd best get back in the house," Hector said. "Dunkeld is pacing by the windows, and one does not try that man's temper." Hector offered me a one-armed hug and jaunted off, thoughts of putting Angelo's out of business doubtless filling his head.

"You are ready to leave?" Sebastian asked when he joined me a few minutes later. He wore riding attire, suggesting that if he and I could not share a coach, he was prepared to seek the safety of the saddle.

"I am ready to leave." I rose, taking one last look around. "The Hall is beautiful in summer, but I will be pleased to get back to my own abode." My house was my own. It might be in London, where I did not particularly care to be, but the house was mine.

I could leave the knocker off the door for days if I pleased to —or not.

"Hector told you about Bascomb?"

"He did. Thank you. I will hold a substantial portion of Bascomb's vowels, and if a hint of a whiff of bad conduct reaches my ears, I will ruin him. He will most assuredly never become a magistrate."

Sebastian paused on the path to regard me. "You won't collapse into another two years of mourning? Won't stitch samplers all in black thread and stare mindlessly at French novels?"

"You have been reading too much Mrs. Radcliffe."

"I worry about you, Violet."

"You need not." Though I was glad he did. A worried Sebastian would hover a bit, and now, I knew enough to let him. The next weeks would be difficult, and nobody could do my grieving for me, but I need not endure the hard days in utter solitude.

"I promised St. Sevier..." Sebastian began.

"I release you from any promises made under duress, Sebastian. St. Sevier and I will manage."

He cursed or offered a short prayer in Gaelic. I did not inquire as to which.

We took my traveling coach on the journey back to Town. Sebastian's presence beside me on the bench was very different from what St. Sevier's had been, but still welcome. I needed a friend, and Sebastian was emphatically, if not always politely, that.

I still had friends. I had family in a way I hadn't realized. I had nieces and nephews. I had love, in other words.

There was love in my life, there were still surprises—such as Hector and Ajax being willing to champion my honor in a very practical sense—and still mysteries to solve.

And if my digestion was upset, and fatigue dogged me at odd moments, that was simply my body adjusting to upheaval, as bodies would. I dozed on Sebastian's shoulder for part of the journey to London, and I was rather pleased that we made the entire trip without once coming to blows or even really shouting.

Much.

When next Sebastian, St. Sevier, Ann, and I encountered one another, I was vexed well past the point of shouting and blows, but that, as they say, is a tale for another time.

TO MY DEAR READERS

Oh, my gracious... When I saw St. Sevier heading for a five-foot fence at a dead gallop in sloppy footing, I had a bad moment. Thanks heavens for sure-footed steeds!

As it happens, though, St. Sevier does not quite keep his promise to Violet, the one about not being too proud to ask for her help. You can read more about that in the excerpt below from book six, **Lady Violet Goes for a Gallop**.

I am hopeful that St. Sevier, Sebastian, and Violet, have more mysteries to unravel after that gallop. The author is sometimes that last to know of such things, but I doubt one more book is going to be enough for these characters.

If you'd like to stay up to date on all my releases and pre-orders, following me on **Bookbub** is a good way to do that. I also have a **Deals** page on my website, where I announce discounts and early releases on the **web store**. For those who enjoy **newsletters**, I put out one about monthly, and I will never, spam, swap, or otherwise give out your personal information, and unsubscribing is easy.

However you like to keep in touch, I wish you, as always...

Happy reading!
    Grace Burrowes

Read on for an excerpt from **Lady Violet Goes for a Gallop,**
Book Six in the Lady Violet Mystery Series!

LADY VIOLET GOES FOR A GALLOP— EXCERPT

Lady Violet has been urgently summoned to the wilds of Kent, by a most unlikely party...

"What can you hope to accomplish, my lady?" My maid Lucy's question held the banked frustration of a woman resorting to reason when she'd rather shout.

"I hope to stop a hanging," I replied.

A relatively mild climate and proximity to London meant Kent as a county was heavily cultivated. Harvest was underway, and thus my coach was frequently stuck behind wagons full of produce or hauling laborers from one property to another. I caught the occasional snippet of song from the crews, but mostly I heard Lucy's fingers drumming on the leather of the opposite bench.

I read the note for the two dozenth time since receiving it that morning.

My lady,

Monsieur is being detained on suspicion of having committed

murder. I did not know who else to ask for help. Please come posthaste.

Madame Ann St. Sevier

The dire implications had not changed, but that Ann St. Sevier would seek my help on her husband's behalf raised her in my esteem. Hugh St. Sevier himself would never trouble another to come to his aid, though he'd promised me to the contrary.

"How can you stop a hanging, ma'am?" Lucy asked. "Interfering with the king's man is a crime. Criticizing the crown is a crime."

"If a murder has taken place, then finding the killer is not a crime."

Lucy muttered something which I knew better than to hear clearly, but the words *rubbishing* and *stupid* might have been mentioned.

"He won't thank you for it," she said a few minutes later. "He'll be all charming and gallant and stoic."

"I do not seek thanks, Lucy. I seek the truth, and the truth is that Hugh St. Sevier would never take another's life." Except possibly in self-defense or by accident.

The coach hit a rut, the thousandth such rut in less than half a day's travel. I was put in mind of the countless miles I had journeyed with Hugh as my escort, the length and breadth of the realm. I had been devastated to think that he and I would never again grouse and cuddle our way across the countryside.

I had found it mortally unfair that I would never again share a morning cup of tea with him, and I had been outraged that another woman would share his bed while I kept company with only memories and regrets.

But I refused, utterly, to contemplate a world without Hugh St. Sevier in it, and woe to any rural magistrate who sought to thwart me.

"Mrs. Bonaventure might not have received your note yet."

"She will receive us, Lucy. Now is not the time to be contrary."

A mulish glower served as Lucy's reply, though her doubts were justified. I did not know Pamela Bonaventure well. She had been widowed several years earlier than I had, and we had some acquaintances in common. At a summer house party the previous year, she and I had struck up a wary association short of friendship, though our paths had seldom crossed since.

In addition to both grain and garden produce, Kent boasted a sizable crop of titles. Because my father was an earl, I knew many of those families, had come out with some of their daughters, and stood up with many of their sons.

I had avoided prevailing on those connections to host me for this journey for reasons having to do with my father's tangled web of alliances, and also because Mrs. Bonaventure had met St. Sevier. She might not stake her reputation on his innocence, but she would regret the death of a handsome, charming fellow on general principles. She was that sort of widow—pragmatic, tolerant, *discreet.*

I had not visited her home previously, but as my coach tooled up a long drive lined with ancient lime trees, I added another adjective to that list: Pamela Bonaventure was *wealthy,* or at least quite well provided for.

The Gauges, her country home, was a three-story temple to whitewashed brick serenely situated halfway up a gentle rise. I counted twenty windows—each one taxed, of course—across the façade. The double front doors and shutters were painted a cheery light blue, and potted red salvia lined the front terrace and steps.

The overall impression was gracious, pleasing, and pretty. The Gauges was large enough to be stately, but small enough to feel inviting. Exactly the sort of country home I sought for myself, and I had a fanciful sense that the house was glad to have a visitor.

A groom rose from the mounting block as the coach came to a halt at the foot of the steps, and a liveried footman marched forth from the house to open the coach door. The groom was tidy, the footman's livery all in order. No hasty buttoning up of his jacket or slicking back his hair.

Pamela Bonaventure knew how to make a proper first impression, even in absentia.

"Welcome to The Gauges, Lady Violet," the footman said, offering his hand.

He was tall, blond, and handsome, as footmen were supposed to be, and he managed to exude cordiality without actually smiling. He handed me down, then performed the same courtesy for Lucy. All quite correct, and by the time he'd ushered me into the keeping of an equally cordial—and equally youngish—butler, my coach had drawn away from the front door.

A frisson of unease came over me as I realized I was far from home, preparing to prevail on the kindness of a near stranger in a matter with the potential for both scandal and tragedy. Then too, for the first time in my life when journeying someplace besides the Deerfield family seat, I'd traveled without a male escort.

I pushed the unease aside and replaced it with determination and a smidgeon of pride. Widows were permitted to travel unescorted, particularly for short excursions. Why not avail myself of that freedom?

"Mrs. Bonaventure will greet you herself shortly," the butler said, taking Lucy's traveling satchel from her. "She is unavoidably detained at a neighbor's, but we expect her home any moment. Mrs. Weaver will show you to your apartment. Please do ring if there's anything we can do to make your stay more comfortable."

He passed Lucy's satchel to another handsome devil of a footman and toddled off, doubtless to oversee the porters unloading my trunks.

"Lady Violet." The housekeeper curtseyed and came up smiling. "It's an honor to claim you among The Gauges's guests. Mrs. Bonaventure said we are to accord you every courtesy and convenience. She's put you in the garden suite, and we will have a tray up in no time."

The tray, through some miracle of domestic wizardry, was waiting on a low table when the housekeeper admitted me to my apartment. I could feel Lucy taking visual inventory of the house and in particular of the sitting room we found ourselves in.

The wallpaper was a soft, marine green, adorned with strutting, jewel-toned peacocks, intricately detailed pink and white camellias, and darker green foliage. The carpet and curtains echoed those colors, creating an impression of a quiet moment in some exotic forest.

The room was beautiful, though its appointments were modest.

"That door," Mrs. Weaver said, nodding at a panel nearly hidden by the pattern of the wallpaper, "opens onto the conservatory. Your balcony overlooks the garden, and you have a fine view of Belle Terre as well."

Lucy opened the French doors, and a gust of country-air-and-stable joined the lavender-sachet scent in the room.

"Belle Terre." Mrs. Weaver gestured to a magnificent edifice in peach-pale stone on a distant rise. "Who knows what's to become of it now, what with the owner behind bars and the squires up in arms? Beautiful house, though. My cousin is housekeeper there."

"Who owns Belle Terre?" An upwelling of foreboding accompanied my question.

"Monsieur Hugh St. Sevier. We never saw much of him—he preferred London or his other properties, but the day Belle Terre fell into the hands of a Frog was a bleak day indeed, my lady. He's a proper enough gentleman, according to my cousin, but we took the war very seriously here in Kent. We stare across the Channel at Calais and well knew who would be first to feel Boney's sword if the French invaded."

Oddly enough, Sussex, Suffolk, and a half-dozen other counties along the southern coast had known the same thing.

"Monsieur St. Sevier served with Wellington," I said. I had anticipated that bigotry would be among the challenges St. Sevier faced on the road to exoneration, but that a housekeeper would disparage a neighbor to a guest was alarming.

"You know him?" Mrs. Weaver asked.

"I do, and I would trust him with my life. He is a highly skilled physician and an exceptionally honorable gentleman." I *had* trusted Hugh with my life, come to that, but kept that fact to myself.

"But he did not *fight* under Wellington, did he?" Mrs. Weaver replied, opening the lid of the silver teapot and peering at the contents.

"Physicians serve in a different capacity," I retorted, "and Monsieur volunteered his services."

She closed the lid on the teapot. "Who better would know how to take a life than a physician, or so they're saying at the Boar's Tail. One must admit the point is valid, my lady."

A tap on the door heralded the porters arriving with my trunk. Lucy shooed them into the adjoining bedroom and disappeared to start the unpacking. I secured from Mrs. Weaver the services of a groom to carry a note to Belle Terre and got a cool visual assessment —or reassessment—in return.

The staff at the Gauges was gracious and attentive, but the house-keeper lacked the perfect decorum of her London counterparts. Mrs. Weaver hadn't exactly gossiped with me, but she'd made it very clear that St. Sevier was not well regarded in the neighborhood.

He owned an astonishingly impressive property, likely provided employment for dozens, and was admitted to be a "proper enough gentleman" who had volunteered to patch up Wellington's injured troops, and yet, nationality alone was sufficient to convict him of murder.

When Mrs. Weaver had withdrawn and taken the porters with her, I poured Lucy a cup of tea and took it to her in the dressing closet off the bedroom.

"This has to be about the prettiest guest room I ever did see," Lucy said, closing the door to a tall cedar-lined wardrobe. "That tea had best not be for me, milady. I have standards, and you do not wait upon me."

"Drink it," I said. "Where do you suppose this wallpaper came from?" The peacock and camellia theme was repeated in the bedroom. The bed, swagged in green hangings and covered in a green, white, and pink quilt, felt like a leafy bower. Afternoon sun slanted through sparkling latticed French doors, and a privacy screen painted all over with peacocks and parrots stood in the corner.

The best touch was a vase of pink roses on the mantel. The flowers emitted a heady, spicy perfume.

Whoever had appointed this apartment had an eye for domestic beauty. I was itching to explore the rest of the house, but first I must send along a note informing Ann St. Sevier that I had arrived in the neighborhood.

Lucy took the cup and saucer from me and sipped. "Could be a little stronger, but plenty hot. You aren't having any?"

"Soon. The coach travel has given me indigestion." That, or the prospect of Hugh St. Sevier's demise at the end of a rope had upset my belly.

Lucy finished her tea and returned the cup and saucer to the tray in the sitting room. "Eat something, and your tummy will settle. I had no idea Monsieur owned a palace."

"It's merely a stately home, Lucy. He's not the king of France." Many an Englishman had found Louis deserving of his fate... until the violence had expanded to include his wife and small children and exploded into years of state-sanctioned savagery. The Corsican had stepped into the resulting chaos, and at the time, many an Englishman had been relieved that somebody had come along to make France settle down.

"Your friend is doomed," Lucy said. "Mrs. Weaver's cousin works for the man, and she's ready to string him up simply for being French."

I wanted to reprimand Lucy for speaking too plainly, but instead penned my note to Ann St. Sevier, informing her that I would call as soon as I had greeted my hostess, before supper if possible.

Lucy took the folded and sealed note from me, promising to see it into the hands of a groom, along with a coin to ensure its immediate delivery.

"You are good to come here," she said, pausing at the apartment door, "and you are good to try, my lady. You've had luck with tough puzzles in the past, but your handsome Frenchman is not long for this world."

She was trying to be kind—and failing. "He's not my handsome Frenchman, and he didn't murder anybody. Be off with you and learn what you can belowstairs, please."

She curtseyed with ironic politesse and silently withdrew.

I considered pouring myself a cup of tea, but still, my digestion refused to settle. Instead, I took myself off on reconnaissance, a pointless exercise that nonetheless appeased my curiosity and gave me an excuse to simply *move*. I needed to familiarize myself with my surroundings, and I needed to dispel the sense of anxiety that was doubtless giving me an upset tummy.

A footman—apparently, they were all gorgeous at The Gauges— directed me to the library, but before I'd gone more than a dozen yards down the indicated corridor, I heard raised voices from behind a closed door. Pamela Bonaventure had returned home, and she was most unhappy with a gentleman who was apparently also quite displeased with her.

Order your copy of **Lady Violet Goes for a Gallop**!